NEW YORK REVIEW'
CLASSICS

TALK

LINDA ROSENKRANTZ is the author of several books of fiction and nonfiction—including *Telegram*, a history of telegraphic communication and *My Life as a List: 207 Things About My (Bronx) Childhood*, a memoir—and is the co-author of *Gone Hollywood: The Movie Colony in the Golden Age*. A longtime syndicated columnist, she was the founding editor of *Auction* magazine, as well as a founder of the popular baby-naming site Nameberry.com. Rosenkrantz was born and raised in New York City and currently lives in Los Angeles.

STEPHEN KOCH is the author of two novels, *Night Watch* and *The Bachelor's Bride*, and of several nonfiction works: *Stargazer: Andy Warhol's World*; *Double Lives: Stalin, Willi Münzenberg and the Seduction of the Intellectuals*; *The Breaking Point: Hemingway, Dos Passos, and the Murder of José Robles*; and *The Modern Library Writer's Workshop*. He lives in New York City, where he is the director of the Peter Hujar Archive.

TALK

LINDA ROSENKRANTZ

Introduction by
STEPHEN KOCH

NEW YORK REVIEW BOOKS

New York

THIS IS A NEW YORK REVIEW BOOK
PUBLISHED BY THE NEW YORK REVIEW OF BOOKS
435 Hudson Street, New York, NY 10014
www.nyrb.com

Library of Congress Cataloging-in-Publication Data
Rosenkrantz, Linda.
 Talk / Linda Rosenkrantz ; introduction by Stephen Koch.
    pages ; cm. — (New York Review Books classics)
 ISBN 978-1-59017-844-7 (softcover)
 1. Friendship—Fiction. 2. Interpersonal relations—Fiction. I. Title.
 PS3568.O823T35 2015
 813'.54—dc23

                          2015003954

ISBN 978-1-59017-844-7
Available as an electronic book; ISBN 978-1-59017-845-4

Printed in the United States of America on acid-free paper.
10 9 8 7 6 5 4 3 2 1

CONTENTS

Introduction · vii

1. Emily Helps Marsha Pack for the Summer · 5
2. Marsha and Vincent on the Beach · 14
3. Emily's First Visit to Marsha's Summer House · 22
4. Emily's Problems Are Discussed on the Beach · 29
5. A Story from Emily's Childhood · 35
6. Watching Tim on the Beach · 38
7. Marsha's Love Story · 45
8. Emily Relates Her Psychedelic Experience to Vincent · 51
9. Emily and Marsha Play a Game · 58
10. Emily and Marsha Compare Childhood Traumata · 63
11. The Clam Dinner · 71
12. Marsha Tells Vincent About Hanging on a Wall · 80
13. Emily Returns · 85
14. In the Shadow of Sick Joan · 93
15. Emily and Marsha Discuss Pleasure on the Beach · 98
16. Emily and Vincent Take a Short Ride · 102
17. Marsha and Emily Talk About Nathan, Philippe,
    Andy Warhol and Nancy Drew · 106

18. Emily, Marsha and Vincent Discuss Orgies · 114

19. Emily Approaches Her Birthday · 123

20. A Difficult Dinner · 132

21. Another Game · 157

22. Marsha Interrupts a Discussion of Herself · 160

23. Emily and Marsha React to an Attack on Vincent · 172

24. Vincent Has a Seizure on the Beach · 179

25. Emily and Vincent Go Out Dancing · 186

26. Marsha and Emily's Last Day on the Beach · 195

27. Marsha and Vincent Drive Back to New York · 204

28. Marsha Unpacks from the Summer · 208

INTRODUCTION

YOU HOLD in your hands a thick, juicy, and above all *authentic* slice of the fabled 1960s, an early example of a literary experiment that worked and is working for us still. The twenty-first century has seen the rise of reality TV; published in 1968, *Talk* is a "reality" novel. None of the dialogue in this book is invented, or vaguely remembered, or a figment of some writer's fantasy. Shortly before the summer of 1965, the author Linda Rosenkrantz had a genuinely original idea: Why not see if life *really* imitates art? Three friends— not fictitious characters but three real people—are spending their summer vacation in East Hampton. How to capture their story?

Tape-record them. Make it real.

"I had the tape recorder running all summer," Rosenkrantz recalls, "even dragging the bulky monster to the beach. At first there were about twenty-five different characters and fifteen hundred pages of single-spaced transcript, which I took close to two years honing down to the three characters and two hundred fifty pages."

What Rosenkrantz fished out of the shoreless sea of sex chatter and beach gossip and summery seafood dinners is a real novel composed entirely of dialogue. The result is a unique document in the annals of friendship and dysfunctional love, filled with irresistible repartee—literary popcorn—that sways between powerful insight and hilarity. This talk is sometimes impressive, sometimes funny. It is never inane. It is always a lot of fun.

Though we hear much more about sex than we hear about art, the setting is the New York art world and its sixties "scene." As the editor of Sotheby's *Auction* magazine, Rosenkrantz was very much part of that scene. The dramatis personae consists of Marsha and her confidante, the hard-drinking Emily. Vincent, a gay male painter, completes the triangle. Marsha has a serious job in New York; Emily is an actress and a brash, brilliant party girl; and Vincent (aka Vinnie) is the gifted, analytical member of the male sex who fills Marsha's mind and usurps her life, displacing every straight contender.

This "reality" novel is a small founding classic which provides a model for television series like *Girls* and *Broad City* and all the many novels and series like them that focus on the primacy of nonromantic peer relationships. It is filled with the same raw talk between independent women friends that gives those series their crackle of excitement. Its picture of intimacy also suggests the earlier series *Friends*. The inimitable banter of two beautiful, much desired, but bewildered women who are each other's alter egos, is capped by a *triste* but classic misalliance—the unrealized, unworkable, but genuine love between Marsha and the homosexual Vincent: a love that despite a lot of outside sex on the part of everyone is— well—all talk.

It's a tight triangle. "You know," Marsha says, "I get a very scary feeling sometimes that I'm pushing myself into a corner—all of a sudden I'm beginning to find everyone except you and Vinnie very dull. We've set up such a stimulating, total, free, hysterical, intimate, intense relationship that I find it impossible to relate to other people, they leave me completely cold."

All three of these "stimulating, total, free, hysterical, intimate, intense" friends find themselves teetering on the cusp of thirty: the dread moment when first youth is at last *finito* and maturity settles in to stay. In fact, the long shadow of maturity hovers over all the talk. How dark is that shadow? What does it portend? Love? Committed relationships? Marriage? Children? Just more talk?

Emily: I've said a lot of very twenty-nine-year-old drunken things this summer. But I can say right now that I don't want any more married men and I don't want any weak men and I

don't want any men that I've ever known before. I think I'm just about ready to find someone who is healthy enough to take the chance of getting married to me.
Marsha: Amen.

Yet Vincent knows his secure place in Marsha's emotions. "You're getting anxious," he confidently tells her on the beach, "because Tim's coming out this weekend. You have to sleep with him and you don't want to…"

Marsha: I *do* want to sleep with him.
Vincent: No you don't.

Like the hapless Tim, the straight men in Marsha's life will never get beyond the sexual bed to reach the intimacy that Marsha shares with Vincent. And the sexual bed is the one place in Marsha's life that Vincent will never go. That conundrum may be the cause of their misalliance. Can it also be the basis of their intimacy?

Despite its crisp freshness, *Talk* is a novel of the sixties—a decade self-consciously immersed in youth. The book was recorded in a climate of change—the epochal summer of 1965—and the decade is woven through the whole text. The world is changing, and our three friends know it. "We're all pioneers," Vincent says to Emily and Marsha, "going through new frontiers, new jungles, we're breaking psychic, social land so that people following us will be able to lead better lives."

Here are some of the new frontiers and new jungles Vincent has in mind.

THE SEXUAL REVOLUTION. Marsha and Emily—not to mention Vincent—either are or recently were busy in bed, and their gossip is all about it. Post-pill, male–female relationships have done a somersault. We are now in what has become a life in which sex is the ubiquitous first step toward what may or may not become a relationship. This is in contrast to pre-pill days, when the sequence was reversed; a relationship might or might not lead to that rarer consummation called sex.

Emily says: "I slept with a lot of men then, Marsha, and they're all like meaningless empty faces now, I don't remember them. I know their names, but they don't mean anything. That was very hard for me, you know," she adds wistfully, "because I'm not promiscuous by nature." There is lots of talk about (female) masturbation; S and M, perversity, penis size; orgies (is anonymous sex tolerable? or does one prefer a comfy ménage à trois among friends?); and at last the basic perplexity of a heterosexual woman bound to a homosexual man.

Speaking of which, THE GAY–STRAIGHT RELATIONSHIP. During the sixties, the integration of gay with straight life had a long distance to go. There was still plenty of shame, suspicion, and secrecy, but the art world was a decade or two ahead of its time. There, gay and straight mingled quite openly and relatively easily.

Other aspects of the sixties are:

ROCK AND ROLL. "Do you realize," Emily says, "that [the new dancing] makes the woman equal to the man for the very first time? She doesn't have to follow him anymore, he doesn't control the rhythms, the music is something they share."

THE DRUG CULTURE. None of *Talk*'s three characters is a druggie in a twenty-first-century sense, but in one of the high points of the book, Emily tells Vincent about her experience on LSD. The passage is pure sixties: "I was intimately a part of every pulsebeat of every sun that came up on everybody's life. There was a huge opening of the sky, I saw God.... I get all the vibrations. You know I called Marsha up when I was under LSD and she said I was talking pure poetry."

THE "SCENE." Our three are on a scene populated by the famous and the almost famous. There is a lot of talk about Andy Warhol and Susan Sontag and who is and is not recognized on the beach. Parties, parties, parties. Literary parties. Art parties. Dinner parties. (The eating that goes on in *Talk* is memorable: see the chapter called

"The Clam Dinner.") We see very little action in *Talk*, but it seems that parties are where the action is.

CULTURE. Emily and Marsha are cultivated, sixties style:

Emily: Let's see, I love Fitzgerald—*Gatsby* is one of my favorite books, and *Tender Is the Night*; the *Autobiography of Alice B. Toklas*, *The Sun Also Rises*, the poem *Kaddish*. I love Proust, Chekhov, Ibsen, Strindberg, Durrell, Robert Creeley, I like Rilke, I like Martin Buber, the idea of I and Thou, even though I don't know much about it. I like Bob Dylan and I love the Beatles.

A more perfect reading list for sixties smarts would be hard to conceive.

PSYCHOANALYSIS. Psychoanalysis is the intellectual touchstone of the book. In virtually every episode, there is talk about relationships and analysts, with a lot of talk about people being "sick" and "major breakthroughs." Every emotion, every fumbled relationship, every moment of bliss, every pang is (sometimes brilliantly) "analyzed." These three think in psychodynamic terms.

The funny thing about *Talk* is that despite being rooted in its time—the youth culture of the sixties, the sexual revolution, LSD, psychoanalysis, rock and roll, and the rest—the novel, seized from that distant moment, does not feel dated. Twenty-first-century readers of *Talk* who are themselves "punching thirty" will be able to hear, in the conversation of people from another generation, ringing echoes of their own lives. Therapy? The "scene"? Rock and roll? The elusive but powerful bond between a heterosexual woman and a gay man? The friendship of two beautiful women pushing thirty and going a little crazy over who is and is not "out there" and "available"?

Does any of this sound familiar?

—STEPHEN KOCH

TALK

Sometimes three is not a crowd

The Supremes, *"Where Did Our Love Go?"*
Album notes

1. EMILY HELPS MARSHA PACK FOR THE SUMMER

MARSHA: Don't forget I *did* sleep with Zeke long after you slept with Michael Christy.

EMILY: You're crazy.

MARSHA: I am not.

EMILY: I slept with Michael about three weeks ago, when I got drunk at that party. So it'll be four weeks this Friday that I slept with Michael.

MARSHA: That's tomorrow.

EMILY: Right, four weeks tomorrow.

MARSHA: Well, it was two weeks for me yesterday, so it's twice as near. By the way, is the thing you brought me a dessert or a snack?

EMILY: Both.

MARSHA: Is it something that goes with milk?

EMILY: Yes.

MARSHA: Oh that's great, just great.

EMILY: I'm sorry, I didn't have enough money to get milk because the thing was so expensive, but I love the question about the milk. What do you think the thing is?

MARSHA: Chocolate-chip cookies.

EMILY: I had to go to two stores to find it.

MARSHA: Brownies, fudge brownies. And there's no tea in the house either. How do you expect me to eat fudge brownies without milk or tea? It was a sweet thought though.

EMILY: Drink water.

MARSHA: Brownies with water. I'm not too keen on how many underpants I have.

EMILY: How keen does one have to be about a thing like that?

MARSHA: I just don't think I have enough.

EMILY: Enough for what?

MARSHA: A summer of drips.

EMILY: Those are my favorite underpants of all time. How much do they cost?

MARSHA: A dollar.

EMILY: Where?

MARSHA: Macy's, Bloomingdale's, one of those.

EMILY: Oh, I *love* them, I love the nudette color. How much money do you think I have altogether?

MARSHA: A thousand dollars.

EMILY: Let me see that bra. I think that's my favorite bra of all time. Can I have it?

MARSHA: No.

EMILY: I want to discuss something with you. I was thinking about it this morning, about Michael. I thought here I am going back into analysis and if I really look at it, I am running after such an utter waste of time, something so destructive to me. I mean can he ever really be a love object at this moment in my life? I decided no, and all my thoughts got very positive, but then I also realized that if I were to take a single drink over it, my feelings would run away from me, I wouldn't be able to rationally deal with the problem and know what was good for me, because the one drink would bring out all my psychotic self-destructiveness.

MARSHA: Do you think every time I call Zeke it's self-destructive?

EMILY: Not necessarily. I don't think calling him has to be self-destructive at all, do you?

MARSHA: Works out that way.

EMILY: Why? He calls you too.

MARSHA: Yah, and I call him very little.

EMILY: Michael hasn't called me in a long time.

MARSHA: Let me ask you—does one carry a gray bag at any time in the summer?

EMILY: Definitely not. Heavy gray leather?

MARSHA: I'm taking it. You never can tell.

EMILY: Now would you explain that to me, please?

MARSHA: What?

EMILY: About phone calls, self-destructiveness. Michael's separated from his wife—it's obviously not a good time to get involved with him. On the other hand it might be a *very* good time to get involved with him.

MARSHA: Well it's not, obviously it's not, it's not working out that way.

EMILY: Oh, I didn't tell you what happened today. The bell rang and I got furious because I'm in the middle of a *gorgeous* rehearsal for a scene in class and in walks this guy I knew in Paris, who told me all about Philippe. He said don't expect Philippe to bring anything over for you when he comes because he's going to have a lot of books on him and he's only allowed twenty kilos. That's about fifty pounds, you know.

MARSHA: On the plane?

EMILY: Now I have been writing Philippe constantly, saying Philippe *please* if you know of anyone coming to New York, *please* give them my things. If he doesn't know I want those properties after all my letters and everything else, if he doesn't bring them when he comes, I'm not going to look at him, I'm not even going to see him.

MARSHA: I don't blame you.

EMILY: Be curious seeing him again.

MARSHA: How do you think you'll react to him?

EMILY: I'll react, for one thing, I'm so fucking immune to him, I don't give a shit about him.

MARSHA: Wait until he comes in and starts to cry. Or do you really think you're completely immune?

EMILY: I won't use the word immune. I'll use one word and that is healthy. I may cry when I see him, I may cry because it's a very sad thing. He did abuse me. We couldn't love each other and that's the end of it. It shows me that I really have terrific problems which I've got to solve. I literally threw out three years of my life on him. That's a long time. You said I was nicer since I got back from Europe. Do you really think I'm nicer?

MARSHA: Yeah, I think you're healthier.

EMILY: I am.

MARSHA: Healthier is nicer.

EMILY: Healthier *is* nicer.

MARSHA: I wonder what Merrill Johnston's doing for sex these days.

EMILY: He's probably fucking someone, that's what he's doing.

MARSHA: The last time I went to him I said what *are* you doing for sex these days? No I didn't. I said you're waiting for me to ask you what you're doing for sex. He said well why don't you ask me if you want to? But I wouldn't give him the satisfaction.

EMILY: You know it's very far out. I had completely forgotten the fact that you do have a Negro analyst. Is he Negro though? Can I ask you a question, *is* he really a Negro?

MARSHA: Oh you *saw* him, Emily, you saw him out there last summer. Did he look Negro to you, sitting in the car with a little blond baby?

EMILY: You mean if you see him you don't know he's a Negro? You can't tell? I didn't realize that.

MARSHA: You looked him in the face—what did you see?

EMILY: Yeah, I looked at him, but I looked at him when I was surrounded by people who were all tan, like from three months of East Hampton.

MARSHA: Well, he looks just as tan now. He looks racially disturbed.

EMILY: I'm serious.

MARSHA: I am too. He looks like some kind of mixture.

EMILY: He looks like a mulatto, you mean. He looks like something beautiful, but he doesn't necessarily look like a Negro?

MARSHA: What's beautiful about him?

EMILY: He's very attractive.

MARSHA: He doesn't look beautiful—I mean he doesn't look Negro. He does, but you don't think of him say if you want to invite a Negro to a party. It's more conceptual than anything else.

EMILY: Do you want some more ice water with your fudge brownie?

MARSHA: Let me ask you something. Is ice lighter than water? How come it floats, how come it's lighter?

EMILY: I don't think it is.

MARSHA: Of course it is. Look at it.

EMILY: It's just more porous. Look, do you think soap is lighter than water?

MARSHA: Soap?

EMILY: Yeah, Ivory soap, it floats.

MARSHA: Do you know why things float?

EMILY: Why? You're telling me they float because they're lighter.

MARSHA: No.

EMILY: Then why does it prove they're lighter?

MARSHA: They *are* lighter.

EMILY: But why is it proof?

MARSHA: It isn't.

EMILY: Okay.

MARSHA: Then why do things float?

EMILY: It has to do with the amount of water they displace in terms of their weight, the ratio to the displacement of their weight, density to displacement. For instance, big Ivory soap, you put it in water and it floats. That doesn't mean it's lighter, it has to do with surface tension, the amount of water that's displaced. Look, *boats* float, don't they? Jesus, are we dumb!

MARSHA: A boat isn't lighter than water.

EMILY: Don't you know anything about surface tension? I'll show you, it's fascinating. It's one of my favorite scientific things. Do you have a bobby pin?

MARSHA: It's holding my head together. Oh no! I cannot stand that phone! I'm hanging up immediately.

EMILY: Absolutely, no matter who it is, absolutely get rid of them.

MARSHA: Hello? . . . Hi, Vinnie darling, what's up? . . . Don't be ridiculous, I'm packing....Who's there?...No! We wouldn't dream of leaving the house.

EMILY: Is he at the Dom? Who's there?

MARSHA: Are we dreaming of leaving the house?

EMILY: I want to know who's there... Absolutely not, we're not leaving, but I have to know who's there.

MARSHA: I'm trying to find out...Who's there, darling?... Who?...Just tell me or you may be killed with your ankle broken... Nobody, right?...Who else?... No Zeke? No Michael?... No, sweetheart, I'm packing and Emmy's helping; we wouldn't dream of leaving the house.

EMILY: What does he want to do?...I hate that fucking Philippe Rocheau.

MARSHA: She says she hates Philippe Rocheau. Who are you with? Clem?...Just the two of you, sitting? That'll get me down there all right....Okay, darling, goodbye, we can't talk now...All right, darling, bye.

EMILY: What did he say?

MARSHA: They're at the Dom, him and Clem Nye. Great couple.

EMILY: Great. Let me ask you something. Would you say Vinnie was very well liked generally? I mean there are some people who are not well liked and there are people who are very well liked.

MARSHA: Well, when he meets new people, they're usually crazy about him.

EMILY: That's not what I mean. I mean is he popular? I would think he'd be fantastically well liked, but at the same time he has a lot of the same faults I have and although I'm very well liked, I'm also very disliked.

MARSHA: Yah, I think you're about equal.

EMILY: We're both very egocentric, like to talk about ourselves, very dominating, aggressive, all that stuff. A lot of people hate it. I guess it's much worse in me though, because I'm a girl and I'm supposed to keep my mouth shut.

MARSHA: What was Diana Reinhardt saying about me the other night?

EMILY: Oh, we were talking about being neurotic. She said she thinks I'm the sickest of the three of us, you, me and Vince. She was watching me at the party and she thought my behavior was very, very sick. She said it looked mad, wild, out of control. She thinks I have a lot of problems. But still I have so many friends who think highly of me that obviously I have some great, really strong things going for me, even though I appear this sick. She didn't say it in a hostile way. In fact, I encouraged her to say it.

MARSHA: It sounds like she was honest and I think that's nice. What about me?

EMILY: I forget exactly what she said. I think she thinks you're the least sick. And I said . . .

MARSHA: That she was wrong.

EMILY: No, I agreed, but I said you weren't so much sick as you were originally, in some traumatic ways, damaged.

MARSHA: Set in my crazy mold.

EMILY: In a freeze. Deep, deep as deep can possibly go.

MARSHA: Originally I was probably the sickest. But I'm healing up. I think my prognosis is good.

EMILY: Certain things about you are still very sick. You know what I think is the sickest thing about you? That never since I've known you have you had a really deep and meaningful love relationship.

MARSHA: I think it is too.

EMILY: But that's about the only thing I can think of. And the fact that Vinnie, the person you love most in the world, is a homosexual. But your relationship to your job and those things, they're not sick at all

MARSHA: No, not the way they used to be. You know it's very funny. I was so worried about public opinion when I decided to go back to my job, but every person I've spoken to has said I don't see why you even wanted to quit—with your long vacations and everything.

EMILY: You never have to worry about public opinion. You know why? Because public opinion isn't worried about you.

MARSHA: I know.

EMILY: Someone said to me the other day—I forget who—they said don't worry, Emily, if you go into one of your drunken reels at a party and you think you made a fool of yourself, don't worry, because people are such egotists and so selfish, they don't even know you're alive. They don't know anybody's alive.

MARSHA: I hate thinking that way.

EMILY: Marsha, when was the last time you wore all those things?

MARSHA: These? I never wear them.

EMILY: Then why don't you throw them out? You have no idea what a marvelous feeling it is to get rid of the things you never wear.

MARSHA: All right, you tell me which ones I might wear. I'll let you decide.

EMILY: First of all, can I pick something for myself if I do all that work? Can I borrow a scarf? I need one desperately.

MARSHA: Okay, make piles.

EMILY: This you don't wear, this you might wear, this you don't wear.

MARSHA: How about this? This I definitely will wear.

EMILY: That is without question one of your more beautiful objects—throw it out!

MARSHA: No, I love it, I'm very fond of it. You want to see the great bargain I got? A big enamel tray for East Hampton barbecues. Don't look at the price.

EMILY: No, I'm not looking at the seventy-nine cents. Is that dress what you're wearing to the Museum tomorrow night?

MARSHA: Yeah.

EMILY: Beautiful.

MARSHA: You don't think it's too dressy?

EMILY: Not at all.

MARSHA: It isn't that dressy.

EMILY: Will you go to the Dom in it though? Everyone's going to the Dom afterwards, you know.

MARSHA: Yeah?

EMILY: I think you should look as elegant and beautiful as possible.

MARSHA: I don't want to be the only one. You know they couldn't go to the Dom last night, Vinnie and Clem, so they had to go tonight.

EMILY: Yeah. If anybody important arrives, they better call us. Michael Christy or anybody.

MARSHA: They're not calling and you're not leaving.

2. MARSHA AND VINCENT ON THE BEACH

MARSHA: So in other words this is really your ancestral family territory.

VINCENT: Yah, these are my sand grains—it's too wet for roots out here. Seriously, it's very important my coming to this part of the island this summer, particularly now, right after my father died and everything. As a matter of fact, my analyst said a very scary thing to me before I left. I had been having a lot of sexual dreams with my sisters near the cemetery where my mother is buried, and my analyst absolutely terrified me, she rephrased the dreams and said you have sexual anxiety about going back to where your mother is. It absolutely terrified me because even though my mother's body may be under the ground somewhere, I don't think of her as present in that place. I mean when all of a sudden someone says to you seventeen, eighteen years after she dies, you are going back to where your mother is, it makes it as if she were sitting out there in a rocking chair or something... Now how do we know when it's ten minutes?

MARSHA: When we get bored we'll ask the radio.

VINCENT: I'm not bored, I like the sun. Why did you ask Merrill Johnston the other day if I seemed homosexual? Is it such a moot question?

MARSHA: No, but what I really wanted to say was isn't Vince attractive, and that seemed too silly, so I said what was your impression of him, did he seem homosexual?...What does your doctor think of our relationship?

VINCENT: She's never said anything about it.

MARSHA: Nothing? What do *you* say about it?

VINCENT: She knows how close we are and everything.

MARSHA: Has she ever asked if I was feminine?

VINCENT: Why, just because you asked your doctor if I was masculine? What kind of question would that be? I mention a girl and my doctor says is she feminine? I say no, she's got a moustache . . . I'm going to lie down and get some sun on my face. I have to leave in ten minutes. Does your doctor, say you tell him a dream at the beginning, and then you go to things which seem to have nothing to do with it, docs he bring it all back to the dream?

MARSHA: Yeah.

VINCENT: That's scary, because it seems like everything you say in there really does count. I mean there's no getting away from it, it's not just theory, it's all true. Because after that I proceeded to talk about your doctor being out here and how you thought he was interested in me at that party or something— I couldn't even remember what it was.

MARSHA: I never said that.

VINCENT: Yes you did. You said he was watching me, studying me, to see what I was like.

MARSHA: I did not.

VINCENT: You did so.

MARSHA: I did not.

VINCENT: You did not?

MARSHA: No. Go ahead.

VINCENT: If you did not, what's the sense in going ahead?

MARSHA: I'd still like to hear what you have to say.

VINCENT: That's all there was. She asked me his name and I said Merrill Johnston. She said she never heard of him. Then I put her down for that, I said many people in New York know Merrill Johnston.

MARSHA: Is she supposed to know every good psychiatrist?

VINCENT: No, is she? Anyway, she said I was using the fact that he was out here and at a party—

MARSHA: Against her.

VINCENT: Against her, because she lives a very stable Connecticut garden life. You know at one point I got very scared. I looked down at her desk and I saw the notes she had been taking on me. There were two doodles—does your doctor doodle?

MARSHA: He doesn't take notes.

VINCENT: Two completely schizophrenic, psychotic profiles, very hard, etched way into the paper. One was a grotesque woman's face. I got terrified, Marshie.

MARSHA: I hate note-taking. Does she laugh?

VINCENT: She laughed a lot until I told her to stop because she was always laughing when I told her sad stories. It's true. Now she doesn't laugh anymore, but I have a riot of a time.

MARSHA: I'm always trying to make Merrill Johnston laugh, to entertain him. Do you laugh?

VINCENT: Never.

MARSHA: Do you smile?

VINCENT: No, I go into funks. I only smile when she says something clever. She's very eerie, you know, she always can tell what I'm thinking.

MARSHA: So can I.

VINCENT: As brilliant as she is, though, I think she gets very upset when I criticize her.

MARSHA: No, that's your projection. I used to think he did too, I used to feel sorry for him and think he'd be crushed. They know it's part of the thing, darling. It's defensive.

VINCENT: Is it really?

MARSHA: Yeah, I always used to tell him he didn't know his business. Remember the time I went to Harlem? Did you ever hear that story?

VINCENT: You did really? Oh that's so *Lost Boundaries*.

MARSHA: I had been feeling that I couldn't establish any contact with him. I left his office and I went to the subway. Now I *certainly* know which subway takes me home! Suddenly I found myself on the A train past 59th Street and the next thing I knew I was at 125th Street. It was a cold snowy night, I was surrounded by Negroes, and I just wandered the streets, looking for my Negro doctor, who's probably never been in Harlem in his life.

VINCENT: Boy, the sun's fantastic.

MARSHA: Gorgeous.

VINCENT: I hate the beach though.

MARSHA: I don't.

VINCENT: So what did you talk to him about for two hours?

MARSHA: I found the time went very quickly. There was no pressure, I didn't look at the clock every minute. Do you look at the clock always?

VINCENT: Never. I don't want to know if she's keeping me overtime because then I'd have to go.

MARSHA: He's never kept me a second overtime, so that's no problem.

VINCENT: Maybe you need that kind of discipline, maybe you need somebody who doesn't give in to you all the time. Your parents would give you *three* hours if they were your psychiatrist. I'm going to teach you how to swim this summer, Marshie. Please, please let me touch you.

MARSHA: No!

VINCENT: They're so beautiful in the bikini. How come you never say anything about me?

MARSHA: I don't see as much as you do.

VINCENT: Look. It's not bad, is it, with a bathing suit on, not hard?

MARSHA: Can I touch it?

VINCENT: No, it might get hard. Marshie, get your hand away— you've never done that before. Are you going to tell your doctor what you just did?

MARSHA: Sure, after all, life is risk.

VINCENT: Life is a bris. Do you know that my life really began for me when it became Jewish? The first part of it was awful when it was only with Christians. It was horrible, I used to hate to come home for lunch, I was afraid of being beaten up by all the rotten Catholics on the street.

MARSHA: But you were a Catholic.

VINCENT: Yeah, but I went to public school and I was Italian. They hated me.

MARSHA: I never knew that.

VINCENT: I was Italian, you knew *that*.

MARSHA: You mean they were Irish.

VINCENT: They were all freckles with blue eyes and I was dark-haired and olive. They hated me.

MARSHA: Were you the only one?

VINCENT: The only one on the block. But my life became terrific when I went to high school and all my friends were Jewish. Now it's sort of balanced out, half and half. Except my psychoanalyst is Jewish, and I'm sure that's all that counts.

MARSHA: They're all Jewish.

VINCENT: There are very few Italians, that's for sure.

MARSHA: Sick Joan's doctor is named Martucci.

VINCENT: Really?

MARSHA: But it's spelled in some Jewish way.

VINCENT: Yeah, it ends with a berg.

MARSHA: No, stein. Martuccistein. Next weekend you aren't having any Jews out, Vinnie. Three Gentiles.

VINCENT: Yes, but the thing is that finally you arrive at a third period, which I'm in now, you go from black to white and then you get gray, and all your friends who are Christian—

MARSHA: Are very Jewish.

VINCENT: Right, are very Jewish. All Italians are Jewish, real Italians from Italy.

MARSHA: Tim Cullen is not in the least Jewish.

VINCENT: No, but he's so beautifully the opposite of it that he becomes algebraically the same thing. Did I ever tell you that when I was in college, I not only wore a Jewish star to seem Jewish, but I would lose it on purpose every month so I could put on the bulletin board "Vince Miano Lost One Jewish Star."

MARSHA: Vinnie, you have terrific fillings.

VINCENT: You mean a lot of them?

MARSHA: No, they're a beautiful copper color.

VINCENT: Look at this. You know how short Alan Ladd is?

MARSHA: Was. Why, is there a picture that finally shows it?

VINCENT: Look at this magazine. You can tell here how short he was. And there's a girl who's half his size. How small can *she* be?

MARSHA: But look how she's leaning on a chair with her legs collapsed.

VINCENT: You know he was my favorite? When I was a child, he was my absolute favorite.

MARSHA: Mine too. Do you have any idea why?

VINCENT: He had a perfect marriage, you know.

MARSHA: Do you have any idea why he was your favorite? I can't understand how we thought he was attractive. I wouldn't look at him twice now.

VINCENT: That's because you've grown up, my hon. You know I'm getting worried about you, Marsh.

MARSHA: Why? You mean lethargic?

VINCENT: Yeah, I think you're getting very lethargic. Maybe it's a reaction to not going in to see your doctor anymore. You're trying to make yourself sick, with your legs aching and everything.

MARSHA: My legs aren't aching anymore.

VINCENT: I think you have a very low sex threshold.

MARSHA: What do you mean?

VINCENT: I mean you're really not very interested in sex, you don't have much sexual desire. I think you just need affection.

MARSHA: No, I just don't show it because the people I'm sleeping with aren't the right people.

VINCENT: Will they ever be?

MARSHA: When there *was* one, I was insatiable.

VINCENT: You were not. Who? Zeke? You were insatiable?

MARSHA: With Zeke I was insatiable: I was totally, perpetually, persistently sexed-up.

VINCENT: Marshie, I think we're in trouble. We've come to a sunless beach. Here it comes, here it comes. Let's shoot it down as it's coming. Wouldn't it be awful if it was the shadow of some monster?

MARSHA: It's only a cloud, hon.

VINCENT: Listen, I'll drop you off and bring the car back later.

MARSHA: No, you can't take the car.

VINCENT: I have to, so I can buy strandbeagles on the way.

MARSHA: What?

VINCENT: Strawberries for my Nico when he comes home. You realize that I won't be going to get the afternoon mail anymore? I won't need to because everything I want will be here. I won't have to be compulsive. I can be restrained and constrained. My Nico's very unneurotic.

MARSHA: What do you mean?

VINCENT: His responses. He's so sure of himself, he's so sure of himself that it's beautiful. He's very good to me, Marshie.

MARSHA: Wait a minute. I'm dropping *you* off because I need cottage cheese.

VINCENT: I know. Do you think the iconography in my painting is slight?

MARSHA: No.

VINCENT: It's everyday material.

MARSHA: I think it's massive. I'm getting very depressed.

VINCENT: You're getting anxious because Tim's coming out this weekend. You have to sleep with him and you don't want to, but getting depressed is not going to solve anything.

MARSHA: I *do* want to sleep with him.

VINCENT: No you don't. I was just thinking about Emily—you know you're getting to be a smoking addict, Marshie—and what she does is perfectly normal.

MARSHA: What does she do normally?

VINCENT: She drinks and gets drunk. It's our response that's abnormal.

MARSHA: No, sweetheart, you're contradicting everything we agreed on, about her abnormal reaction to drink. She loses her whole reality.

VINCENT: I'm saying she's an alcoholic but it doesn't matter.

MARSHA: She just better be good this weekend. There are going to be a lot of Fourth of July parties and she just better be good.

VINCENT: What did you just do? Is it an age we're getting to that we're all belching? Clem kept doing it last time I was with him.

MARSHA: Emily too. Are they older than we are?

VINCENT: Certainly, if you measure it by glasses of wine.

MARSHA: How old is Clem?

VINCENT: Clem is seven thousand eight glasses of scotch.

MARSHA: No, how old is he?

VINCENT: Thirty-one.

MARSHA: And how old am I?

VINCENT: Thirty-one.

MARSHA: And Emily?

VINCENT: Thirty-one, two.

MARSHA: Twenty-nine.

VINCENT: Is she really? Oh, that's doubly tragic. She's going to commit suicide when she's thirty.

MARSHA: Oh shut up.

VINCENT: You don't think she could commit suicide?

MARSHA: Never.

VINCENT: I don't really think so either. She could have maybe a year ago, but she won't now.

MARSHA: She never would have.

VINCENT: Why? Is she too weak or too strong?

MARSHA: Too strong.

VINCENT: You're sure?

MARSHA: I know my Emmy.

3. EMILY'S FIRST VISIT TO MARSHA'S SUMMER HOUSE

EMILY: I'm putting a little gorgonzola into the salad dressing to brighten it up. Is there any sour cream or anything like that?

MARSHA: Nothing of that nature.

EMILY: The salad has to marinate.

MARSHA: It's marinating in water at this moment.

EMILY: Could you limp it out of the water, helper that you are? Marinating in water, pretty funny. That's one of your real cul-de-sac remarks. Hey, I haven't told you about the big breakthrough I had last week. I had a very big breakthrough.

MARSHA: What was the breakthrough?

EMILY: I did a scene in class, that's what it was really all about. I had to do a monologue and I picked the end of *La Notte*, where she reads the letter. And it was fantastic, it was the best work I've ever done for myself. I was able to beat a problem that I've never been able to beat before. I won't go into the whole complicated nature of it, but it had to do with like when you're all alone and you have certain kinds of private thoughts, maybe you read a love letter and you cry, in a way you could never cry if anyone was with you. Well I was able to do that on the stage, with all those people watching me, absolutely purely, with *no* concern for the audience. It was an incredible thing—I think very few actors ever do it. You see, as I read the letter, I personalized it as if it was from Philippe, I recreated our little apartment in Paris. The scene starts and as I read this letter, the tears begin to fall down my face, it was the most intimate private thing. Acting-wise it was a very big breakthrough and everybody loved it. They had tears in their eyes too.

I was marvelous, not marvelous the way I might be at a party, but pure, private and pure, simple and moving. And what I did was right scene-wise, it was right for the interpretation of the character and everything else. So anyway, the next night I went to a party where Michael Christy was, and I was completely calm. And then I realized what it was all about. It wasn't that I had suddenly gotten healthier, it was that in the acting I was able to put my feelings where they belonged. Those feelings, those hysterical feelings for Michael Christy, they're not really frantic, hysterical feelings. They're damaged, abused love feelings about Philippe, and I brought them to my acting, I was able to feel them at the right place about the right things, about Philippe, so they weren't repressed, neurotic, to be pushed into other channels and played out with Michael Christy. It was the first time I was able to do it on the stage and it had a real effect on my life. It's not as moving to translate it verbally.

MARSHA: Yes it is.

EMILY: So how do you like my big breakthrough story?

MARSHA: I like it. And I love this salad dressing.

EMILY: You and your love, love this and love that.

MARSHA: Hello this, hello that. Can I take this wing?

EMILY: Yes, it's for you. I was going to give you both of them but then I got interested in one myself. I'm getting interested in myself myself lately. You promised to discuss that with me. When you masturbate, how do you do it?

MARSHA: Some dinner talk. All right, I lie on my stomach, I have to be wearing some clothing.

EMILY: You do? Why?

MARSHA: I don't know, I can't stand my naked flesh.

EMILY: That's so sweet. You have to have a nightie on or something?

MARSHA: Anything. If worse comes to worse, I use the sheet.

EMILY: And what do you do? You rub your clitoris until you have an orgasm? How many times can you do it in a day?

MARSHA: Once.

EMILY: I can do it up to ten times.

MARSHA: I can't even do it once anymore. It bores me, I cut off. Except sometimes when I'm reading something sexy in a book, I have to make a dash for the bed.

EMILY: That happens to me constantly.

MARSHA: It does? Do you have to have some inspiration?

EMILY: Like what?

MARSHA: Literature or something.

EMILY: Never. I don't even use fantasies, I don't need a thing.

MARSHA: I used to look at Zeke's picture. How do you do it?

EMILY: I do it any way at all.

MARSHA: Yeah, even on the toilet.

EMILY: I masturbate on the toilet, when I'm wiping myself I get all hot and I masturbate. Everybody does, more or less. I masturbated at Philippe's parents' once. I went to a dinner party at their house and I got horny for no reason at all, went to the bathroom and jerked off one two three. Standing up.

MARSHA: Girls don't jerk off.

EMILY: I did.

MARSHA: You know what was the sickest thing I ever did? I must have told you.

EMILY: What?

MARSHA: On Eliot Simon's bathroom rug. There were some other people there, we were sitting and talking, and suddenly I got a fantastic, powerful wave.

EMILY: To masturbate.

MARSHA: To anything. I went into the bathroom and—I never did this before or after—it was a small bathroom with this red shag rug on the floor, and I lay down on it and masturbated. And the horrible thing was that when I got up, I was full of that red shag. It was very embarrassing. I couldn't pick it off, it would have taken an hour. And I kept thinking how will they think she got the rug on her?

EMILY: Fell down.

MARSHA: Fell down! And then rolled all over?

EMILY: You fell down and you liked it there. Let me think. On the train to Paris when Kennedy died, I masturbated. I masturbate sitting in a chair talking on the telephone, I masturbate in bed, on my side, on my back, on my front, any way at all.

MARSHA: On the telephone? What do you say? Excuse me please while I come?

EMILY: I don't say a word.

MARSHA: You keep the conversation going while you're having an orgasm? Must be some wracking experience!

EMILY: No, I keep the conversation going while I'm *masturbating*, then I shut up while I'm having the orgasm.

MARSHA: I don't believe you. How often have you done it?

EMILY: Maybe twice.

MARSHA: With who?

EMILY: I don't remember.

MARSHA: If you've ever done it talking to me, I'm hanging up.

EMILY: Never did.

MARSHA: You have an orgasm every time you masturbate?

EMILY: I wouldn't masturbate without having an orgasm. But how long does the whole thing last anyway?

MARSHA: Well I'm sorry, I have to concentrate. I can't even have the radio on.

EMILY: I'd say it lasts about three seconds, that's all.

MARSHA: I have to have the utmost concentration. You leave the radio on and everything? I can't stand the rhythms of the music.

EMILY: Marsha, do you think there's anything sick about our friendship?

MARSHA: It's unusual.

EMILY: It *is* unusual, it's unique. I'll tell you what my sister said; she said if you meet a man and have a relationship with him, do you think you're going to share it with Marsha and Sick Joan? I said the nature of my life is to share a lot, I share almost everything.

MARSHA: Yeah, but you won't share as much then as you do now about someone you're not having a real relationship with.

EMILY: What do you mean?

MARSHA: I mean that you can share more about a Michael Christy *this* way than if you were living with him. Your loyalties would switch.

EMILY: Not the loyalties, the needs.

MARSHA: The loyalties too. You should have a deeper loyalty to the man. You can't go running around telling everything, that he's impotent or this or that.

EMILY: You're right, I can't. I remember you never talked about how Zeke was in bed.

MARSHA: That was something else, I wasn't as close to you then, darling. I was *willing* to tell anyone who would listen.

EMILY: No, when we *were* close, when we got close again, you didn't want to talk about it.

MARSHA: When I was seeing Zeke, you were very sick.

EMILY: How sick was I?

MARSHA: I couldn't talk to you, man.

EMILY: Could you talk to me woman?

MARSHA: Woman to woman, one to one.

EMILY: You couldn't talk to me? But you were calling me and making sure I was okay when you were with Zeke and making spaghetti sauce. His children were there, you were spreading the tablecloths for them.

MARSHA: So I called you, so what? You never knew the depths of what was happening to me. . . . What's on this? Just butter? Great. Do you like cabbage?

EMILY: Adore it. I didn't even know you liked it.

MARSHA: It's underplayed.

EMILY: Definitely. And fantastically healthy, that's what I like about it.

MARSHA: It is?

EMILY: Oh God, it's the healthiest thing in the world. You know it's interesting, I can't get over the relationship of three human beings, you, Vinnie and me. The only three people I know who I really think might possibly be able to do something together. What can you do in three? Take a trip or something like that?

MARSHA: I don't know if we could.

EMILY: I don't either. We're all so difficult.

MARSHA: I'm much more comfortable alone with either one of you. I don't really like it in three.

EMILY: Really? I love being with you and Vincie. But then you're always more comfortable in twos.

MARSHA: I really am. Are you finished with the eating?

EMILY: No, I have to have a little more cabbage. You know I just realized something about Vinnie. With certain exceptions, Vinnie surrounds himself with inferior people.

MARSHA: The exceptions being me, Nico and you?

EMILY: Yeah, he has very ineffectual friends that he completely dominates.

MARSHA: I would say that there are three major relationships in Vinnie's life. Do you know who they are?

EMILY: His analyst aside, right?

MARSHA: Yeah.

EMILY: You and Nico. I'm putting myself aside also, because I'm too recent.

MARSHA: Yeah, now what's the third key relationship? Do you know?

EMILY: Would I know? Should I know?

MARSHA: Yes.

EMILY: It's not an ex-lover?

MARSHA: It is.

EMILY: Then it's Clem?

MARSHA: Right, Clem is still one of his key relationships. He has so much love-hate left for Clem, Clem calls him on the phone and no matter what happens, he's shaken up for three days—by Clem's successes, Clem's failures, every action of Clem's is fantastically important to him. He might even be more important than Nico or me in the effect on his life. You know Clem thinks of himself as one of the great sado-masochists of our time.

EMILY: You mean as a Genet?

MARSHA: Yeah, he has a real Genet image of himself. He's got in a way a very criminal mentality, he's very death oriented. He picks

up these rough truck-driver types and they have *ménages à* any
number you can mention.

EMILY: He seems very vain.

MARSHA: Very vain, very bright, and he's funny, he's talented.

EMILY: Is he good?

MARSHA: You mean is he a good person? I don't know. He's vulnerable.

EMILY: Vinnie's very vulnerable too.

MARSHA: I don't want to get into Vinnie for the moment.

EMILY: But does he want to get into you? The one thing I don't understand is his relationship with Nico. You don't either, do you?

MARSHA: No.

EMILY: I just don't get it, Marsha, so help me God. Listen, have you
seen *any*one out here so far who's available?

MARSHA: No one.

EMILY: If I find out about an interesting-sounding party tonight,
are you interested in going?

MARSHA: What about Vinnie? Did he say he was coming over?

EMILY: No, I think he wants to be alone with his Nico before the
weekend guests arrive. Look, Marshie, we're two beautiful
women and we have to start making inroads.

4. EMILY'S PROBLEMS ARE
DISCUSSED ON THE BEACH

EMILY: I have multiple involvements and I think I always will. But I don't really want to discuss it.

VINCENT: Do you feel any of them have come to fruition?

EMILY: No.

VINCENT: That's the point. I don't mind multiple involvements if a couple of them are fulfilled. My whole point is that you expend all your creative energies on your love objects.

EMILY: You think so?

VINCENT: I know so.

EMILY: Let's discuss it. Tell me about my love objects and tell me why Michael Christy's a waste of time.

VINCENT: He's a waste of time, my dear, because he doesn't love you. He's just a sexual interest.

EMILY: No, he's a *love* interest, he's not a sexual interest.

VINCENT: He *is* a sexual interest, because your only relationship with him is sexual.

EMILY: You are *insane!*

VINCENT: Are you going to tell me it's a talking, caring, affectionate relationship?

EMILY: When we're together, it certainly is.

VINCENT: Then why do you both have to get immediately drunk every time?

EMILY: That's not because it's sexual, it's because it's emotional.

VINCENT: It's because neither of you can relate emotionally. You always pick people, situations, which cannot give you any sort of return. You pick twisted trees to nourish, instead of giving your fertilizer to new young ones.

EMILY: Wait a second. What about Philippe Rocheau? Philippe Rocheau on the surface, at least on certain levels, is a very feeling, emotional kind of person, although he's not really. My picking him was not because I'm afraid to give and afraid to love.

VINCENT: That was five years ago, I don't know about that. I'm talking about now.

MARSHA: We know about now, let's talk about the future.

VINCENT: All right, let's talk about *her* future. How do you see yourself in the future? The future, you know, is what you're doing about the present.

EMILY: Of course the future's the present.

VINCENT: The future is like the next word I'm going to say, which then immediately becomes the past. There is no present, only the future and the past. Marshie, you're getting a terrible sunburn. I would cover it up.

MARSHA: I have nothing to cover it with.

VINCENT: Take off your bathing suit and cover it with that.

EMILY: You know you criticize me, but you don't understand certain things in my background. Do you know my father had an entire library of Indian philosophy, life after death? My father was a fantastic moral, spiritual person who wrote letters to the Pope which were printed in *The New York Times* and everything else. My sister thinks my father was a hero.

VINCENT: I've heard all that before.

MARSHA: So have I.

EMILY: But you must understand where it all comes from.

VINCENT: All right, so that's where it all comes from. Does that mean you have to hold on to it forever?

EMILY: Okay, what *am* I supposed to believe?

MARSHA: Just that there is good and bad in people.

EMILY: Don't you think I believe that? That's the most simple-minded thing I ever heard in my life.

MARSHA: But you don't believe it in a realistic way. You think they're all good, they're pure, they're deep, they're this, they're that. You don't basically believe that either Zeke or Michael could be anything but good and pure and sweet.

EMILY: I really do believe that Michael is pure.

MARSHA: I don't for a minute, and I hardly even know him.

VINCENT: The thing is, Emmy, you are a product of the nineteenth century: you believe that sadness implies goodness and suffering implies purity. And you think that when you find someone who is sick in the head, they must be good because they've suffered.

MARSHA: Yes, you're always saying that deep underneath all the shit, somewhere at the bottom of the left toe, they're good. Zeke has ruined the lives of his wife and his children, and I'm sure Michael has ruined the lives of *his* wife and child. That's not being so good, is it, Vinnie?

EMILY: But I know all that. I don't get what you're telling me that you think I don't know.

MARSHA: I'm saying that most people are not nice, that they're selfish and *that's* their main motivation in life, to get what they can for themselves.

EMILY: Well let me ask you this then—why is Michael Christy *very* well loved?

MARSHA: Because he's all fucked up and he's suffering.

VINCENT: All right, and who are the people who love him?

EMILY: The people who love him are the people who've had the opportunity to really know him.

VINCENT: Yeah, but what are they?

EMILY: Fucked up.

VINCENT: Exactly.

EMILY: Some of them aren't.

VINCENT: There are very few people in that whole art world who aren't fucked up, darling.

EMILY: Well, Zeke Sutherland may be an idiot and everything else, but he does love Mike.

VINCENT: Is he some sort of love meter? You say to me people love him, then you point to somebody who's got not one bit of love in him.

EMILY: Now you're saying something which philosophically just doesn't hold water. You're saying if someone is really very well loved, then you have to examine all the people who love him and think oh my God, they're so *manqué* and they're so deficient emotionally that of course they could love him. I'm sorry, there's something beyond that. If someone is well loved, he is well loved.

VINCENT: I think lots of people are well loved who are very unlovable. Just look at idols, public idols.

EMILY: Darling, public idols are not well loved. Who? L. B. Johnson? Besides, there are all kinds of sensational public relations things going to elicit love for these people.

VINCENT: Oh what's love anyway? Love is a very subjective thing, don't bullshit me.

EMILY: Who's saying it isn't subjective?

VINCENT: Well you're making it like some ultimate truth. You know it's possible to love people for their defects as well as their virtues. And don't get arrogant just because we happen to be talking about the man you love. What you're saying is that because people love him, he's not defective.

EMILY: I'm not saying he's not defective.

VINCENT: You know I love little dogs that have hurt themselves much more than ones that can run and have a good time.

EMILY: I still think there must be a basic goodness in someone who is loved by a lot of people. I'm sorry, I really do.

VINCENT: I think there's a goodness about the people who can love, I don't know about the object. There's more goodness in *you* ... You see you can't admit it because that would mean you're completely wrong. I'll tell you something, your love is really very egotistical, because it's always for people who are fantastically less than you and destroyed and distraught. And by loving them, you're helping them; it's egotistical because it makes you something more than you are. Love someone equal to you and see if you can give something to *that* person.

EMILY: Well I'll go along with that, but I don't understand how it relates to what you want me to learn about people being bad.

VINCENT: Oh listen, I didn't say that, it was Marsha. I certainly don't think Michael Christy is a bad person.

EMILY: I think Zeke Sutherland is like fifty times worse than what's-his-name, Michael. I really do.

VINCENT: That's like taking two defective apples out of a bushel and saying one's better than the other.

EMILY: I think Zeke socially is one of the most evil people in the whole world. He makes anyone who speaks to him feel like a piece of shit.

MARSHA: I agree. He's awful. And yet he's loved too. Believe me, I love him still, even though I think he's evil.

VINCENT: You see, Emily, I'm not talking about Christy, I'm not talking about anyone specific. I'm talking about you; I'm talking about setting up situations in which you cannot have a positive love relationship, you can only have a negative one.

EMILY: What is a negative love relationship?

VINCENT: One in which there is no return.

EMILY: Oh Philippe loved me, darling, he really did.

VINCENT: I'm not talking about him. I'm talking about this past year, about *you now*, the length of time I've known you, and it seems to me a year is a long enough time to use as a barometer about one's life, particularly at this crucial point, when you're thirty years old.

EMILY: No, because this year has still been all about Philippe.

VINCENT: All right, so maybe we should put off this conversation until next summer.

EMILY: Is that true or isn't it, Marshie, about this whole year?

VINCENT: Well that's saying a lot about you, because this goes back again to how you let men completely destroy you and activate your whole life. The idea that someone you stopped seeing more

than a year ago determines everything you do the whole following year, that makes his role in your life very positive. So when
you talk to me about Philippe being a rat and weak and everything, I say Philippe's a pretty genius of a kid.

EMILY: Darling, Michael Christy is about Philippe, he's not about
Michael.

VINCENT: I don't think Philippe or Michael are about anything, I
think it's all hang-ups about your father. That's what's negative
about these relationships. Love should be in terms of you and the
other person. You know, there are certain people, like Genêt and
Bacon, who probably can't love, but they still function and have a
strangely positive perverted kind of life. Your life is not that positive. And you know I wouldn't be saying all this if I didn't think
you had fantastic potential. You're like a gigantically big bud that
you look at and say oh my God, this is going to make a big beautiful flower some day. But you know the thing about that bud? It's
got funny little bugs crawling all over it.

5. A STORY FROM EMILY'S CHILDHOOD

EMILY: I'm trying to think how old I was. I guess between the ages of five and twelve. I went to this school for very bright little girls and boys, and they had this bus that used to pick us up, called Jaybees.

MARSHA: The bus had a name?

EMILY: Yeah, it was a private bus that used to pick you up at your door. I lived at 10 East 79th Street, and I was picked up about a quarter of nine every morning, as the bus went along its selective route, picking these high-minded children up for school. All my friendships were formed on that bus. For instance I had one friend who was horrible, he was very rich and very fat, and his mother made him a lunch which he promptly ate as soon as he got on the bus.

MARSHA: What did he eat at lunchtime?

EMILY: Bought a school lunch. So he had breakfast, then he had his bag of lunch on the bus about a half-hour later, and then he had his regular lunch during lunch period. Also I remember there was this guy named Ernest Enfield who was absolutely madly in love with me. He was a shy, retiring boy and also a brat. But really very nice. He used to antagonize the teacher, Barbara Mulligan.

MARSHA: The teacher?

EMILY: Yes, I had a teacher named Barbara Mulligan. She used to bring liverwurst sandwiches that were mixed up with mayonnaise and chopped pickles and she would eat them on this strange kind of tired-looking bread. It was very sad, she wrapped them in waxed paper. I couldn't stand it. She was very skinny and she

wore those heavy brown cotton stockings. One day she slapped
Ernest Enfield across the face and I cried, because I really liked
him. Anyway, I had all kinds of friends on that bus. There were
twin girls who were both fat, Florence and her sister. I don't know
if they were twins or just looked like twins, but they had long
blond hair that kept getting longer and longer. I saw one of them
a couple of years ago in Central Park and she still had the long
blond hair, I think it's been growing ever since. So. The girl who
got on the bus with me, who lived in my house, was named
Wilma. She was very pretty because she was already mature, in a
way that I didn't know anything about. Her mother wanted her
to be a little lady and she was very feminine. She used to wear a
certain kind of cologne and she had short little hair that was in
Shirley Temple ringlets. She was very sweet. She had a much better time usually than I did because her mother was very good to
her. She had a doll collection. I had only one awful doll, and
whenever we played dolls, she naturally always had the better
doll. Finally one day, her mother said listen, I'll take you two girls
to a wig house and you can buy wigs for your dolls. So I went with
Wilma and she picked out a wig and I picked out a wig. She
picked out this absolutely gorgeous wig with red hair that you
could wash and set.

MARSHA: Um.

EMILY: You could braid it, you could put it up or wear it down, you
could have bangs, you could curl it, you could wear it straight,
you could have a ponytail, anything. And I picked out a really
ugly wig. I mean I didn't know any better. I picked out this sad
little wig and when we got home and started playing with our
dolls, I began to realize how fantastic her wig was, Wilma's wig.

MARSHA: Yeah.

EMILY: We kept playing and the weeks went by. Wilma had always
coveted this collection I had of glamour girl trading cards. I had
all those *Esquire* girls and Varga girls. There was one called *The
Lace Shawl*, which was sort of a very old-fashioned girl wearing a
lace shawl except she was nude. And Wilma really liked my col-

lection. It was the only thing I had that I was proud of, that I had made an effort on, that was individual, that was mine. She really wanted it and I really wanted that gorgeous doll she had with the red hair. So one day, we were playing in her house, we made the trade: I gave her my whole collection of glamour girl trading cards and she gave me the doll with the red hair. I took that doll upstairs, I washed its hair, I set it, I combed it out, I set it again, I gave it this hairdo and that hairdo, and when I went to sleep that night I put the doll on the pillow right beside me. I was madly in love with that doll. The next morning the phone rang, I was getting ready for school, the phone rang and I heard hello? It was my mother. Oh yes, Mrs. Hargarther.

MARSHA: What was her name?

EMILY: No, maybe she called her Estelle. It was Wilma's mother. Yes Estelle, yes she does. Oh. Oh, it's Wilma's doll. Oh, I see. No no no, I'll tell her. That's fine. Of course. Terrible. Yes I will. 'Bye. My mother told me that Wilma's mother said Wilma wanted her doll back and she would return the trading cards. So my mother scolded me and sent me downstairs by myself with the doll in my arms and I waited for Wilma to come down. While I was waiting—I was out on the sidewalk looking for the bus—I forget if it was winter or spring or whatever the hell it was—I kept looking at the doll and looking at the post that held up the canopy, and at a certain point, I found myself bashing the head of the doll against the post. I started to stamp on the face, I completely destroyed the doll. I took the hair and I chewed it up.

MARSHA: Some story.

EMILY: Very sad story, isn't it?

MARSHA: Yup.

EMILY: You should have seen what happened then. Wilma became hysterical, she called her mother, her mother called my mother, my mother came down and told them how terrible I was and everything else. Very sad story. I have so many sad childhood stories I could tell you.

6. WATCHING TIM ON THE BEACH

EMILY: Look at Tim over there. Doesn't he look Persian, with the dark glasses and the moustache and the towel on his head?

VINCENT: He wants to do a work of art with me. A major American work of art—that's the only kind I do.

MARSHA: Yes, but he can't paint, you know. Although he used to do fantastic *trompe l'oeils.*

EMILY: Fool the eyes.

VINCENT: Foulards? Oh, I used to do those too, and also paisleys.

MARSHA: What could you do together?

VINCENT: I could paint on one of his white sculptures. Why not? They're both real life.

MARSHA: No, yours is real-life pornography, his is abstract.

VINCENT: Mine is the most pornographic art in New York.

EMILY: Yours is obscene, to quote Dr. Fass.

VINCENT: Yes, Nathan Fass, major American art critic, says Vincent Miano's work is obscene.

EMILY: And Emily Benson, major-major American art critic, says that's not what it's about at all. It's about a juxtaposition of images, which arouses upsetting anxieties.

VINCENT: I want that piped into subway johns all over New York.

MARSHA: Subway johns, that's where Tim said Clem hangs out. And funeral parlors. You know Clem told him he's a necrophiliac?

VINCENT: He's a negrophiliac? Clem makes love to Negroes?

MARSHA: No. They were talking about subway johns.

EMILY: That's not negrophilia, that's subwayphilia.

MARSHA: That's metrophilia.

VINCENT: Feelyaphilia.

EMILY: Fellatiophilia. Did you hear what I said? Fellatiophilia.

VINCENT: What ever happened to plain old Ophelia?

MARSHA: He also makes it with many spades.

VINCENT: Well now that *is* perverse. I tried it once with a hoe, but never a spade.

EMILY: Look at Diana working with her needlework over there.

VINCENT: That family unit, it's just like Coney Island.

EMILY: She's sewing a cock cover.

MARSHA: A what?

EMILY: A cock cover.

VINCENT: He needs it. You know coming in contact with the art world again brings out all my anxieties and everything, it's just fantastic. Tim *is* the art world, you know. Emily, how does that guy get such a tight body?

EMILY: It's because he's tight spiritually. You know it's very interesting that Emil never comes over and says hello to anyone.

MARSHA: Yeah.

EMILY: Why do people always expect us to do the going over and saying hello? I'm sorry.

VINCENT: We'll wave to them when we leave.

MARSHA: You know Tim said this collector said that Oliver Haupt thinks he's the hottest young sculptor in town.

VINCENT: Really?

MARSHA: I think he should try to get a show with Oliver Haupt.

VINCENT: My doctor told me I could get dandruff on my penis.

EMILY: From what?

VINCENT: I have dandruff in my hair, I can get it on my eyebrows, on my chest, under my arms.

MARSHA: Come on, what about Oliver Haupt? Do you think Tim should go to him and be honest and say he's looking for a new gallery?

VINCENT: I think he definitely should. It might be good for Zinner to know he's thinking of leaving. The thing is, there are just a handful of galleries that would pay him a monthly salary.

MARSHA: Yeah, and he owes Zinner money too.

VINCENT: He does?

MARSHA: He owes them four thousand dollars. At least.

VINCENT: He should marry a rich girl. He should marry your father.

MARSHA: He could tell Oliver Haupt he'll go with him if he pays off his debts.

EMILY: Or tell Zinner he has some hot information worth four thousand dollars. Like he'll tell the world Dolph Zinner is queer. By the way, Vinnie, I found out in this book that masturbation is completely homosexual.

VINCENT: Masturbation is no good. I don't do it anymore.

EMILY: Don't be ridiculous, darling, it can be very important. It prevents social crime, because a criminal lives out a fantasy life when he masturbates. With the risk of unsettling you a little bit, Marsha, I'm going to lean my head on your leg.

MARSHA: Vinnie, she's threatening me.

VINCENT: Marshie, you're getting an erection.

EMILY: She's been masturbating too much.

VINCENT: Or not enough.

EMILY: Vinnie, you have beautiful hands.

VINCENT: Thank you, and you have a beautiful face. You know, I can get away with all sorts of physical things with women.

EMILY: Vinnie, I do not like erotic behavior on the beach.

VINCENT: Why? It's a good answer for social crime. It all depends how you do it. Style is everything. That's why most actors are lousy, because they're not intelligent. I was telling Emmy that before. I told her she's got everything: she's got looks, talent, she's got that special something to make her the intimate star of the theatre.

MARSHA: I don't think she wants to be a star.

VINCENT: She doesn't. She doesn't even want to be in the theatre. You know what she wants? She wants when she's out here in three years to come on this beach and for everyone to know who she is.

EMILY: I've *always* had that need.

VINCENT: I have it too.

MARSHA: I would love to be famous.

VINCENT: I want to go to the laundromat, come out with my bag, and have all the people waiting for the bus in front of it know who I am.

MARSHA: Famous artists don't become that much of a star.

EMILY: Famous actors do.

VINCENT: Andy Warhol is.

MARSHA: What about writers?

EMILY: Rona Jaffe, people don't know her.

VINCENT: Mary McCarthy they do.

MARSHA: No, not on the street.

VINCENT: Susan Sontag's gotten pretty famous. But I don't want just *anyone* to know me, I don't want to be like an Andy Griffith or an Andy Williams.

MARSHA: I do.

EMILY: Can't we be serious for a minute? Can't we all interpret the meaning of something? Like what does it mean that this beach ball is between my legs? Beyond the obvious, what do you think it means, Vinnie?

VINCENT: I think it means that it's a boring idea. What do you think it means?

MARSHA: That she's trying to simulate one of Tim's sculptures.

VINCENT: Okay, what does it mean what Marsha thinks it means?

EMILY: That I'm trying to make one of his sculptures?

VINCENT: Simulate does not mean make. Simulate means to get along with all groups.

EMILY: My analyst says that I interpersonally relate quite well.

VINCENT: Let's try not to talk about you for thirty seconds and see if we can survive.

EMILY: Okay, what can we talk about?

VINCENT: What book was I reading recently? Oh yes, it was Mailer, *An American Dream*, and the strangest thing, he fucks a girl in it, it was his wife, and they both know that they made a baby right in that second.

EMILY: I've heard that before.

MARSHA: I've felt it but it hasn't been true.

EMILY: I've known it and the guy's known it, but the baby hasn't known it.

VINCENT: Let's pretend we don't see them.

EMILY: Why, what are they doing? What are they doing?

VINCENT: They're leaving.

EMILY: We're not saying goodbye to them. Did you say hello to them?

VINCENT: No.

EMILY: I think that was the height of rudeness, their not saying goodbye.

VINCENT: Darling, they're very corny, cheap people. Why don't you get it through your head?

EMILY: He's corny and cheap and he's also the man I gave up my husband for.

VINCENT: Tell me, this Roy Husband of yours, I'm very curious about him. Was he a wonderful person?

EMILY: Fantastic.

MARSHA: No he wasn't.

EMILY: No he wasn't.

MARSHA: He had no soul as far as I could ever see.

EMILY: He had a soul.

MARSHA: Is there any more lemonade?

EMILY: Yeah, tons.

VINCENT: What was your responsibility to him? Your relationship?

EMILY: We were in love with each other, we were both our first loves.

VINCENT: What was the age?

EMILY: The age was twenty.

VINCENT: Was he good in bed?

EMILY: As a matter of fact, he wasn't bad for that age at all.

VINCENT: Are you kidding? That's the age when they're supposed to be good. Passion. I consider passion the important thing, not know-how.

EMILY: I don't. I consider sensual involvement.

VINCENT: That's passion.

EMILY: I have terrible regrets about it at this point.

VINCENT: About the divorce?

EMILY: Yeah, because even though never in a million years would I have wanted to stay married to Roy, he was rich.

MARSHA: Oh God, if you have one single regret about that, you don't deserve our friendship.

VINCENT: You know the thing about you, Emily, you really want to be rich. But for all the wrong reasons, for comfort and security.

EMILY: I want to be rich for one reason only: money. Not so people will think of me as rich, but so I can have whatever I want.

VINCENT: Like what?

EMILY: There's a certain kind of Jaguar car I've always wanted, that has a wooden inside, four doors, it's very, very small.

VINCENT: I know the car.

EMILY: Well I want that car, I really love that car. You know what happened to me, Vinnie? I was at someone's house the other night and a girl offered to drive me home. She was a lesbian, she had just been rejected by some woman, and I said fine. She told me to wait a second while she went down to the garage. She was a very simple girl. She came back up in this car, it wasn't even black, it was so fantastic, it was very, very dark blue. I said where did you get it? She said my boyfriend gave it to me for my birthday.

MARSHA: Maybe you should become a lesbian.

VINCENT: If you were rich and I was a homosexual, you could buy *me* a car. You know something, if we had money, we'd all be very good to each other.

EMILY: Hey, look at that handsome creature over there. Hi, Mister Man, want to be my new hub-hub? I would now like to make some announcements. The month of September is going to bring important tidings for all: the opening of a show of a fine young painter, Vincent Miano, and the publishing of a major breakthrough American novel by Miss Marsha Zoxbaum. More important will be the month of October when Zinner Gallery will surrender cunning Timothy Cullen to another gallery higher up on the artistic spectrum. Then in November we will have the death of Miss Emily Benson, because she just couldn't face all her friends becoming so famous.

VINCENT: There isn't an iota of truth in that, is there, Emily, my darling?

7. MARSHA'S LOVE STORY

MARSHA: My average relationship with a man, actual talking to each other, loving each other, relating to each other, sleeping with each other, is usually one to two weeks in duration. The amount of time I spend feeling rejected, crying over it, not seeing him but living it out, is three to four years.

EMILY: When I was going over the Emil Reinhardt affair with my doctor, he said it sounded like a threepenny novel.

MARSHA: My doctor says my life is a soap opera.

EMILY: Mine said threepenny novel.

MARSHA: Soap opera.

EMILY: His grasp of dialect is different. Anyway, the point is that my syndrome is just the opposite of yours. The most important thing for me is what I trump up before I sleep with a man, like what was going on when I met Emil Reinhardt, the perfumed missives and secret assignations and the ricochet rendezvous. When we finally did make it, it was great, but I really liked the foreplay better than the act itself. Then I went on for two years moaning and groaning for all I was worth. And it wasn't worth that much.

MARSHA: I'm more involved in aftermath and afterbirth; you're involved in the pregnancy.

EMILY: What does it mean? Take Timothy Cullen. You met Timothy Cullen, you said this might be a healthy specimen, I'm giving him a chance. He's Irish, he has a moustache.

MARSHA: Dark glasses.

EMILY: French clothes. He dances. You had a whole thing about how healthy you thought he was. Soon as he met you he wanted to go to bed with you, you wouldn't go to bed with him, right?

MARSHA: Then I started building up a dread.

EMILY: The actual pattern is the first week he loves you, you don't love him. Second week he gets the idea you don't love him and he stops loving you. You get the idea he's not loving you and you start loving him. Third week: zero.

MARSHA: Where are we now, six months later?

EMILY: It ends with you're still in love with him, because it's unresolved. He feels rejected, he finally gets the message you don't want any dirty part of him, cunning as he is.

MARSHA: You know what sticks in my mind? Do you remember there was one night in the Dom, it was in the first week when he was in love with me, and his eyes didn't leave the nape of my neck the whole entire evening? Every time I sensed him coming near me, I zooped up and sat somewhere else.

EMILY: As long as you didn't Zeke up, you're okay.

MARSHA: I couldn't stand the pressure, the clinging.

EMILY: *He* was clinging?

MARSHA: He was clinging. He was calling me up constantly, what are you doing tonight, where will you be tomorrow, where are you every minute of the day?

EMILY: Remember the night you called him twenty-five times? *More* than twenty-five times. He was out all night, you didn't know where, and you kept calling him every two seconds?

MARSHA: The next morning was the big break-up. He found his Marie.

EMILY: Marie the dawn is breaking. Marshie's heart. Go on.

MARSHA: Where? He'll be coming back any second.

EMILY: What if Zeke Sutherland fell in love with you, what would happen?

MARSHA: Even Zeke Sutherland made me nervous when he liked me. But I couldn't get *too* nervous because *he* got nervous so fast I didn't have time.

EMILY: I got nervous to death with Michael Christy. I rejected him.

MARSHA: Then you have the *same* pattern, that the actual relationship is minimal in the gestalt of the whole thing. For me, the actual relationship is something to get over with so I can drop into the mud and my heart can pound dialing a certain number I'm not supposed to dial. That's the essence of it.

EMILY: So all they really are are vehicles for acting things out.

MARSHA: Instruments on which to play my problems.

EMILY: Who said that?

MARSHA: Me.

EMILY: Very good. If art makes visible that which is invisible, you can imagine what problems do. Seriously, what if Zeke Sutherland at some point *really* turned around and did an about— I mean an a-belly face?

MARSHA: Well the classic example of that was Eliot Simon. Our relationship lasted about three weeks of love.

EMILY: Real love? Mutual give and take?

MARSHA: Mutual love. We met and we were stunned and knocked out by the presence of each other. Fantastic opening night scene: we stayed up until dawn and talked, getting to know you, getting to know all about you.

EMILY: Fantastic closing morning scene. Did you go to bed with him right away?

MARSHA: No, I was recovering from an abortion, I wasn't allowed to. All right, so soon after he rejected me, and for two years I was moaning and groaning for all I was worth.

EMILY: It was worth two years.

MARSHA: I'm not so sure. Finally, at some point after years and years of this, he suddenly decides he's in love with me. I must have told you that story.

EMILY: One morning he decides you're the person he's loved all this time?

MARSHA: He just looked at me and saw an entirely new person and fell in love with me.

EMILY: Who were you sleeping with at this point?

MARSHA: All his best friends.

EMILY: Oh. What number is he on the list?

MARSHA: About seven. So he wakes up that morning and he says a very strange thing has happened to me, Marsh. I said what? He said I fell in love with you during the night.

EMILY: All alone?

MARSHA: I was with him. So I said *what*? You're pulling my leg, you're not serious, you're joking. And he said I mean it, I mean it more than anything I've ever meant. Please don't go to work today, don't get out of bed, don't ever leave me. I want to be with you the rest of my life, I want to marry you.

EMILY: And you said—

MARSHA: I said sorry darling, you know I have to go to work.

EMILY: You can't give up your job.

MARSHA: Right, I can't risk my position in life. So I went to work and he called me I might say nine or ten times during the day. I have to see you tonight, I have to be with you, blablabla. I said I'm supposed to have dinner with my father. He said cancel it. I canceled it. I came home, and you know I had made him all these fancy gourmet dinners before—well that night I didn't even feel like cooking an egg, I didn't want to do thing one for him. I just wanted to be alone. I was very nervous.

EMILY: What were you nervous about, Marsha? Here the person you've always loved is finally loving you back.

MARSHA: Oh, guess I didn't realize that. So when he came, I managed to cook some flimsy dinner, and he just sat there, staring at me all through it, he could hardly eat, telling me how he had never had such a fantastic day of work in his life, he had had this giant erection all day and he couldn't wait to see me, but he had worked at fever pitch because his life's dreams were all resolved now.

EMILY: Did you tell him there was only one catch?

MARSHA: I was ready to crawl into the wall. There was no fighting, nothing going on. He's not baiting me, he's very serious, very sober. We had absolutely no idea how to entertain ourselves.

EMILY: Why didn't he simply put his arms around you?

MARSHA: He was just in love with me and I didn't know how to deal with it so I took a bath. I said okay, I'm taking a bath now, a long bath. I go into the bathroom, and you know my tub, how it takes two hours to fill.

EMILY: Is it your bathtub or his?

MARSHA: Mine. He's in my house, everything is for me.

EMILY: Life has changed.

MARSHA: Finally the bath is ready, the water has dripped in, and I get into it. My idea is to stay there as long as I conceivably can, for the rest of my life if possible. Then he walks in with a huge tray of snacks for me to eat in the bath.

EMILY: I though you already whipped up such a terrific dinner.

MARSHA: This was after dinner. He's bringing me peaches and peeled grapes and everything else. Then he comes and sits and stares at me while I'm taking the bath.

EMILY: Did he give you bath salts and peppers? Go ahead, he's staring at you in the bath.

MARSHA: He's staring at me as I wash and I'm hiding myself among the bubbles. The next night, the same thing happens.

EMILY: Wait a second. Did you fuck?

MARSHA: Yah, and I think he even looked at me while we fucked.

EMILY: Why did you fuck?

MARSHA: Yah, while we fucked, he even glanced my way.

EMILY: *Why* are you fucking, *why* are you doing it? Not while: *why?*

MARSHA: Are you kidding? This is the love of my life, he finally falls in love with me, what do you want me to do? Keep taking baths? The next day it's the same thing, he's calling me up at work, I come home, repeat performance at night, he doesn't want to see anyone but me.

EMILY: He just wants to sit and stare.

MARSHA: He's still staring at me.

EMILY: Even on the phone?

MARSHA: So for about two days he doesn't want me to go to work, staring on the phone and everything. The third day I go to work, I'm waiting for the normal ten calls, I get . . .

EMILY: Zero.

MARSHA: And I panic. Finally, as I'm ready to leave work, I call *him.*

The service tells me where he is, at one of his basketball friends'. I call him there and he says darling—he's crying—darling? Just the way it came, that's the way it went. Our love.

EMILY: Did he really say that?

MARSHA: He really did. I breathed a huge sigh of relief, went home so I could suffer in private, and lived happily ever after.

EMILY: And that was it? You never loved him again?

MARSHA: Of course I did, immediately thereafter. Picked right up, took me about twenty minutes: he never loved me, I love him so much.

EMILY: And you believed it and felt it and everything?

MARSHA: Sure.

EMILY: So sad. You know you really were mad about him.

MARSHA: There are still some vestiges, like I just realized looking at that Spearmint gum—that's the only kind of gum I can chew, because it was his favorite.

EMILY: I saw you sneaking some Frosty Mint in the supermarket today.

MARSHA: That was for you, darling.

EMILY: It was for me, all for me? How come there seemed to be a couple of pieces empty and gone when we got home?

MARSHA: I chewed them for you too.

EMILY:

8. EMILY RELATES HER PSYCHEDELIC EXPERIENCE TO VINCENT

EMILY: You know I've taken LSD. And let me tell you, at a certain point—it's really impossible for you to understand, you might be able to comprehend it in your head, but you can't experience it—all of a sudden my mind was where this boyfriend was, where that best friend was, all of a sudden I didn't *understand* their sickness, I *had* it. I was there, right where they were. If I took it now I could go maybe where Michael Christy is. It's incredible. I for instance thought of Jonquil. Jonquil my cat: instant tears, instant total emotional value of the thought. My mind the next moment is on that bathing suit on the line and it's hysterically funny to me that the bathing suit is drying there, and I can feel the pull, the water going into the air.

VINCENT: My God! How fantastic!

EMILY: The next thing I'm a mother in her loneliness, and there's a whole kind of gloomy feeling, but there's no working yourself into, it's instantly touching all the notes of the instrument.

VINCENT: Then when you talk about love, you're talking about like total empathy and compassion.

EMILY: No, not compassion, because compassion is to a certain extent identification and a kind of tolerance. This was feeling that my blood wasn't the blood that made up Emily Benson and the cells that were all locked inside her life; it was an extension of humanity, like I was part of Marsha, we weren't separate people, we were all part of each other, somehow sliced off by maybe a knife.

VINCENT: Right.

ILY: But that everything was touching and I was intimately a part of every pulsebeat of every sun that came up on everybody's life. There was a huge opening of the sky, I saw God, I had a tremendously mystical experience. I was deeply moved, deeply in love. And when I say love, it's not like on the level we know from analysis. It was the absence of all anger, the absence of all conflict.

VINCENT: But that's what you're working toward in analysis.

EMILY: No no no, that's not what you get from analysis. Analyzed love is not the absence of all those things, it's after dealing with them. Under LSD, they didn't even exist. You see it wasn't a love in which there was *present* such-and-such, but rather an *absence* of anger, of aggression, of conflict, of identification, of need, of unfulfillment, of frustration—all those things we feel go into love, because love is based on so much else. I don't think love is some kind of pure fucking quality, you know. Actually, the only thing that comes close to expressing the kind of feeling I had is "Seymour, an Introduction" by Salinger, that's the only thing that approaches it. It has nothing to do with thinking things out. It's like if you're in a warm bath, your reality is that the body is in warm water.

VINCENT: I know.

EMILY: Yeah, you get it, darling.

VINCENT: But I think you can also arrive there in other ways.

EMILY: I've been there, but only under the most extraordinary circumstances, the most temporal.

VINCENT: After you come down, is the experience very meaningful? In other words, do you think I should take the trip?

EMILY: The LSD trip? I don't know, a lot of people have asked me that. I'll tell you, Vinnie, the experience was fantastically extraordinary, and I would never undo it.

VINCENT: That's good.

EMILY: I would never undo it, but I would never tell you to do it.

VINCENT: I'd be afraid of the cataclysm, the black depression coming in on me. I've had enough of that.

EMILY: I had blackness then like I've never known blackness in my life, because when I started coming down, and I saw I'd written all over Philippe's body and on the walls with a ballpoint pen *This stone is love, God is in this pebble*, and I really knew when I wrote it what the fuck I was talking about, and then I started to come down and I said who wrote this?

VINCENT: Oh my poor darling.

EMILY: And all of a sudden I said my mind, I'm losing my mind. There's nothing more frightening. Like no matter how drunk you are, how insane, there's always some core that you know in yourself to be you?

VINCENT: Right. And you lost that.

EMILY: And that went. But if you could take it with a doctor, then I'd say definitely take it.

VINCENT: Actually, truth is both those things, you've got to accept both that huge love and the total absence. One is no more true than the other.

EMILY: You know I'm not at all sure, Vinnie—this is a very strange thing I'm coming to—I'm not at all sure that the way it's worked out socially, in terms of civilization, I'm not so sure that men and women *can* love each other and grow families, that naturally these things work out.

VINCENT: Civilization is completely artificial, I've always said that.

EMILY: The working out of structure is a decision and civilization surviving is a decision.

VINCENT: And even love isn't natural.

EMILY: I'm not sure it is. Not that it's strictly synthetic, but I'm not sure it's a built-in thing, that whole marriage system of society our lives are based on. Even yours.

VINCENT: Is it out of your LSD you're talking now or are you jumping?

EMILY: I'm jumping.

VINCENT: Oh, jumping. Because I don't want to go off into marriage, that's a whole other discussion. I want to stay on what you learned out of your LSD experience.

EMILY: I'm not a pragmatic person, so I can't say that it had a use. I only know that the only time I've ever gone beyond any point of identity in terms of Emily Benson was then.

VINCENT: But now, when you look at reality, has it made a new imprint on you? Do you see things in a different way? Do you feel more religiosity? I sound like David Susskind.

EMILY: No, but you asked me about the religious part. First of all, in a crazy way, I don't want to use the word religious, but you know that from my father I have a mystical side to my mind, my nature. And I'll tell you, Vinnie, the phoniest thing, the Zen koan at the beginning of *Catcher in the Rye*—I really love Salinger very much, I'm very hooked up with him—it says we know the sound of two hands clapping, what is the sound of one hand clapping? Now that's a very kind of trite thing, it's pat, but I really get it and I get all the vibrations. You know I called Marsha up when I was under LSD and she said I was talking pure poetry.

VINCENT: Really?

EMILY: A child is crying in the wall. You know the idea that flowers cry when they're picked? Well the sensitivity was so great that if the flower *was* picked, I could hear it crying. I didn't identify with the flower, I *was* the flower. And it wasn't like I'm such a sensitive person or anything, it was simply that the power or the chemistry of the mind reached a certain level. I remember pouring a glass of milk, and as I did, I experienced myself being poured into the glass. The milk was part of me, an extension, that's what I mean by mystical.

VINCENT: Incredible.

EMILY: I shouldn't really say mystical, because the word evokes a whole mysterious realm of associations, whereas this was absolutely logical. Say for instance right now we both look up: we both see a certain kind of blue sky, a certain kind of star, and it makes a certain kind of sense, so that if we each sat down to paint it, the paintings would correlate to a great degree. But if we both took LSD, the art would instantly change. That's what pre-Columbian art is all about, you know, because those guys weren't straight, they were chemically different, and the whole distortion of style was just a reflection of what they saw. The reality of the landscape is completely determined by the people who see it.

VINCENT: Of course.

EMILY: Like when a madman on the street says get away from me, it's because he sees a person with a knife trying to kill him. It's not that he's a lunatic seeing a mirage; he actually, for his own mind, sees it. It's completely real. That's why the word mystical is misleading. You know, Vinnie, I really believe that the nature of the fucking sands would change if the chemistry was a little bit different in all our heads. For instance, if *my* chemistry was different, I might see that this sand wasn't sand. Look, I'm going over to it right now, I'm walking to the sand and I'm going to the LSD experience. I'm getting canyons, and these little things that dip in all of a sudden become miles dipping in. The top becomes sunbaked peaks, and these specks become arid plants growing.

VINCENT: No kidding!

EMILY: And the white becomes illusions of clouds floating on top. All kinds of things start to happen if I let my mind go. I don't associate just sand is sand, like I've always seen sand and I know it because I'm secure that that's sand. All the security is taken away from everything. Suddenly I've never really seen sand before— and I haven't, because my eyes have changed, the retinas.

VINCENT: But isn't that flirting with the psychotic? Isn't it like a psychotic interlude? I'm scared, Emmy.

EMILY: Of course, it induces a false psychosis, that's what the drug is all about. But the term psychotic means a flight from reality, and the reality, as I just said, is based upon what we all define it to be. If we took those limitations away, a psychotic would just be someone on another level.

VINCENT: Why *don't* we take them away?

EMILY: Why don't we? Because we have to function within orders, within laws, within rules of society, whatever it is people say we have to function in. You know that as well as I do.

VINCENT: You're brilliant, Emmy. But look at the sand. You *know*, when you walk over there it's not a canyon.

EMILY: Why isn't it? Because I know all about sand, I've walked on it since I was a child, I know you can walk on it and you're not going to sink. But if you never have walked on sand before . . . .

VINCENT: So you're saying you have to go back to the innocence of not knowing.

EMILY: Back to a total innocence of not knowing.

VINCENT: And if you were on LSD and you walked over to that sand, you might feel you were sinking?

EMILY: I could feel that the sand might be a grave beginning to open.

VINCENT: In other words, you don't really believe that there are objective limits.

EMILY: No, I don't believe that we, who are all sane, know all there is to know about that sand. I think that if we took LSD right now, we'd know something else about it. The thing is, if we were babies, we couldn't say what we felt about it; we'd just have a certain kind of feeling about the sensation. We couldn't articulate it, right?

VINCENT: Yah.

EMILY: And it wouldn't be the same for both of us. Maybe for me it would be dirt or shit and for you it would be some kind of cream like your mother used or hair or what it feels like to touch your clothes. Whatever these things are, they wouldn't become sand right away, with a word.

VINCENT: Look, I understand that under LSD, I might experience this coffee cup in huge, monumental fashion; I just wonder if there isn't a reality outside that. I mean I can make this into a thousand bigger or different qualities, but after all it *is* porcelain, it *is* four inches in diameter, and it *can* hold maybe half a pint of liquid. Aren't those limits that exist outside any potential it has in our psyche?

EMILY: Yes, but those limits are absolutely infinitesimal.

VINCENT: What do you mean?

EMILY: That the possibilities are infinite, whereas the limitations are infinitesimal; that this is porcelain, that it weighs half a pound,

that it holds half a pint, these qualities, confronting the possibilities of it, are minute. They're *nothing* to what it could possibly be.
You know that Marsha, for example, would never take LSD.

VINCENT: I know she wouldn't.

EMILY: She's terrified of all drugs. She needs her controls, she can't
give them up. Of course she will someday.

VINCENT: You think she'll take LSD?

EMILY: No, I think someday she'll surrender, she'll love.

9. EMILY AND MARSHA PLAY A GAME

MARSHA: Okay, Sidney Greenstreet or Peter Lorre?

EMILY: Sidney Greenstreet.

MARSHA: Joe DiMaggio or Arthur Miller?

EMILY: Joe DiMaggio, he went to the funeral.

MARSHA: He arranged the whole thing. Jack Kennedy or—

EMILY: What about me?

MARSHA: Wait a second, you'll have your turn, you'll be asking me. Jack Kennedy or Fidel Castro?

EMILY: That's very close. When you first said it, I didn't think so, but it's really very close.

MARSHA: Neither did I when I first said it.

EMILY: I think Fidel.

MARSHA: Fidel Castrated.

EMILY: Jack Ruby or Lee Oswald?

MARSHA: Lee Harvey.

EMILY: George Washington or Abraham Lincoln?

MARSHA: Are you kidding? George Washington with his teeth coming out every night and the wig coming off?

EMILY: Lyndon B. Johnson or Harry S. Truman?

MARSHA: Harry Truman.

EMILY: Barry Goldwater or Larry Rivers?

MARSHA: Barry or Larry? Larry.

EMILY: Bob Dylan or Bob Rauschenberg?

MARSHA: Rauschenberg. They have sort of the same face, in a way.

EMILY: Henry Geldzahler or Andy Warhol?

MARSHA: Henry Geldzahler. You?

EMILY: Henry, he's sweet.

MARSHA: Sweet little porky, porky-pie.

EMILY: Robert Mitchum or Robert Creeley? You'd get more out of the experience with Creeley.

MARSHA: Yeah, but Robert Mitchum's not stupid. I heard him on the radio. Wally Cox or Henry Geldzahler?

EMILY: I think I'd rather sleep with Henry than anyone. Henry's a winner.

MARSHA: I got one. Sam Snead or Harry Truman?

EMILY: Well one's a swinger.

MARSHA: So's Harry, he shoots in the sixties.

EMILY: Harry Truman.

MARSHA: Ava Gardner or Eva Gabor?

EMILY: Ava Gardner. Eva Gabor or Zsa Zsa?

MARSHA: I think they're the same person. John Lindsay or Bill Buckley?

EMILY: John Lindsay. You can't help being influenced by ideology.

MARSHA: Vittorio DiSica or Vittorio Gassman?

EMILY: Gassman as he is in Italy, not here.

MARSHA: Allen Ginsberg or Gregory Corso?

EMILY: Allen.

MARSHA: Sonny Liston or Glenn Gould?

EMILY: Sonny Liston.

MARSHA: Hoagy Carmichael or Stokely Carmichael?

EMILY: Black power. Allen Funt or Bert Parks?

MARSHA: Allen Funt. He's sort of cute, in his voyeuristic way. Harold Rosenberg or Clem Greenberg?

EMILY: Clem Greenberg.

MARSHA: Roy Lichtenstein or Claes Oldenburg?

EMILY: Roy. Paul Thek or Beni Montresor?

MARSHA: Beni.

EMILY: Really? Not me.

MARSHA: Susan Sontag or Marisol?

EMILY: Susan Sontag. Marisol would be too passive. Hubert Humphrey or Lyndon B. Johnson?

MARSHA: Hubert.

EMILY: Either way. H. H. either way or Lyndon B. either way. Okay, I got a great one. U Thant or the guy who plays Charlie Chan in the movies?

MARSHA: U. Morey Amsterdam or—

EMILY: Who?

MARSHA: Morey Amsterdam.

EMILY: Never heard of him. Bill de Kooning or Claes Oldenburg?

MARSHA: De Kooning. Oldenburg or—we need some new blood. Let's think of some serious people. Marlon Brando or Paul Newman?

EMILY: Paulie. Miles Davis or Ornette Coleman?

MARSHA: Miles. Menotti or that guy Gino from last night?

EMILY: Menotti.

MARSHA: Yves St. Laurent or Leo?

EMILY: Steinberg?

MARSHA: No, Leo Castelli.

EMILY: Who was the first one?

MARSHA: I don't remember. Who was it?

EMILY: Yves St. Laurent. Then it's Leo Castelli, definitely. Paul Newman or Henry Geldzahler?

MARSHA: Henry! Yay!

EMILY: Zeke Sutherland or Michael Christy?

MARSHA: Are you serious? You know we can't use people we're involved with in real life.

EMILY: Right. Who aren't we involved with? Bette Davis or Betty Grable?

MARSHA: I'm involved with Bette Davis, I think she looks like me. Norman Mailer or Philip Roth?

EMILY: I've never met Philip Roth.

MARSHA: It's an interesting choice.

EMILY: Yeah. I've never met Philip Roth, but I think it would probably be Mailer.

MARSHA: It would. Jonas Mekas or Gregory Markopolous?

EMILY: Gregory Markopolous. He might make me a superstar.

MARSHA: John Chamberlain or Ivan Karp?

EMILY: John Chamberlain.

MARSHA: Edward Albee or Henry Geldzahler?

EMILY: Henry! Yay!

MARSHA: Hey, I got a whole new thing, the Beatles, Dionne Warwick, Leslie Gore, Gore Vidal, the whole rock n' roll contingent.

EMILY: Okay, Ringo or Paul?

MARSHA: Paulie. Dionne Warwick or Leslie Gore?

EMILY: Dionne Warwick. Gore Vidal or McGeorge Bundy?

MARSHA: Oh, I'd much rather make it with McGeorge Bundy, just to be able to whisper the name McGeorge.

EMILY: Baby Jane Holzer or Tuesday Weld?

MARSHA: What ever happened to Baby Jane? Sinatra or Belmondo?

EMILY: Belmondo. Up to very recently it would have been Frank, but he's gone just a little too far, the mafioso.

MARSHA: Yeah. Robert Trout or Walter Cronkite?

EMILY: Robert Trout. Cardinal Spellman or Menasha Skulnik?

MARSHA: That's disgusting. I'm not going to answer.

EMILY: Bobby or Teddy?

MARSHA: I think Teddy.

EMILY: No, Bobby, definitely.

MARSHA: Which of your two brothers?

EMILY: David. Your father or Henry Geldzahler?

MARSHA: Henry! Yay!

EMILY: You know this game can push you into a whole new feeling about people.

MARSHA: You're right—I can hardly wait until I see Henry again.

EMILY: Who else is around?

MARSHA: Hedda or Louella?

EMILY: Whichever is still alive.

MARSHA: Goebbels or Goering?

EMILY: The fat one.

MARSHA: Huntley or Brinkley?

EMILY: Brinkley.

MARSHA: Jules or Jim?

EMILY: Jim.

MARSHA: Funny, I thought you would have picked Jules.

10. EMILY AND MARSHA
COMPARE CHILDHOOD TRAUMATA

MARSHA: I had this image all through my childhood that my mother was a saint. She never raised her voice, she never hit me, she was a complete goody-goody. One day I was standing on my canopied bed in the Bronx—my mother had made me a beautiful princess's room and I had this very high bed with white ruffles on top. Now you *know* I was a model child—the only time I ever was bad was when I'd ask for glasses of water and sing and dance to avoid going to sleep and this one night I must have been particularly rambunctious. Finally my mother really got angry. She came in and said Marsha, you are a little stinker. Well! You can't imagine what it meant for me to hear that vile obscenity come out of my mother's pure mouth. It shot the whole image to hell. I started to cry and weep and scream. She tried to wiggle out of it by saying she just meant I smelled because I didn't take a bath that night, and that stinker was a perfectly good English word—but I knew it wasn't.

EMILY: She meant you were a bitch or a bastard, isn't that what she meant?

MARSHA: Yeah, and I never got over it.

EMILY: No kidding. It's interesting, but God almighty, it's really not much in terms of traumas.

MARSHA: Sorry, that's all I have to offer. It was a very big thing to me, believe it or not, because of this incorruptible image I had of her. She never raised her voice to my father, she was just this gentle, giving, loving, flowing indulgent mother with flesh like silk.

EMILY: I don't remember my mother raising her voice either. Flesh like silk?

MARSHA: Satin, old-fashioned satin. Probably I'm remembering her nightgowns. But I used to get the creeps, her skin was so soft and smooth—like marble—I thought there was something wrong with her. She never shaved her legs, under her arms, she had no hair.

EMILY: Really? Sounds like a Chinese.

MARSHA: My grandfather is the same way.

EMILY: What about your sister? Does Rochelle have hair under her arms?

MARSHA: She's hairy with eyebrows that grow all over. In fact when she was about six and getting a little fuzz, I used to constantly tell her how hairy she was.

EMILY: You were so jealous of her!

MARSHA: I made her feel disgusting—that was one of *her* lifelong traumas. I think I *was* jealous of her, but I would lie to myself and say what bothered me was that we just didn't have much in common, she wasn't the type of person I liked to be with, she was phony. But I wasn't *jealous*, of course not—I just didn't happen to care for her personality. That was when she was about three. Because don't forget she had suddenly appeared after twelve years of my only child-dom, this pishy little kid who could do everything I couldn't do, not only manual things with her hands and athletics, but she could talk to people, she wasn't shy. I mean all she did was get born and two minutes later she's doing all the banes of my existence, flushing mice down the toilet and everything else.

EMILY: I bet she couldn't do it now. I have a story about my mother too. I had this best friend named Judi who had a fantastic wardrobe. Of course all my friends always wore beautiful clothes and I had nothing, because my mother spent my clothes allowance on herself.

MARSHA: Nice mommy.

EMILY: Very nice mommy. I didn't know about it until one day a friend of my sister's went into my mother's closet. I was a small little girl of ten and my sister was very very tall. I was wearing her hand-me-down skirts—half the skirt was a hem.

MARSHA: Why didn't your mother cut some of it off?

EMILY: Because she didn't give a shit. When I tried on clothes, everything looked good on me, according to my mother. Naturally. So anyway this girl took one look at my mother's closet and she said what's going on? Look at the Christian Dior suits and the Pauline Trigère dresses and the Bergdorf Goodman shoes, piles upon piles.

MARSHA: You mean you never looked in your mother's closet?

EMILY: Who knows at ten years old what's good and what's not? So here my mother has fifteen thousand basic black dresses, basic black suits and basic black shoes, all from the best places. She has two mink coats and a Persian lamb coat, a gray fox, all these crazy coats, while I'm going around with the skirts with the hems. So anyway, my friend Judi and I were going to a dance. I had to go stag, I had nothing to wear, so she lent me a blouse. I loved this blouse so much I could have died. I wore it and I got ink on it.

MARSHA: Ink at a party?

EMILY: Somehow, wherever I wore it, I got ink on it. I was desperate. And of course I could never turn to my mother with any problem. I was so guilty and felt so terrible about it, I put it into the laundry. It came out still with the spot, so I hid it in my closet. My mother found it and she said how did you get ink on Judi's blouse?

MARSHA: She knew it was borrowed?

EMILY: Of course. I gave her a long song and dance and then I broke down, I told her the truth. She said that is a *lie*. She called Althea in, the maid. Althea, did you find these spots in the laundry? Oh no, ma'am, it was clean as a mother-fucker's ass, as clean as clean could be. The two of them against me. Tell the truth, tell the truth, tell the truth, and she started smacking me across the fucking face until finally I broke down and told her what she wanted to hear, which was a lie.

MARSHA: What was the point?

EMILY: She didn't want me lying to her. No lies. My mother was a very big liar.

MARSHA: How come you went stag without a date?

EMILY: I was the wallflower of all time.

MARSHA: I was a terrible wallflower. With my glasses and my curly permanented hair.

EMILY: But you were very pretty.

MARSHA: Yeah, but don't forget when you see pictures of me at that age I have my glasses off. I have a couple at home with the glasses on.

EMILY: Those don't go in the album.

MARSHA: Those don't go in any album. I *was* always pretty, but what I did to myself with the shyness and everything else was unbelievable, I mean I was so gangly and awkward. And you *know* that I used to bandage my foot.

EMILY: What do you mean you bandaged your foot?

MARSHA: I used to put a bandage around my ankle and tell people I hurt my foot because I was afraid to dance.

EMILY: You mean you always went to parties with the bandage? Didn't people begin to wonder about it?

MARSHA: I only did it a couple of times. And there was this one story—I don't know why it sticks in my mind—but there was a boy in my class named Bradley Greenberg who had a crush on me, glasses and all, and he had a whole gang of boys living in his building who called themselves the Handlers. They were called the Handlers because their names were Harvey, Alan, Norman, Danny, Lester, Ernie, Ray and Sheldon, and that's what their initials spelled out.

EMILY: You remember all those names?

MARSHA: Sure do. When I'm eighty, I'll remember them. They were all gorgeous. I was fourteen and they were seventeen and I kept telling Bradley Greenberg that I wanted to go out with them.

EMILY: But he wasn't a member—his name started with B.

MARSHA: He idolized them. And he quoted them to me saying fifteen was the bottom of the barrel—they would *never* go out with anyone fourteen. So I was put in my place, at the bottom of the barrel. Finally I got to be fifteen and one of them condescended to go out with me, Lester. We had a long romance, we went out every Saturday night for a month and a half. He was short and pudgy.

EMILY: I thought they were all gorgeous.

MARSHA: All except Lester. Anyway, one time my friend was baby-sitting at a woman named Mrs. Bespaloff's. How many years ago was this? Seventeen years ago, and I still remember the woman's name. So we went over there, I had my foot bandaged on the chance there might be a little dancing to the Frank Sinatra records, and the boys kept putting the lights off. Those boys loved to kiss.

EMILY: Was Mrs. Bespaloff there?

MARSHA: Of course not, we were baby-sitting with her kids. Then something happened, I don't remember what, but I got terrified, I guess I was terrified of the necking. And somehow or other I found myself on the couch with Lester, and I was sitting on my hands.

EMILY: Why?

MARSHA: I don't know, but the word got out that I sat on my hands and it was passed around from Handler to Handler and they all made jokes about Marsha who sat on her hands. I didn't go out much after that.

EMILY: I love these stories.

MARSHA: I have another *horrible* one that was really traumatic. You know I grew up in this slummy section of the Bronx. My mother was fanatically clean, but in spite of it, because the woman upstairs was a slob, we had cockroaches in hordes. And mice. Cockroaches, as you may know, are afraid of the light. They start to play around when it's dark. And we had a white, what do you call that material that tables used to be made of? Old-fashioned kitchen tables?

EMILY: Formica.

MARSHA: No, before it was invented. Metal! A white metal table! Well, one night I came in with my boyfriend Marty Halpern and the white table was black, it was completely covered with bugs. I screamed.

EMILY: Marshie, I would have gone out of my mind.

MARSHA: Also my mother would make me take the soda bottles back to the candy store for the deposit, and before I went, I'd have to turn them over and dump out the bugs so I wouldn't be embarrassed in the store. One time when I was standing at the kitchen sink washing my hair a mouse ran over my foot. Another night I was baby-sitting with my sister, I had had a fight with my boyfriend Marty Halpern, we weren't seeing each other, so I was alone doing my homework when suddenly a fuse blew. The lights went out and I knew, in a matter of minutes, it would be the cotillion ball of the cockroaches and the mice. I was petrified. I couldn't leave the goddamned kid, this brat who was ruining my life anyway. I couldn't leave her alone. It was about twelve o'clock. I looked out the window and just luckily, there was Marty Halpern coming home from a date. I completely swallowed my pride, I didn't give a damn, and I screamed out the window you have to come up, just stay with me, bring me a flashlight. So he came. And then this crazy embarrassing thing happened, one of these things you can remember for thirty years and the other person didn't even notice? When he came in, he put his jacket on the back of the chair I later sat down in, and when he finally was leaving, he came over to me, and I thought he wanted to make up, be my boyfriend again, marry me, but he was just going for the jacket. It was the most humiliating moment of my life. And he didn't even know what I was thinking.

EMILY: Did you put your arms around him or anything?

MARSHA: No, I just started to get a warm feeling. I was so naive. I was fifteen and we used to neck at the door every night and he would get a hard-on? I used to think it was his wallet that had somehow worked its way over, I thought he had very peculiar pockets. Until I was twenty-five years old, I thought it was his wallet.

EMILY: Maybe it *was* his wallet. What did Tim say? Is he coming over?

MARSHA: Yeah, I can't believe he's really coming back after what I did to him last night. I thought he'd be furious.

EMILY: Do you understand why you threw him out?

MARSHA: Of course I do—it was all about Merrill Johnston, it was the first time I've ever seen my doctor with a woman. I was much more jealous of *that* than of Tim Cullen and his little lip-reading flirtation with another girl, but he was the only one around to attack.

EMILY: You know it's interesting, talking about last night, that story you told before about your goody-goody image of your mother, it's interesting because it upsets you so much when I get drunk and everything. Did you ever analyze that?

MARSHA: I just don't think it's nice.

EMILY: You don't think it's nice. Precisely.

MARSHA: Emily, don't try to make it into a thing of mine. Everybody gets as upset.

EMILY: Joan doesn't.

MARSHA: Joan is an alcoholic, you can't take her as a criterion. Do you get upset when she drinks?

EMILY: Very upset.

MARSHA: There you are, because you're normal. How would you feel if I did what you did last night, if I didn't recognize you when I got drunk and behaved that way? Would you think it was a peculiarity of yours if you got upset?

EMILY: No, but I'm not sure how upset I *would* get.

MARSHA: Believe me, you'd get fantastically upset if you saw someone as sick as you. It was incredible. You did not know who I was.

EMILY: Did Tim get upset?

MARSHA: He was ready to leave you on the beach. Everybody was. I had to fight them to go get you—even Vinnie, and then you treated me like your jailer, you told me to leave you alone.

EMILY: Did I really?

MARSHA: That's what infuriates me, that you don't even remember. I really can't take it, Emily.

EMILY: There's no reason why you should. I don't think I'm going to be coming out for a while, Marshie. Maybe I'll take Sick Joan and we'll go to Woods Hole for a little rest cure—the two sickies.

MARSHA: I think maybe you should.

11. THE CLAM DINNER

VINCENT: Do you have any bread?

MARSHA: Only white.

VINCENT: What kind would you want with clams? Don't you know the Italian color way of eating? White and white and white: the white wines and white clams and white bread, it's gorgeous. Were you sitting out here when I pulled up?

MARSHA: I was hovering by the door, I was afraid something happened to you. You took such an inordinate length of time.

VINCENT: You told me to drive slowly, I went purposely slow so you wouldn't be nervous.

MARSHA: Well I was. I felt like I was waiting for my daddy.

VINCENT: What time did your father used to get home from work?

MARSHA: About six-thirty.

VINCENT: Mine got home at seven-thirty. That's too late for a young kid to wait up.

MARSHA: Didn't he work in the neighborhood?

VINCENT: No, but it's funny, he worked not far from the hospital he died in.

MARSHA: That was near your house.

VINCENT: No it wasn't. Brooklyn is an enormous long place, it's a big graveyard.

MARSHA: Don't eat that black stuff, the foreskin. Peel it back as if you were giving it a bris.

VINCENT: You know when I was sixteen, my mother was dead and I made a New Year's dinner for a girl at my house. I made her this, but she couldn't eat it.

MARSHA: Why?

VINCENT: The sight of the penies got her so upset.

MARSHA: You don't eat that, Vinnie.

VINCENT: Of course you do, are you kidding? It's the combination of this softness and that hardness that's the great thing.

MARSHA: I love them. I love seafood.

VINCENT: They're really exquisite. Don't ever eat any raw clams though.

MARSHA: I like raw clams.

VINCENT: Okay, get hepatitis.

MARSHA: Boy, I'm glad the weekend's over.

VINCENT: When's Timothy coming out again?

MARSHA: I don't know. I'll tell you, when I threw him out, I was sure that was the last I'd see of him. The next day, when I finally found him at your house—

VINCENT: As though you were even looking.

MARSHA: No, after I explained to him what had happened, the pressures on me of Emily's drunkenness on the beach, seeing Merrill Johnston with that blonde, but that it was still very bad of me and I was sorry, and he forgave me, I was really taken aback because most people I know aren't forgiving.

VINCENT: Catholic. Priest.

MARSHA: You never heard the whole story. On the phone I said you know you left your bathing suit here and everything, Tim, do you want to come and get it? He said yes and then I got very nervous. I thought it was going to be awful, I mean I still thought he must be furious with me. I was doing the dishes when he came in, I had my back to the room.

VINCENT: Were you aware he arrived?

MARSHA: I guess so, but I really didn't know how to handle it, so I just kept washing the dishes. And he came up behind me and kissed me.

VINCENT: On the neck?

MARSHA: On the cheek. He took me in his arms and held me, and I got fantastic waves of love. I mean I really loved him and he really loved me.

VINCENT: Your father forgiving you.

MARSHA: We talked a little bit and it was very very beautiful, very loaded. I didn't want him to leave, but he was determined to go.

VINCENT: You're almost in tears, you know.

MARSHA: I was very sad, but in a deep, wistful, loving way. I walked him out to the car and we talked some more. His last words before he drove off were "sometimes I think I care about you more than I know."

VINCENT: That's a beautiful story.

MARSHA: I'll tell you the weirdest thing though—he said he wouldn't be at all surprised if the next time he came out you and I were married, and that he didn't even think it would be so sick.

VINCENT: Don't you think we should have some white bread?

MARSHA: If we're getting married, we should definitely have some white bread. I think it would be very sick, don't you, Vinnie?

VINCENT: I wouldn't sleep with you, but it would be an interesting experience.

MARSHA: I wouldn't either.

VINCENT: Why, because I'm too much like a brother?

MARSHA: No, I just wouldn't. I told my doctor I wouldn't.

VINCENT: What does that mean, what you told your doctor?

MARSHA: It means it's the truth.

VINCENT: You told your doctor you wouldn't to defend yourself against the possibility of being attracted to me. That's how sick you are, Marsh.

MARSHA: Is this good?

VINCENT: No, it's a bad one. How did you know?

MARSHA: Because the last one I had was so bad and it looked like that. Oh, all of them are that way.

VINCENT: That's the inside, stupid. It's their shit, but it tastes good. Psychology I'm using so I can finish the whole thing.

MARSHA: You know I think it's terrible the way you get upset at

Nico every time he has to go away for a weekend. You're completely hypocritical, with your *liaisons dangereuses* and your thises and your thats, saying people can screw whoever they want.

VINCENT: But Nico never does screw around; he's a good boy.

MARSHA: I don't mean that specifically. He just doesn't have the least bit of freedom to go away without your starting to sulk. In the end you're as possessive and jealous as any ordinary person. They're very unreal and idealistic, all your highflown ideas, because jealousy is basic to love, I don't care what you say.

VINCENT: No it's not, darling. Jealousy is basic to insecurity.

MARSHA: Well, everyone is insecure.

VINCENT: What you don't understand about having a one-to-one adult relationship with another human being is that it's *not* one-to-one, it's A-to-ah, two things which are similar but different. The beauty is not in finding the mirror image, like you're looking for with Tim, but complementary things. I think the ideal relationship is when you look into the other person and realize things you couldn't possibly realize alone or with anyone else. That's my success, in a humanistic way, with Nico, because he's so very different from me, and that's one of your basic problems with Tim.

MARSHA: You think we're alike?

VINCENT: I think you're very similar. The only thing is that you're stronger and that's bad because you need someone more powerful than you.

MARSHA: That's the problem—to find one.

VINCENT: They exist. And as *you* get stronger, through your analysis, through living, you'll be able to deal with them. I think Tim would actually make you a perfect first marriage. And I don't mean that to be cynical, I mean it in a very realistic way. I think you'd each learn a lot from being married to each other. Tim has great capacity.

MARSHA: He has great potential, let's face it.

VINCENT: He really does, that's what I'm afraid of in your involvement with him, that he'll reach his potential through you and then—

MARSHA: Drop me.

VINCENT: And then drop you. But that's what life is, that's what all first marriages are about. And just because you're thirty-one doesn't mean it still can't be a first marriage. You've never lived with anyone full-time, and he hasn't either. Just if you were to live in his studio and have to buy him food on your way home from work and cook for him and bring his dirty underwear to the laundromat.

MARSHA: That's still not a commitment. It's a step further, but it's not a commitment. I want to have children.

VINCENT: You will. Besides, having children's becoming a different thing now; it's becoming that you make them and look after them, but not necessarily in a family atmosphere. I mean the parents can be split, like with all the kids on the beach.

MARSHA: That's the way it is becoming. You know we have to be very brave people.

VINCENT: It's becoming that way because of the nature of giving women their independence. The reason marriages lasted before was women were put down, they were in the kitchen and out of the question. Now women find that they need more than one man in a lifetime. We're each too many people for one mate to satisfy. Look at the symbols of man and woman—the man's arrow points up because he isn't monogamous, he wants to screw and move on. But I'm not sure women don't want exactly the same thing. If they do bend aside and choose one man, in order to make it work over a long period of time, they've got to be very very independent and have, not affairs necessarily, but the sort of freewheeling thing Emil and Diana have.

MARSHA: But they're very unhappy people.

VINCENT: You know why? Because they're pioneers, we're all pioneers going through new frontiers, new jungles, we're breaking psychic, social land so that people following us will be able to lead better lives.

MARSHA: I don't think Emil and Diana have the guts really to do it.

VINCENT: You know, when I think of myself having a child, in a way I'd love to have one, but I also feel very selfish about it. I always remember what I think it was Motherwell said, he had these two sons or something, and he said when he takes them to the zoo, he feels guilty about not staying home and painting, and when he stays painting, he feels guilty about not taking them to the zoo. I see men on the beach embracing and caring about their children, and that's what you really have to do, give yourself up to them.

MARSHA: Only for about ten years.

VINCENT: The thing is the older we get the less energy we have. An artist is already an accelerated, intensified human being and you cannot spend eight hours painting and then be a good, creative father.

MARSHA: Well you're not ever going to be a father, so what are you talking about?

VINCENT: Who knows? Anyway that's not the point. I said something to my analyst and she said you're right, or did I say it to Nico and he said you're right? I think I said it to Nico and he said I was right. But when you're going through a good creative period, you have very light sexual needs and when you're going through a bad creative period they're very strong. That is to say the creative act is sexual and the sexual act is creative.

MARSHA: The fun of this dinner is reaching over and pulling the clams out.

VINCENT: If Tim asked you to marry him in September, would you?

MARSHA: No, I'd say I'd try living with him.

VINCENT: You *would* live down in his dirty loft?

MARSHA: No, but I'd see him a lot and test it out. I couldn't rush into marrying him, Vinnie.

VINCENT: I wouldn't want you to, hon, I don't think you should.

MARSHA: I mean it's dangerous.

VINCENT: When I was a little boy, each child in my family was allowed to have whatever they wanted for their birthday dinner and—

MARSHA: You had clams?

VINCENT: I would have steamed clams and something else, I don't remember what, and then pineapple upside-down cake.

MARSHA: Let's not talk about pineapple upside-down cake.

VINCENT: Why, don't you like it?

MARSHA: You only threw one in my face after I made it for your birthday, if you recall.

VINCENT: Well, you didn't make it the way I wanted, and I was almost dead with hepatitis, which you didn't even appreciate.

MARSHA: Who cares? I baked you a cake and it was beautiful, there was absolutely nothing wrong with it.

VINCENT: It wasn't right, it wasn't upside-down.

MARSHA: It was so!

VINCENT: It wasn't like my mommy's.

MARSHA: Well maybe *she* made it wrong. Do you realize that I used to come see you every single day when you were in the hospital?

VINCENT: God, if we talk about that some more. So what if you did? You worked just down the street.

MARSHA: It was still a drag.

VINCENT: You didn't enjoy seeing me?

MARSHA: No, you were nasty and abusive.

VINCENT: I was not. You were my girl—I wouldn't have gotten better if it hadn't been for you.

MARSHA: Yes you would have.

VINCENT: I would have gotten better differently. Do you know why you lose men, Marshie? Because you completely hang on to them.

MARSHA: I know, but I can't help it.

VINCENT: You've *got* to help it, darling.

MARSHA: My religious adviser, Merrill Johnston, will guide me through it.

VINCENT: You just said something very profound and you didn't even realize it.

MARSHA: Emily once told me she couldn't marry anyone who hadn't been analyzed and I said that reeked of fanaticism.

VINCENT: Analysis is the substitute for religion.

MARSHA: Oh God, we've known that since time immemorial. Don't sexual organs look clammy?

VINCENT: That's the silliest thing I've ever heard—it's the other way around. There are more sexual organs than clams in the world.

MARSHA: Oh no.

VINCENT: Oh yes. You have to plant clams, you don't have to plant sexual organs.

MARSHA: Yes you do.

VINCENT: You have to tune them up, that's all. Actually, you know, this should be a first course.

MARSHA: Did you ever stick flowers in your nose when you were a child, so you'd have that sweet smell with you all day?

VINCENT: That's right, Marsha, encourage the bugs and animals to come.

MARSHA: I'm feeding the flowers a few crumbs. That's more than you do—you pull them out by the roots. That was sinful; you really destroyed a landscape today. You may have created something on canvas, but you destroyed a landscape.

VINCENT: You have to destroy in order to create beauty.

MARSHA: That's a pseudo-intellectual cliché.

VINCENT: Sure, call Picasso and Nijinsky pseudo-intellectuals. Listen, we could still go and buy more clams.

MARSHA: Why do we want more clams?

VINCENT: Because we're not satisfied with our dinner.

MARSHA: Yes we are. Do you like this lettuce? Doesn't it taste fresh? You don't get this in the city.

VINCENT: No, but I'm not crazy about this brand.

MARSHA: This Campbell's lettuce?

VINCENT: Do you like my laugh a lot?

MARSHA: Do *you*?

VINCENT: It's a ripple.

MARSHA: It is. Oh—I got a card from Emily this morning. They're having a nice quiet time in Woods Hole, her and Joan, and everyone's in love with her.

VINCENT: Emily does think everyone likes her.

MARSHA: You know I once made up a classic analogy about that. Say I wake up in the morning with a big pimple on my face. I'd say oh my God, I can't go out of the house, I look awful, the whole world will be looking at me. She wakes up with the same pimple. She looks in the mirror and she says hmmm, I look rather Italian today.

VINCENT: She does have a fantastic mechanism for turning negative things to positive.

MARSHA: Yeah, but when she finds out the truth, it hurts her doubly.

VINCENT: No it doesn't, because she never accepts the truth, or if she does it's only for a slight second, then she'll put it completely out of her mind. And in a percentage way, she's right. Because most people are too timid to say hello to anyone first, so when Emily is friendly to everyone, the people who might think she doesn't like them and in turn not like her, when she comes over to them, they like *her*. So in the long run she probably wins out and has more people liking her. If that's what she cares about, and it *is*.

MARSHA: Here, finish it up. The last one is the best.

VINCENT: That's nice, it's very positive that you like the last one, Marsha. Most people only like the first.

12. MARSHA TELLS VINCENT ABOUT HANGING ON A WALL

MARSHA: What's the most perverse thing you've ever done?

VINCENT: Sexually?

MARSHA: Of course sexually.

VINCENT: Going to bed with a pair of twins and an animal.

MARSHA: What kind of animal?

VINCENT: No animal really, just a pair of twins.

MARSHA: That's not so perverse.

VINCENT: They also happened to be in love with each other. I know what yours was, my poor darling—hanging up on the wall, that bastard Eliot.

MARSHA: Let's not mention any names, but it's true he may have had something to do with it.

VINCENT: How did he ever get you to do it?

MARSHA: He didn't get me—I got him. He had told me about this terrible hang-up hang-up of his which I just couldn't reconcile with my sweet Jersey City loveball Elie. Then, on New Year's Eve, which wasn't long after he rejected me for no reason at all, I called him up and said he was really missing some great action. He had a girl at his apartment—it was even her birthday, the poor thing. He kept calling me Arthur on the phone, can't we possibly wait, Arthur, and work on the case tomorrow? I said no because I couldn't bear to be alone on New Year's Eve and I was desperate enough to do anything. So he ditched the girl and came running over with a briefcase full of legal briefs and took me back to his house.

VINCENT: Where did he live?

MARSHA: East End Avenue. And he had this whole apparatus set up on the wall, these hooks at the bottom and the top.

VINCENT: Did he put them in himself?

MARSHA: Well the apartment didn't come equipped, if that's what you mean. The thing was you would stand with your legs stretched apart, with your feet on piles of books. He tied your ankles with ropes, he attached the ropes to the hooks, and then he took the books away, so that you were all completely stretched, trying to touch the ground.

VINCENT: Really? And you would hang up there?

MARSHA: Yeah, and he tied ropes around the wrists too, so your arms were stretched out, just like Christ. It was really very interesting.

VINCENT: He tied you with ropes?

MARSHA: Yah.

VINCENT: Did he pad them so they didn't cut in?

MARSHA: You seem to be missing the point, sweetheart. He *wanted* it to hurt. He put golf balls in my mouth too but I kept spitting them out and they bounced all over the floor. It was very funny. I mean here I was in this ludicrous position and he's going through all these things, he had lotions and potions that he rubbed on all my sensitive areas, wintergreen oil that athletes use, and he's running around very busy, busy, busy. I was laughing—I though it was the most hysterical thing I ever saw—until all of a sudden I realized my God, my body is being stretched to death! So I passed out. I went totally unconscious.

VINCENT: Was anyone else there?

MARSHA: Of course not.

VINCENT: What about the sexual part?

MARSHA: To tell you the truth, I didn't find it that sexual. I mean of course it was, the ecstasy of the pain and everything, but I didn't really get the feeling he wanted me to have of being his slave girl. I had it much more once when he tied me up in bed and made me totally passive—I knew I couldn't do any of my sick clinging behavior and I was glad; I was relieved of all aggressive possibility. I

was there, I was a woman, a female object—he had to do everything. And in that moment I understood the whole dynamic.

VINCENT: He tied you in bed and then? Did he beat you up?

MARSHA: Yeah.

VINCENT: With what?

MARSHA: A leather strap.

VINCENT: Really hard?

MARSHA: As hard as he could.

VINCENT: And then?

MARSHA: And then I got up and had a glass of milk and a chocolate
brownie. One time he told me he was going to beat me ten times
and I said go ahead, I was being very stoic, like when my father
used to hit me and I wouldn't let myself cry. He couldn't do it in
the same place twice, because it would hurt too much, so he went
down my back with these ten strokes. When he finished, he said
I'm sorry, Marsh, but you didn't react enough, I'm going to have
to do ten more. Then I burst into tears, I knew I couldn't take it,
so he stopped. When it was over I felt very elated, filled with joy.
But then all of a sudden I said oh my God, I just remembered that
my mother's coming tomorrow for me to try on some bathing
suits she bought me—what should I do? She'll see the welts all
over my back. He said that's your problem, darling. So the next
day, sure enough, I wake up and there's this systematic series of
red brutal-looking welts down my whole back. What am I going
to do? My mother's coming in from Westchester just to bring the
bathing suits, there's no way I can get out of trying them on. So
she arrives and I go into the bathroom and get undressed. I try on
the first bathing suit and sort of edge out so she can't see my back.
I show her the front, I say I don't like it and I edge back in. I'm
dying. I don't know what to do.

VINCENT: How many bathing suits?

MARSHA: About four. Suddenly I get a brilliant, intuitive idea. I'm
in the bathroom and I scream Mother! What is this? My God!
There are these marks on my back, I must have some horrible dis-
ease! I come out very upset, she looks and she says what are you

getting so excited about, Marsha? It's nothing. You must have sat near a venetian blind or something and gotten sunburned. She completely brushed it off, because I was so upset.

VINCENT: How did you know she would fall for it?

MARSHA: It was a desperate stab.

VINCENT: It's the most gutsy thing I've ever heard you do, Marshie, it really is.

MARSHA: If she had seen them by herself, she would have become panic-stricken. Once Eliot tried to tie me up in my apartment with stockings and scarves and things because I didn't happen to have any ropes on hand. He hung me up on the bathroom door and I was terrified because it kept swinging. You know I'm afraid of heights.

VINCENT: I think it would make me laugh.

MARSHA: I'm telling you, I laughed so hard the golf balls were bouncing out of my mouth.

VINCENT: Did *he* laugh?

MARSHA: No! He was dead earnest.

VINCENT: Did he get an erection watching you in pain?

MARSHA: Yeah, the bastard.

VINCENT: And what would happen?

MARSHA: It ended up in fantastic fucking. The time I passed out, we wound up in the shower together and it was very very wild ecstatic lovemaking, one of the great moments of my life. Except I was worried about my hair getting wet.

VINCENT: With your mother coming the next day.

MARSHA: He also had a pair of handcuffs, and one night he was kidding around and he handcuffed my hands behind my back. Then he said he was going out for the evening. I said you can't leave me like this. He said just go out and ask someone in the street to unhook them. When he left, my reaction was so abnormal, you know I immediately forgot about the handcuffs? I remember there was a *New Republic* lying there, and first of all I got a cigarette into my mouth somehow and lit it with my foot, completely calm. Then I started reading an article about Medicare, turning the pages of the *New Republic* with my teeth, as if it were the most natural thing in the world. It's really amazing.

VINCENT: It really is. What is he doing now, Eliot?

MARSHA: He's still prosecuting perverts in court.

VINCENT: They must have written that song for him—"Beat me Daddy, Eight to the Bar."

13. EMILY RETURNS

VINCENT: Emmy, can I imitate how I got when I thought about your coming? I'd be with Marshie in a room and I'd burst out MY EMMY'S COMING FROM WOODS HOLE! HI EMMY! HI! I've been doing it all week and now here you are completely different, serious and sober, just sitting and saying I have something interesting to discuss with you.

EMILY: You don't like it that I'm calm.

VINCENT: I love it that you're calm, but I've been practicing my HI EMMY all week.

EMILY: I'm glad, sweetheart. I'll be up tomorrow, give me a little time.

VINCENT: Before we go any further, can I just say one thing, Emily, because it involves you? The steak, the onions and the cucumber salad are fantastic things. Okay, Em.

EMILY: I want to know what you think of Emil Reinhardt, Vinnie, just from seeing him on the beach. Do you find him attractive?

VINCENT: Not at all. I know you both do, but I find him totally unattractive, I really do. Big fake, with that long cigarette holder.

EMILY: Vinnie's saying something that's very true. He *is* a terrible phony.

VINCENT: You're always talking about how elegant he is. I'm sorry. To me he is physically one or two steps above a pharmacist in a fancy Madison Avenue pharmacy, involved in whether or not he has the right amount of candies on the counter next to the cortisone. I mean courtesans.

EMILY: He's a deeply elegant man.

VINCENT: Don't make the mistake of thinking that every man you've been to bed with was something special, Emily.

EMILY: Vinnie darling, Emil Reinhardt wasn't a casual meaning in my life. He was very important.

MARSHA: Do you know what Joan calls him? That poor, poor soldier.

VINCENT: Prussian soldier, that's exactly what he is.

EMILY: You're actually judging him on a very pure level, Vinnie. His insecurities are so fantastic that he projects this pose, and I can understand your seeing it.

VINCENT: That's an excellent word; it's all pose.

MARSHA: A lot of your men have that quality in common.

EMILY: Michael Christy has a pose?

MARSHA: Philippe does.

EMILY: Michael Christy doesn't have pose one.

VINCENT: Look, I don't want to encourage any sentimental feelings of Emily Benson toward Michael Christy, I really don't, because I think he's bad news for you, but he is *not* posed, he's the real thing. Change the subject, Marsh, before she goes into a reverie. Let's talk about really elegant people.

MARSHA: Okay, do we know any?

EMILY: Emil Reinhardt is an elegant person.

VINCENT: Well then we can't have this conversation, because I'm sure he's not.

EMILY: If he isn't, I don't know who is. Vincey, I don't want your corn to get burned. Take it off the fire, darling. Who do we know who's elegant? Nico is very elegant.

VINCENT: You know who I really think is elegant? That British wife of Reinhardt's, Diana. You meet her and you know she could be the highest royalty.

EMILY: Throughout their whole marriage, she has made his life elegant, that happens to be true, although Emil *is* an elegant man.

VINCENT: I was looking at it from the other angle, how he may have put oil into her pure water. I find him so absolutely vulgar, I mean he could be a German.

EMILY: He *is* German. Vinnie, I have to tell you something. I've known Emil Reinhardt for a long time, through some very strange things. I gave up my marriage for him. I have a weird relationship with him now, I can't say we're friends, I can't say we're lovers, but he is an exceptional man. I can still see him as someone I could marry, have a life with. But I also see what you see in him and I don't like that either. I'm not *going* to marry Emil, I'm never even going to sleep with him again, I know that. You know what he told me one night? He's such a peculiar mixture of being elegant and also very frank.

VINCENT: You see, that's where you're wrong. You think that façade is elegance; I'm talking about it as an inner thing.

EMILY: My father, by the way, was a very elegant man, in relation to certain sensual needs, like his food, his newspaper, his cigars.

MARSHA: Can I have more steak?

EMILY: Yes, I saved you a certain centipede centerpiece. Pass. I must say, in his light linen suit, Philippe was very elegant. He was raised by a fantastically elegant mother. I mean that woman's got elegance in her fucking toes. Philippe, when I watched him eat an artichoke or cut his meat or read a book, he did have a kind of elegance. You know what elegance is?

VINCENT: What?

EMILY: It's a certain great sensual respect for the essence of things. That's really in a way how I could define it.

VINCENT: That's very good.

MARSHA: I never get involved with elegant men.

EMILY: No, you don't. You know who the most elegant *was?*

MARSHA: Zeke?

EMILY: Zeke.

MARSHA: Yeah, I think of Zeke as elegant. He's got that sensual thing—whatever you said.

EMILY: Deep sensual respect for the essence of things. He also needs a particular kind of steak, a particular kind of brandy, a particular tobacco.

MARSHA: Everything has to be perfect.

VINCENT: You know who's very elegant up to a point? Clem Nye. Let me put it this way—he's aristocratic, he's got aristocratic strains in him.

EMILY: You can tell a great deal by the way the hands handle things. Did you find Philippe elegant in any way? I found that no matter what low-grade thing he did, there was a certain kind of class.

MARSHA: Not that last time we saw him at Leo Castelli.

EMILY: Yeah, he showed up in a coat down to the floor and five days' growth.

VINCENT: Are you serious?

EMILY: He came with a barefoot Indian beatnik and they were all junked up.

MARSHA: I hadn't seen him in three years. Want to hear the greeting I got? *Ciao*, so you could hardly make it out, then he walked right by.

EMILY: She was ready to kill him.

MARSHA: I wanted to scream.

EMILY: You were ready to *kill* him.

MARSHA: Hey, don't eat those cookies up, you fat pig, I need them for my stews.

VINCENT: Look, Em, I'm eating a lot—she can't stop me.

EMILY: Nathan Fass thought *I* was very elegant when he first met me.

VINCENT: You are.

MARSHA: I think you're split.

EMILY: I think I'm definitely split.

MARSHA: You're also split, Vince. I have *no* elegance, do I?

VINCENT: Oh, listen to her.

MARSHA: I don't.

EMILY: No, I don't think Marsha's elegant. By the way, you know, I don't think elegance is the great quality. Joan is also very split.

MARSHA: Everyone's split but me.

EMILY: In terms of my definition, Joan certainly has a sensual respect for the essence of things.

VINCENT: Let me put it this way, darling, your definition may or may not be correct. You know who was elegant? Lawrence of Arabia.

EMILY: I think Marlon Brando's fantastically elegant.

VINCENT: Jackie Kennedy is not elegant. She's got good taste and good intentions, but she's not elegant. Neither was Jack, none of those kids are.

EMILY: Franklin Delano Roosevelt was elegant.

VINCENT: Menotti is fantastically elegant, he's the meaning of the word. Tim Cullen is not elegant, the way he picks his nose. I don't know what Julie Harris is like, but she gives me the feeling that she would be elegant.

EMILY: By the way, Elizabeth Taylor has absolutely zero in elegance.

VINCENT: I ate many cookies and they were mighty good.

EMILY: How come you had those cookies in the house, Marsha? They're not your style.

MARSHA: For cooking, gingersnap gravy. Can't we talk about something a little more universal than these personalities?

VINCENT: We're talking about elegance, what do you want? It's unbelievably universal.

EMILY: You know, if we had more of an escort, we could go to that party.

VINCENT: I'm Marshie's escort all the time.

EMILY: Where have you been going?

MARSHA: Oh, we go to the supermarket and back, and we do laundry almost every day. You know some people only go to the laundromat once or twice a summer?

VINCENT: That's not very elegant.

MARSHA: Haven't we exhausted the subject?

EMILY: We could also find out what it is by the people who pretend toward it. Is Andy Warhol elegant?

VINCENT: No, but he's got style. He's so fake that it becomes real. I would say that in nature the sky is elegant, but the ocean isn't. However the ocean is much more exciting than the sky.

MARSHA: Don't knock the sky.

EMILY: Don't knock the sky that feeds you rain.

VINCENT: You know if that diet pill made you high, I'd hate to see you when you're low.

EMILY: You think I'm low? I'm just serious.

VINCENT: No you're not—you're sad and depressed and somewhat cut-off. You know what she is, Marsh? She's on the brink of knowing that she's got to make her move in life, and she's getting up the energy.

EMILY: I just made a face that a friend of mine makes, Mike Christy.

VINCENT: That's what got her all depressed, you know, just the mention of his name before. I was trying to be objective, I thought she could take it. The terrible thing about Mike Christy is that he's probably full of all the right things, he comes very close to her and then he goes pssssssssst.

EMILY: I'm not too fond of him on that level either. You know most people in the art world are totally inelegant.

VINCENT: Thank God you realize that.

MARSHA: Who has sex appeal?

EMILY: I think Emil does, wow.

VINCENT: No, as a matter of fact he's the only person who I ever heard had a big penis and still didn't find attractive.

EMILY: I can't understand why you're so negative about him.

VINCENT: I don't know, but I am.

MARSHA: You'll work it out, darling. He probably looks like somebody you once hated.

VINCENT: Oh no, it's too embarrassing to put everything on that level.

EMILY: Who *is* sexual? I think Marsha's sexy, I think you're sexy. I don't find Nico sexy, exuding sex—I'm just telling you, Vinnie.

VINCENT: I *want* you to be honest.

EMILY: I think Emil's sexy.

VINCENT: You *know* he's sexy because you know he's good in bed.

EMILY: I don't call a person sexy just because he has a big prick.

VINCENT: It helps.

EMILY: If someone is small, I can still find him very attractive. Listen, Michael Christy's much sexier than a lot of these people, and his penis isn't that special.

VINCENT: I bet Norman Mailer's very good.

MARSHA: I've always thought that. What is sexual? Let's talk about what sexual is.

EMILY: I think sexual is the least distance between yourself and the object of gratification.

MARSHA: She's got these ready-made fires.

EMILY: My mind is a steel trap. The first time I slept with Nathan Fass, which lasted seven hours, it was the most incredible thing in my life. That man is so tight and so crazy, he went out of his mind wild, like some kind of soldier goes beserk one day?

VINCENT: You know that's the second time you said soldier tonight.

EMILY: No, Joan said it the first time.

VINCENT: And she isn't even here.

EMILY: Marshie's falling asleep.

VINCENT: I am too. It's got nothing to do with you; I've been up since six o'clock.

EMILY: What about the party?

VINCENT: We could pass by it. I'm going to read my Willa Cather, but the two of you go.

EMILY: We can't go without an escort.

VINCENT: Don't be silly—two girls *are* an escort.

EMILY: You just said we could pass by.

VINCENT: Yes, because it's on my way home, but I'm not going in. Oh come on, don't make me out to be a rat. I just want to read my Willa Cather and then go to sleep and wake up early so I can get three hours of painting in before I go to the beach with my girls.

EMILY: I'm sort of interested in the party because I've been in seclusion in Woods Hole for three weeks.

MARSHA: I've been in seclusion in East Hampton for six weeks.

EMILY: But I certainly don't feel about parties the way I did the last time I was here. I just want to go and see what the men are like.

MARSHA: You know my nature is similar to Vinnie's. I'd like to go to bed early and get up early.

EMILY: I wish you'd stop in for five seconds, Vincie. If we walk in
and hate it, we'll leave.

VINCENT: No, I'm not in the mood. I haven't been in the mood for
parties for about four months, particularly if there's no dancing,
so please leave me out of it. But the two of you should go. Put the
dishes in the sink and we'll leave.

MARSHA: Don't start pushing me.

VINCENT: I could *walk* home, actually.

MARSHA: No, you'd get raped.

VINCENT: I think the two of you should go.

EMILY: It's a stupid literary party.

MARSHA: I don't want to talk to people I don't know. I can hardly
talk to the people I do know.

14. IN THE SHADOW OF SICK JOAN

EMILY: I'm not saying a word until the car pulls away.

MARSHA: She can't hear.

EMILY: I'm waiting for the absolute departure. Okay. Now, first of all, there are certain things about Joan that I cannot stand. I cannot bear the suffering, the alcoholic waste bullshit. They make me feel rage and anger and fantastic contempt. Her sickness scares me, darling, because I get scared for myself. I mean Jesus Christ, she's my oldest friend and if she ruins her life, I'll feel very responsible. I don't have to identify with her, I don't have to feel her pain, but I'm an intelligent person who loves her and I should certainly be able to give her something constructive as a human being. But I can't be her mother, sister, therapist, brother, father.

MARSHA: You can't, especially if you start getting healthier this winter, which I'm sure you will, and get interested in doing something for yourself—you're going to find out that a person only has a limited amount of energy.

EMILY: Marsha, I know I only have a limited amount of energy, and instead of it being for myself, it's always for other people.

MARSHA: You're not going to want to do that much longer.

EMILY: No, I'm not.

MARSHA: You know what keeps coming back to me about Joan? When her mother said that her tear ducts were going to dry up. It's incredible. That girl has an absolutely unlimited supply of tears. I don't know where she keeps them.

EMILY: An emotional gangster, that's what someone once called her. Brilliant, isn't it? By the way, have you seen how I've changed in relation to her? She still affects me emotionally, but she has absolutely no power over me anymore. I feel sick things stirring, but they're completely in control. But I'll tell you something, last night, after she went into her crazy hysteria over nothing, I was lying in bed, just a touch high from the wine because I haven't been drinking at all lately, and the mind started filling up, you wouldn't believe it, with who is there for me to get, to love, the utter desperation. But as that's happening, I check it, because I'm strong enough now at least to know how fucking sick it is. But one drink brings all the pain and loneliness in on me, the feeling of emptiness and being alone, and I try to fill it with some man who's completely pointless—just escape, fly, flee. The thing that's hard for me to believe is that this is Emily Benson and that it's in *my* head and *that* I think is part of why I act so strangely when I'm high. I mean I always have anxieties, but I don't think about sleeping with Emil. He came right popping into my skull last night; go out and look for him, round him up, track him down.

MARSHA: That's how I used to get, but last night when Joan got so hysterical, I had only one thought in my mind: to get to the typewriter. I walked out on the whole scene, I had no interest in discussing it for the rest of the evening.

EMILY: Neither did I. I'm not interested in discussing anything for the rest of *any* evening. These sick things are fucking boring.

MARSHA: It's bad enough we let them happen. You asked me why I got so upset—it was because these were someone else's problems being dumped on me, and I don't need them or want them.

EMILY: But that's part of life, darling. Life is being dumped shit on that doesn't necessarily belong to you.

MARSHA: And being healthy is standing up and brushing it off. You know something else? I never realized before the totality of Joan's lack of humor. She doesn't get anything we say.

EMILY: She's too paranoid.

MARSHA: She takes everything literally.

EMILY: Give me an example.

MARSHA: You say, Joan, I'm getting sick of seeing your face around.

She'd answer all right, Marsha, I'll leave. *You* would answer you're getting sick of seeing my face? I'm getting tired of seeing your cunt, or some such ladylike remark. That's one reason I find it impossible to deal with her. If you can't joke about these things, you're absolutely lost.

EMILY: But she's not lost.

MARSHA: I hold very little hope for her.

EMILY: She was very good in Woods Hole.

MARSHA: You know what that adds up to, don't you?

EMILY: Zero, zero amount of zero. You know when I said Joan should kill herself, which is a terrible thing to say, I really felt it, that at this point she's incurable. She needs drugs, she should be on tranquilizers twenty-four hours a fucking day.

MARSHA: And what does that accomplish? She goes druggily through life and then what?

EMILY: Look, darling, first of all if you're on drugs for a year and a half and you go off them you're not back where you started because the whole chemistry has changed. Drugs are therapeutic. Don't forget Joan has had six years of analysis and she *has* responded to it, she's not completely lost. I think there should be no more ports in the storm for her; at a certain point in your life you either sink or swim. There should be no more crutches, no father's money, no good mother handing out money—which there still is. You know Joan and also you—it's ironically not true of me because of the circumstances of my life—have never—

MARSHA: Been loved?

EMILY: *No!* Have never had the doors closed. Her father dies, terrible tragedy, blablabla, but she had money—sixty, seventy thousand dollars. She insisted on going through every penny of it, every cent. She insisted on going through it and then her mother came to her rescue, different men came to her rescue. She lived very well, she didn't give a shit, and now she's crying poverty.

MARSHA: She doesn't know what she's doing. Vinnie asked her if she was really going to enroll in Columbia this fall to become a social worker and she said she can't. She said she has to go the hilt

of the way with acting, she has to go the hilt of the way with becoming a whore, she has to go the hilt of all possible ways, and if
she dies doing it, then she will. Then, if she still survives, and they
don't work out, maybe she'll go to Columbia and become a social
worker.

EMILY: Go the hilt of the way with becoming a social worker.

MARSHA: Let me ask you something. Do you think you're going to
start drinking again?

EMILY: You mean back to that alcoholic behavior stuff?

MARSHA: Yeah.

EMILY: Do *you* think I am?

MARSHA: No, do you?

EMILY: I obviously don't. Look how thin I am, look how everything
I'm doing.

MARSHA: Yeah, but it can be very hard to hold on.

EMILY: It can be. You know I had a terrible feeling, I was looking at
myself in the mirror and it suddenly occurred to me that maybe
I'm a loser.

MARSHA: You're not basically a loser, but I think you can be one if
you don't start moving right now.

EMILY: As a person, I'm a winner.

MARSHA: Yeah, and as a person, *I'm* a loser.

EMILY: Why?

MARSHA: Because for so many years I got myself into those put-
down positions, I slept all the time, I had a loser job—but I'm
getting out of it, I'm not going to end up a loser. A loser doesn't
work as hard as I am now.

EMILY: You're not a loser, darling.

MARSHA: No, but I could have been, at a time when you *couldn't*
have. Now I think I can't be one and you *can*, if you choose to.

EMILY: You don't think I'll choose to, do you?

MARSHA: Would I be wasting my time on you if I did?

EMILY: It's funny because I don't really doubt myself, I just know
how fucking difficult life is and I know the nature of my sickness,

the psychotic way I behave when I'm drunk. I finally owned up to all that, I finally fessed up.

MARSHA: You certainly were denying it before Woods Hole. I didn't know who you were the Fourth of July.

EMILY: That's part of the superego thing you do and Joan does too and I *never* do. You can doubt a friend, you can all of a sudden question and I can't question at all. I never, never, never question.

MARSHA: What?

EMILY: Loyalty or who that person is. I would know it was you no matter what crazy things you did, and I'd know you'd come back.

MARSHA: I knew you'd come back too, but I didn't want to be around in the meantime.

EMILY: I've got news for you, Marsha, I'm going to make a tremendous effort in the fall.

MARSHA: I think you have to do it *now*, get some ideas in your head right *now*, when it's warm and you can lie on the beach and think about it and not have to take the time in the fall.

EMILY: I know all that, but I'm very paralyzed. I really need the therapy to help me out of this fucking paralysis. I'm not saying I'm a weakling, but I do need it. You know I'm really wondering, when I talk about myself and my life, I'm wondering who would be able to love a crazy person like this?

MARSHA: Me too. That's why I was very depressed at the beginning of the summer, because I have come face to face with myself, listening to the tapes and all.

EMILY: *Vis-à-vis*, as they say in French?

MARSHA: One to one.

EMILY: We really have.

MARSHA: Yeah, and it's pretty scary.

15. EMILY AND MARSHA DISCUSS PLEASURE ON THE BEACH

MARSHA: I would put them in two categories: sort of basic, fundamental things, and then the secondary pleasures.

EMILY: No, I don't want to say primary and secondary, I'll just list the things that give me real pleasure, simply that. Like being massaged, I love to be massaged.

MARSHA: I do too.

EMILY: I love to be kissed.

MARSHA: Just kissed, any old way?

EMILY: No, I love to be beautifully and deeply kissed.

MARSHA: By someone you're fond of.

EMILY: By anyone at all. And there's a certain kind of man's body I love—it's a body on which clothes just hang because he doesn't care about them, but that looks beautiful in bed. It's a secret body. I love people with secret bodies, secretly beautiful.

MARSHA: I love mayonnaise on my arm, that's one of my great pleasures.

EMILY: Leave it there, it's good for suntan cream.

MARSHA: What do I love? I love to laugh more than anything.

EMILY: I haven't quite finished with me. I love to watch nice men's bodies walk down the beach.

MARSHA: I love hair, men's hair. I love to touch it, all kinds, thick and wiry like Timmy's, thick and soft and curly like Zeke's.

EMILY: And your Daddy's, perchance? I love lying on my back and also lying on my stomach. I love lying near the blue-green waters of the Mediterranean, looking up at some town like Positano and knowing that I'm going to have a glass of cold white wine in about half an hour.

MARSHA: I love mountains that go right into the sea, Taormina, all those corny things.

EMILY: Corny things are the most beautiful. Like rich tropical islands.

MARSHA: I love to dance when I'm high, *hate* to dance when I'm sober.

EMILY: I like to screw when I'm high too.

MARSHA: I like to be high, a certain amount of high.

EMILY: Right, I like that very much. I love to write well, I love to act well, I like to dance well.

MARSHA: You like to do things well?

EMILY: I like to do things well.

MARSHA: Everyone does.

EMILY: I like to go to a party where I know a lot of people and go around saying hello. That gives me a lot of pleasure.

MARSHA: I like it when people remember me because they usually don't.

EMILY: I love, *love* to see a good movie, a good play.

MARSHA: I love the sun right this minute.

EMILY: I love good acting. I think I love good acting almost more than anything else.

MARSHA: I love good writing—it really gives me orgasmic pleasure. But there's very little good writing in the world.

EMILY: Let's see, I love Fitzgerald—*Gatsby* is one of my favorite books, and *Tender Is the Night*; the *Autobiography of Alice B. Toklas, The Sun Also Rises*, the poem *Kaddish*. I love Proust, Chekhov, Ibsen, Strindberg, Durrell, Robert Creeley, I like Rilke, I like Martin Buber, the idea of I and Thou, even though I don't know much about it. I like Bob Dylan and I love the Beatles. I like Frank Sinatra. I have a couple of favorite songs in the word, I think one of them is "Speak Low" by Kurt Weill.

MARSHA: I love Zeke Sutherland's eyes when they're not cut off.

EMILY: I like Christy's eyes even when they *are* cut off.

MARSHA: I love Vinnie's voice.

EMILY: *Love* Vinnie's voice. His may be the greatest voice. Beautiful voice, so does Michael.

MARSHA: So does Zeke. I love the way Tim Cullen dances.

EMILY: I love the way Tim Cullen's getting famous.

MARSHA: I love your gestures of kindness.

EMILY: You do? Isn't that the sweetest thing?

MARSHA: It's one of my great loves.

EMILY: Do I make gestures of kindness?

MARSHA: Of course, you're very kind to me. I also love it when Vinnie has faith in me.

EMILY: I love it when Vinnie has faith in himself and can accept criticism.

MARSHA: I love Vinnie's paintings.

EMILY: I love Vinnie's paintings.

MARSHA: I love Cimabue.

EMILY: I love certain people being disliked.

MARSHA: What do you mean?

EMILY: Just that.

MARSHA: I love getting tan. I love my body when it's tan. And thin. I like my body generally.

EMILY: I like myself, actually.

MARSHA: Me too. We're lucky we do.

EMILY: We're not lucky; that's a prime requisite.

MARSHA: I love it when I'm able to talk in public places.

EMILY: I love to relate to people and I love to laugh. God, I love to laugh.

MARSHA: You laugh all the time; I hardly ever do.

EMILY: I laugh a great deal.

MARSHA: I love the end of a dinner out of doors, with the candle-light, after you've had wine, and you're smoking a cigarette, you've just had a great meal, and you're with people you love, listening to the country noises.

EMILY: There's nothing like a group of people who love each other and are having a good time.

MARSHA: I also love to be alone.

EMILY: I love the vision of Venice, by all my dreams attended.

MARSHA: I love Venice, I love Sicily.

EMILY: I love Sicily and I love Venice. I love New York.

MARSHA: I don't, I hate New York.

EMILY: What people do I love? Who do I feel for? I love Joan, I love my sister.

MARSHA: I used to love my sister a *lot* until she deserted me for her husband. I'm crazy about my parents.

EMILY: I love my father, I think that's a very important thing in me. He didn't take care of me, he didn't prepare me for life, and that's probably why I do have such a strange love for him. I love my mother, I love my brother Barry, I feel a different kind of love for my brother Arthur. I love my old analyst.

MARSHA: I don't love Merrill Johnston.

EMILY: I love you and Vince, I love Tim, I love anybody who makes me feel warm. I don't love Zeke anymore, I don't think.

MARSHA: You didn't say Joan.

EMILY: Of course I did, she was the first one. I love Michael, I love Nathan Fass.

MARSHA: Maybe Tim is right when he says we have too many loves.

16. EMILY AND VINCENT TAKE A SHORT RIDE

EMILY: He's real low-class, isn't he?

VINCENT: No, he goes to college.

EMILY: He's looking at you, did you get that?

VINCENT: My feeling is this: all summer long I've been attracted to that boy.

EMILY: Is he the one you've been having hard-on dreams about? You're really attracted to him, with that Butch-Jenkins-who's-never-grown-up face?

VINCENT: What do you want? He's only eighteen.

EMILY: Butch Jenkins was four.

VINCENT: I'm just saying that I haven't gone near him all summer, I've reserved myself, completely disciplined myself, I didn't even go near the store he works in.

EMILY: You mean you could have picked him up.

VINCENT: I could have gotten involved with him.

EMILY: Is he queer?

VINCENT: Yes.

EMILY: Is he a nice healthy boy?

VINCENT: Yes.

EMILY: Then what's wrong with it?

VINCENT: It's jail bait.

EMILY: There's my car. Someday I'm going to ride in a fucking car like that. Do you know where that line comes from? Do you have any grasp of literature whatsoever?

VINCENT: Emmy, Marsha and I were talking about how well you are.

EMILY: How well *am* I? I should be well, I've spent thirteen thousand on my analysis.

VINCENT: Was it worth it?

EMILY: It's been an awful lot of sacrifice and pain, darling, but I had no choice. All of a sudden at one point in my life I was having a fucking breakdown, I didn't have a husband, I didn't have a love, I didn't have a dime and I had lost my father—I lost everything in one fell swoop. I couldn't stand on my fucking feet.

VINCENT: When was that?

EMILY: I was married in 1959, then my father died, then Roy went away to summer stock and I fell in love with Emil Reinhardt. As soon as that happened, I knew my marriage couldn't survive. Not because I was going to run off with Emil, but just because it was all wrong. I told Roy and he got violent, he went crazy, he was ready to murder. After that I couldn't see Emil anymore, I couldn't stay with Roy and my father was dead; I had no one to turn to and I started falling apart. Roy got very alarmed, he wanted to keep the marriage together, so he took me to a doctor and the doctor said I should go away, to rally my forces.

VINCENT: Be put away?

EMILY: Yeah, he diagnosed the beginnings of a breakdown. You didn't know me then. If you think Joan is bad, I had involuntary tremors—my entire body was spastic, completely shaking. So I went to Bermuda and when I came back I started seeing this doctor five times a week.

VINCENT: That cop is coming towards us.

EMILY: Vinnie, I'm very upset. I have no license and neither do you.

VINCENT: I know. Listen, you're Marsha Zoxbaum. He's coming straight towards us.

EMILY: Towards *you*, not me—he saw that crazy big fat face of yours.

VINCENT: He's very attracted to us.

EMILY: He's Marsha's boyfriend, he always says hello to her. You know, I don't get why you and Marsha suddenly think I'm healthy. Our whole relationship is based on the premise that you have to take care of me because I'm so sick.

VINCENT: Are you getting sad? Go slow. Tell me about your feelings.

EMILY: I'll tell you about one thing that happened the other day when I saw my mother.

VINCENT: I wish you would.

EMILY: My mother called me three times in one week, asking me to come over. I never see her, you know, she makes me very sad. She said I realize you're very ambivalent towards me, if I could only undo all the wrongs I've done you, but I do love you very much and I really want you to come. So I said okay. I haven't been there in about five months. I walked in and the television set was on. I told this to Marsha—the television set was on the entire time and she didn't deal with me once. When I sat down to smoke a cigarette, the ashtray was gone the next minute into the kitchen.

VINCENT: Meaning?

EMILY: Meaning that her need for neatness was greater than her sensitivity to my need to smoke and feel relaxed.

VINCENT: Maybe she wanted you to follow the ashtray into the kitchen where she was preparing you some lunch.

EMILY: She wasn't preparing me anything, she was sitting in her room watching television. Listen, I'm telling you, I know the possibilities, I know the truth. But the thing was I didn't think my mother has her own problems and she has to have that television set—I just felt, for the first time in my life that I've ever really been aware of it, I felt all those feelings I had when I was a little girl of needing something from my mother and not getting it. The need was there and it was overwhelming. It drove me to look at *Vogue* magazine, it drove me to talk to my mother about some movie, but the need, that little-girl need, still remained. But you see I've been in analysis, so that the anger and the hurt, even though they were there, they didn't cloud me and push me under. The feelings were very pure and I acknowledged them, I understood them. I think a girl like me—it's not as true of Marsha, Marsha's more complicated because of the relationship with the father—but my being unsuccessful and my passivity and hopelessness in that cheap little apartment, it's all about remaining faithful to my mother. If I went out and got the things I want and really need, you know what I'd be admitting? It's a very profound thing. I'd be admitting that I'm losing my mother's love.

VINCENT: Why?

EMILY: Because now I'm living out exactly what she wants from me.

VINCENT: She wants you to be a success?

EMILY: No.

VINCENT: She wants you *not* to be a success.

EMILY: She wants me to be just what I am, full of dreams about what I *could* be.

VINCENT: You mean she wants you not to be more than she is.

EMILY: No more than she is. Because my mother was never a mother, she never distinguished between herself and what she gave birth to. I'm only an extension of her ego. What I know about love for my mother is remaining true to what she needs from me; that's how I get the love, that's how I recognize it. No matter what kind of defiant life I may lead, sleeping with men, doing all kinds of things she doesn't approve of, I'm remaining basically true to the love pact between us. As soon as I go out and get the things for myself that I was never given, I lose her love. I gain the real one, the true one, I gain a love for *myself* which I never had. What's this moron doing? Look at this moron.

VINCENT: You're so brilliant, Emmy. Tell me what I should do about that boy.

EMILY: I don't know.

VINCENT: How do you truthfully feel about my relationship with Nico? Be absolutely honest—I can take it.

EMILY: As far as I can see, you have a very beautiful and deep relationship with him.

VINCENT: But I mean, don't you think it's strange that I'm here with you today talking about that boy and he's off in Salt Lake City?

EMILY: I believe life is very complex and no one person can fulfill the needs of any other, it's that simple.

VINCENT: That's my philosophy exactly. I don't think my psychiatrist understands that.

17. MARSHA AND EMILY TALK ABOUT NATHAN, PHILIPPE, ANDY WARHOL AND NANCY DREW

EMILY: Should I get it?

MARSHA: No, it's not going to be for you. Hello? *Qui est-il?* Which *moi?* Who? Oh, Nathan, what are you doing out here? Yeah, she is. May I ask you one thing first though? Did Emily by any chance ever leave my sneakers in your house? I need them very much. All right, just a second, here she is.

EMILY: Nathan? Hi. What are you doing in East Hampton, darling? It's very strange, Marsha and I were just talking before about if we were faced with the ultimatum of spending our lives on a desert island, who would we choose to take along? We were just sitting around and it was a nice topic to relax with. I said Nathan Fass would be excellent because he'd figure out how to make the salt water sweet, he'd have rational deduction at his fingertips. Zeke Sutherland would also be great, he'd knock down the trees and build up the houses and everything else. What? Yeah, sure, okay, bye.

MARSHA: What's up? What did he want?

EMILY: I don't know. He's going to call back later, he wants to talk to me. He's so nuts. You know what Nathan is? Nathan Fass is *the* supreme authority on everything. For instance, say you have to buy an icebox, he knows you don't go to Korvette's for it, you go to someplace on 86th Street and Third Avenue where you get the best buy in the city. If you want to have a drink, you don't go to the Plaza—he knows a bar where they make the best Bloody Marys for the best value. If someone comes in from out of town and they need a hotel, you don't send them to the St. Regis—he knows the best hotel. You never heard of any of these places, and that's the point—you get the best value *because* nobody ever heard of them. I cannot stand it. He knows *everything*. There's never any—

MARSHA: *Dubbio.*

EMILY: Never any *dubbio*. Except that you always must buy a brand name. I asked him about getting my icebox? You have to get an American make, you have to do this, you have to do that. There's only one mayonnaise to buy, there's only one brand of frozen food, there's only one diet cola that's really diet cola.

MARSHA: How does he know? Does he read Consumers' Union or something?

EMILY: That's right. I couldn't have a paint job on my apartment until I read *Consumers' Report*. Absolutely.

MARSHA: I don't understand the *Consumers' Report*.

EMILY: It makes no sense to me whatsoever. I can't stand the people who consult it either. I understand the reasons for it—it's all got to do with paranoia, checking out every possibility because they're so positive they're going to be done in. There's so much attack from the outside, in order to really get yourself ready for it, you have to make sure you're not going to be anybody's sucker, you're not getting your prick and your balls snipped off. Snip, snip. I told you what Nathan once said to me. He said our relationship would be so simple, Emily, we wouldn't have any problems at all, if I just made a small incision right here. That's what he said. Wasn't it strange, him calling me here?

MARSHA: I know, with that whole French business.

EMILY: He's a very weird guy. He was coming on to you too, darling.

MARSHA: Oh no.

EMILY: Big fucking come-on, I'm telling you. I know him deeply, I know his whole schtick.

MARSHA: Don't be silly—he knew you were here.

EMILY: I don't see how.

MARSHA: You think he was calling *me?*

EMILY: No, he was calling for me.

MARSHA: What does desert island mean anyway? A *desert* island.

EMILY: That's not it, is it?

MARSHA: It's called a desert island.

EMILY: Deserted?

MARSHA: *Desert* island.

EMILY: Remember that time Nathan found a tampax under my bed and he said who did you fuck last night? My analyst said what did he mean, who did you fuck?

MARSHA: Making you the active one.

EMILY: Now is that true? Does it work that way?

MARSHA: I think it's just a figure of speech.

EMILY: What *am* I supposed to say? Last night I got laid? Last night someone put his prick into me? What's the correct way of phrasing it?

MARSHA: I don't know. I say I got fucked.

EMILY: You mean the man fucks and the girl gets fucked?

MARSHA: Don't people fuck each other? What does fuck mean anyway? Does it mean to put your penis in or to make love?

EMILY: That's what I'm asking. Look it up in your dictionary of slang, it's very interesting.

MARSHA: Okay, wait a second: "Fuck, an act of sexual connection, verb transitive only of the male."

EMILY: No kidding. Verb transitive only of the male. What's a transitive verb?

MARSHA: I forget, something about an object.

EMILY: It means it takes an object.

MARSHA: So women take objects and men don't?

EMILY: Yeah, so when Nathan Fass says who'd you fuck last night, he's wrong. When a girl says I fuck around, it's wrong. Then what *do* you say? I went to bed with, I slept with?

MARSHA: That's what I always say, I slept with. How do you know when something's sautéed?

EMILY: It becomes transparent and honey-colored. I like your cooking spoon, it's very nice. A measuring spoon she cooks with.

MARSHA: You know, talking about coming on, I never mentioned it, but I really don't like those long phone calls you have with Eliot.

EMILY: I don't blame you, I don't like them either. But they aren't sexual.

MARSHA: They are for him—talking out is his big kick, and I don't think he should be allowed to do it.

EMILY: Why was he always so interested in calling *you* after you broke up?

MARSHA: Probably because I was the one person in the whole world who really knew who he was.

EMILY: Yeah, it's amazing, isn't it, when you *know* that you know someone? There's nothing more painful than to be with a person who doesn't know who the fuck you are, and to like see him coming towards you, making love to you. It's so sad.

MARSHA: Tim doesn't know who I am, that's the whole thing.

EMILY: That really *is* the whole thing. Eliot knew who you were.

MARSHA: He knew who I was then, but I wasn't myself.

EMILY: Yes you were, you were yourself *then*.

MARSHA: No, I was too neurotic to be myself.

EMILY: Yeah, Eliot doesn't know who you are. Vinnie does. Merrill Johnston? No, it's almost impossible for an analyst.

MARSHA: Very few people do know who you are.

EMILY: I'm putting these dishes in the sink because they're making me nauseous.

MARSHA: Which of your abortions was your favorite?

EMILY: My Puerto Rican one, I loved it.

MARSHA: We had a great time with that abortion.

EMILY: Made-to-order vacation.

MARSHA: Cut-to-order, you might say.

EMILY: Very safe, no pain. Except that I was really scared shitless because it was my first. I was very brave, do you remember?

MARSHA: And I was very good to you, I played the husband. You didn't even know me when I had mine.

EMILY: Philippe was a scoundrel. He was the father of my child, he had lived with me for almost three years, and on the night of my abortion he was screwing someone else. Do you think you can just throw out three years of your life? Yes.

MARSHA: Are you asking the right person? Yes.

EMILY: If someone who didn't know Philippe asked you to describe him, what would you say?

MARSHA: I'd say he was a broken coil.

EMILY: That's very good, because he's so tense and yet so completely ineffectual. Those are the two biggest things about him, his tension and his passivity.

MARSHA: And this was your ideal man.

EMILY: Mentally tense, muscularly tense. I've seen him shake, he's so fucked-up. Whew. It scares me how fucked-up he is. I think he could kill himself, don't you?

MARSHA: Yeah.

EMILY: I *know* he'll die before I do and I know how it will hurt me. But as close as I was to Philippe, he's a complete stranger to me now.

MARSHA: You were never as close to him as you are to me.

EMILY: No, I wasn't.

MARSHA: Of course it's a different kind of intimacy in a love affair, it grows in the bed.

EMILY: Yeah? The bed was a little bit barren in our relationship, a lot of rocks in there. You should have put the milk in the can, Marsha—then you get all the extra goodies.

MARSHA: I got the goodies.

EMILY: I would suggest you put some fresh dill in the soup.

MARSHA: No, fresh parsley maybe.

EMILY: I'll cut it up for you.

MARSHA: Just a little bit. I don't want parsley soup.

EMILY: All right, give me a glass and some scissors, I'll show you a great thing I learned.

MARSHA: I don't call that a little.

EMILY: From Calder's wife.

MARSHA: Very little.

EMILY: I wonder what possessed them to paint this ceiling red.

MARSHA: I like it.

EMILY: Marsha, what books did you read when you were a child? Did you like Nancy Drew?

MARSHA: Yah.

EMILY: I did too, I loved her.

MARSHA: Also Linda Carlton, Air Stewardess, I liked.

EMILY: Linda Carlton, Air Stewardess? Sissy shit like that you read?

MARSHA: I also loved dog books, Albert Payson Terhune. I had a thing about dogs, I had a whole collection of porcelain dogs.

EMILY: You and Laura Wingfield.

MARSHA: I also loved Negro books, Ann Petry. And I adored Sinclair Lewis.

EMILY: I never read Sinclair Lewis.

MARSHA: *Main Street, Arrowsmith, Babbitt, Dodsworth, Kingsblood Royal.*

EMILY: Isn't this a marvelous way to cut parsley? Calder's wife taught it to me. Actually it should be in a glass that's half the perimeter.

MARSHA: How about turning down that Dionne Warwick?

EMILY: I love these lyrics.

> *And when you feel you*
> *Can't accept the abuse you are taking,*
> *Reach out for me,*
> *I'll see you through,*
> *I'll be there.*

It's really about us, it says to the guy when you're broken in two, when you're weak and abused and you can't pick your fucking feet off the floor, you're a total washout flunky failure, what then? Just come to old Emily Benson, she'll nurse you, she'll pick up all the pieces. Right? Take Michael Christy, perfect example. I'm telling him reach out for me, I'll see him through, if he wants a little bit of a drink, I'll perpetuate his drunkenness and give him one because he can't accept the abuse he is taking. Doesn't it make sense?

MARSHA: It makes sense.

EMILY: I'm getting hot, I think I'll put on my favorite outfit of today, the Emmett Kelly.

MARSHA: Oh God in heaven, please don't put that on.

EMILY: I'm sorry, I'm putting on my Amagansett outfit.

MARSHA: Your Elmer Gantry?

EMILY: Let me ask you about something. I want to know exactly what you think of the new dancing. I've been sitting here trying to analyze it. Do you realize that it makes the woman equal to the man for the very first time? She doesn't have to follow him anymore, he doesn't control the rhythms, the music is something they share.

MARSHA: So she can express herself.

EMILY: Right, they're now separate but equal, the dancing is all about individual style. Also, popular opinion to the contrary, I think it has more to do with relating than the old kind of dancing did.

MARSHA: You know those imitations you do of people dancing, you couldn't have done them with the old dancing.

EMILY: No. Now there's a rhythm and a generalized style to follow, but still the way Timothy Cullen does something and the way Nathan Fass does it are completely unique. Whereas if they were fox-trotting or whatever the fuck it was we used to do, even the twist, it wouldn't have been that different. Okay, what else is involved? The woman is dancing; is she dancing for the man?

MARSHA: No, I think she's dancing for the public. And they're dancing out their relationship, if they have one.

EMILY: This is very interesting. For instance you know Andy Warhol won't dance.

MARSHA: Yah, and some people, all they *do* is dance, like Tim. It's the only way he relates, he doesn't talk.

EMILY: Would you please give me a cigarette? I feel very lonely in my Elmer Gantry outfit.

MARSHA: Emmett Kelly.

EMILY: I feel lonely too in my Emmett Kelly outfit, even lonelier. And loneliest of all in my Amagansett outfit. Does anyone have a light for a lonely clown? I'm suddenly getting tears in my eyes.

MARSHA: Stop it, Emily, you're making me nervous. Light your own cigarette.

EMILY: By the way, when I was in the Amagansett supermarket today, I saw one of my earliest childhood loves, a guy named Wallace Balfour. Do you remember the first person you were ever in love with? My first was a boy named Stevie.

MARSHA: Were you, as a child from about the age of six, constantly thinking about marriage?

EMILY: Never.

MARSHA: That's all I thought about as I grew up, I was completely marriage-oriented.

EMILY: Maybe that's why you never got married. But I'd like to get back to *me* now, if you don't mind. I was around four, I was mad about this little boy named Stevie and I had him pee in a bottle for me. I loved it so much I put it on the dining-room table.

MARSHA: And your parents knew what it was?

EMILY: I put it on the table and then I got scared and dumped it down the toytoy. We also got undressed once and climbed into the bathtub together.

MARSHA: I never did any of those things.

EMILY: We were investigating each other's genitalia when my mother came in.

MARSHA: What did she do?

EMILY: Nothing. She said, Emily, what are you and Stevie doing in there? So we pulled up our panties, jumped out of the tub and ran out of the bathroom. I have a picture of us at that age.

MARSHA: Together in the bathtub? Polaroid snap? My first real love was a girl, Meg Kaplan. I wrote her a letter saying I'd never forget her no matter what happened, what paths our lives took, whether they stopped crossing or what, I would always love her.

EMILY: Maybe *that's* why you never got married.

18. EMILY, MARSHA AND VINCENT DISCUSS ORGIES

EMILY: Vinnie, wouldn't it be great when Clem comes out if the three of us went to bed together? He must have a beautiful little penis.

VINCENT: What makes you think it's little?

EMILY: No, you're right, it's probably a sweet fat cowboy punchy midwest free penis.

MARSHA: You're always talking about the size of the penis.

VINCENT: Oh Marsha! That's what people talk about these days.

MARSHA: Only you.

EMILY: And *me*. I talk about it with Joan all the time.

VINCENT: Everybody does.

MARSHA: Well, here's where I get left out of the conversation then. Can you dig my clock out of the bed?

EMILY: Can we dig the ashtray out of the gum?

MARSHA: Okay, if you two are all set with Clem, where does that leave me?

EMILY: Is it a put-down for a woman to sleep with those two men?

VINCENT: What a horrible thing to say! Both happen to be straight interiorly.

EMILY: Let me ask you about the dynamics of an orgy. What really happens?

VINCENT: Are you talking about an orgy or a *ménage à trois*?

EMILY: What's the difference?

VINCENT: Orgies are completely anonymous.

MARSHA: I thought a *ménage à trois* had to be a whole household setup. *Ménage* means living together.

VINCENT: Not anymore, darling. Don't forget I lived in Rome, so I know.

EMILY: Okay, then what are the dynamics? For instance, I wouldn't want to sleep with Marsha and someone else no matter how drunk I get. Who would you like to have the ideal orgy with?

VINCENT: I'm very interested in three men.

EMILY: What are you interested in, Marsha? Orgy or *ménage?*

MARSHA: *Ménage.*

EMILY: Me too.

VINCENT: I don't like the idea of an orgy because for me the personal thing is very very important, and with a *ménage à trois*, you still retain it. And the reason I'm interested in two other men is that it's a beautiful thing to have two penises in your mouth at once.

MARSHA: My God, how big a mouth do you have?

VINCENT: Enormous, but I pick very small penises too. You can also have three balls, two from one person and one from the other.

MARSHA: Do you have to hold your mouth open with your hands?

VINCENT: No.

MARSHA: Why is it so beautiful to have two penises in your mouth?

VINCENT: It's a fantastic extension of experience.

EMILY: That's what I'm interested in, extending my sexual experience.

MARSHA: Wouldn't you like a couple of tits in your mouth at the same time, Vinnie? A ball in the hand is worth two tits in the mouth.

EMILY: Two tits in the bush. You know when I was under LSD, I could have done anything, I was so tuned-in sexually, so aware on so many psychic levels.

VINCENT: I'm really surprised you don't want to go to bed with Marsha. You can't face up to that, can you? Are you able to go to bed with anyone at all?

EMILY: What do you mean, darling?

VINCENT: I mean is sexuality to you so special that you can only go to bed with a specific person, or when you need it can you go with anyone?

EMILY: No, I can't go to bed with anyone. I'm much more selective than Marsha, actually. I've had my promiscuous periods, but...

MARSHA: What do you mean? I can't go to bed with just anyone either.

EMILY: No, but it doesn't mean as much to you on that promiscuous level. But why are you so surprised that I don't want to go to bed with Marsha?

VINCENT: Because you seem very open to me sexually.

EMILY: I *am* very open sexually, but I'm not interested in going to bed with Marsha. I love her but I don't feel any desire for her.

VINCENT: If I had a chance to go to bed with my best friend, I would.

EMILY: Well you're very different from us. For one thing, we've never had any homosexual experience. I did when I was twelve or thirteen, but I haven't since. And the only thing that involved was necking and touching breasts, that's it.

MARSHA: What else is there?

VINCENT: Licking cunts. That's something I'd never do. Have you ever had men lick your cunt?

EMILY: Of course.

VINCENT: Every time you go to bed with a man does he do that? Did you ever stick your tongue up a man's ass-hole?

MARSHA: Sure, hon, we can do anything boys can do.

EMILY: No, how does a *ménage à trois* work? Doesn't it make you feel competitive?

VINCENT: Yes.

EMILY: I don't like that.

MARSHA: What's wrong with a little healthy competition? It's the American way.

VINCENT: Oh please let me keep holding it.

MARSHA: Please darling, don't.

VINCENT: You really feel I'm wasting you, don't you? And Emily's absolutely stunned.

EMILY: I can't even see anything, Vinnie, because her knee is there. It looks very sweet; though it's average, but full average.

VINCENT: No it's not. Let's not make it more than it is. But you know something? It's got an enormous head on it.

EMILY: That's what counts.

VINCENT: With a good set of brains.

MARSHA: We got pretty far with our orgy talk.

VINCENT: It's because we're sitting in the bedroom. It *is*, darling. Believe me, I know all about all things. In the living room, everything was crystallized and crystalline.

EMILY: I know nothing about nothing, but I will say—

VINCENT: Who would *your* ideal be?

EMILY: Well I wouldn't want to share Michael Christy with anyone because I love him so much.

MARSHA: Even with another man?

EMILY: Possibly with another man.

VINCENT: What if he was sucking him? Then you'd be jealous.

MARSHA: I'd like that, I'd be interested.

EMILY: I'd be very interested, I'd be fascinated.

VINCENT: Jonquil's a very special cat.

EMILY: She's brilliant.

MARSHA: I would take Zeke.

EMILY: I'd take Michael Christy and maybe Nathan Fass.

VINCENT: What about Zeke, me and you? No, let's be honest, you're not attracted to me, Marshie, you don't want to go to bed with me.

MARSHA: No.

VINCENT: I *would* like to go to bed with Zeke though.

MARSHA: Who can I have in my parlay with Zeke?

VINCENT: This is getting stupid. You know what it is? It's just repeating that old game of yours, I'm sorry. Instead of picking one man to go to bed with, you're picking two.

EMILY: I *would* like to go to bed with Michael Christy and see a man suck him off and everything else.

VINCENT: You'd be very jealous.

EMILY: Darling, I am *fantastically* curious. I'd like to go to the beach with you right now and watch a whole scene.

VINCENT: You want to hide in the back seat, I'll pick up someone and you'll hear us talking and everything?

EMILY: Yeah, I really would. Who are you more attracted to, Marsha, Joan or me?

MARSHA: Joan.

EMILY: I love Marshie, she's getting so open.

VINCENT: Please, just let me see it.

MARSHA: Absolutely not.

EMILY: It's sweet that he wants to see it. Let him see it, I want to watch him see it.

MARSHA: Close your eyes and I'll show it to you.

VINCENT: Okay.

EMILY: Do you know that I'm embarrassed?

MARSHA: All right, I showed it to you.

VINCENT: Show me again.

MARSHA: Close your eyes.

VINCENT: It's beautiful, it really is. I'm sorry, Emmy, it is.

EMILY: It's beautiful because she has a nice body. She's holding her stomach in and everything.

MARSHA: That's enough.

VINCENT: She's the best sport of any girl I know.

EMILY: I love her very much. Can I say something?

VINCENT: Now I'll show you mine.

MARSHA: Okay. It's pretty. Look Emmy, just the hair.

EMILY: The hair color is very pretty.

VINCENT: Now let us see yours, Em.

EMILY: Oh no, I am *not* showing my twat. I want to say something. Can I say something please?

VINCENT: Go on.

EMILY: When I'm in the movies and there's a scene where people kiss, the first feeling I get is I'm flooded with sexuality. The second feeling is I get very embarrassed. You don't feel any embarrassment?

VINCENT: That's probably the reason you're so promiscuous, because you're very sick.

EMILY: And yet I'm dying to see two people make love.

VINCENT: Would you like to watch me do it this weekend with a woman?

EMILY: I'd love to.

VINCENT: I'll tell you of the women I know which ones I'd like to go to bed with, okay? I'd like to sleep with Marshie, but I couldn't because emotionally I'm too pent up, it's too loaded. I'd go to bed with Emmy in a minute. Does it always have to be women?

EMILY: No.

MARSHA: Yes! That's what the list is.

EMILY: Could you fuck with Nathan Fass?

VINCENT: Only if I could tie his hands behind his back and really slap him. No, you know what I'd love to do? I just got the whole image. I'd like to put him down on his knees, tie his feet to a pole, have him kneeling in front of me, then slap him until the blood started creeping out of his ear, and then take his dick and slap him silly.

EMILY: Sock the dick?

VINCENT: No, just hold onto the dick and slap him silly.

EMILY: Nathan used to play with me in front of the mirror, and make me masturbate for him.

VINCENT: What's wrong with that?

EMILY: Nothing, I'm not putting it down. I'm talking about sensibilities. How many men have you been to bed with?

VINCENT: About a hundred.

EMILY: And how many women?

VINCENT: About seven.

EMILY: So you haven't really been promiscuous at all.

VINCENT: No, I haven't. Why is my green lady painting in here crying instead of in the living room?

EMILY: She's related to the green in the box on the bureau. Isn't it brilliant that I picked up on it?

VINCENT: You know for having a father who was as loving and mystical as yours was, you're remarkably insecure.

EMILY: My mother, Marsha knows about my mother.

VINCENT: Your mother had a hard life, darling.

EMILY: Oh, yeah, my mother had a *very* hard life. She had a nurse and a maid, she never took her children out herself.

VINCENT: Look, I don't even know this woman, but she *is* going to die within ten years.

EMILY: Wait a second, Vinnie, I don't like that, I swear to God.

MARSHA: He always says that to me and I can't stand it.

EMILY: Please don't do that, it's very upsetting.

VINCENT: You know something? You have a lot to work out in your analysis.

EMILY: Don't even do it in jest.

VINCENT: I'm *not* doing it in jest. How old is she? Sixty?

EMILY: She's almost seventy and it's very upsetting. I don't want you to do it.

VINCENT: I'm saying something very objective which one can say about older people. She's almost seventy years old and you don't accept the fact that she's going to die in ten years. It really panics you.

EMILY: First of all, my grandmother died at ninety-five and my mother probably will too.

VINCENT: And if she doesn't? What's the difference to you if she's alive or dead? One less person you can call up? I mean it, what's the difference really? What are you doing for her now?

EMILY: Look, there's one thing about me, I don't care what kind of anger I have about her, I'm very good to my mother and I love her way out of proportion to the amount she loves me.

VINCENT: Don't forget it's one thing algebraically for a child to love his mother, but for a mother to love four children is different.

MARSHA: It's the same.

VINCENT: No, Marshie, you're wrong. I understand all things like this.

MARSHA: Oh stop saying you understand everything about everything.

VINCENT: I'm just trying to get at the bottom of things and you're both getting angry.

EMILY: I happen to be capable of tremendous love. I'm very loyal and very loving, which comes from my mother.

VINCENT: But you must admit you've got a problem when I say that a woman of seventy's going to die within ten years and you panic. If I say Marsha's mother is going to die within the next fifteen, it doesn't panic you, does it?

MARSHA: It certainly does.

EMILY: What are we in analysis for if we can't panic about our mothers dying? You're telling me I have problems? I'm devastated.

VINCENT: You just said something so self-indulgent, you really said a terrible thing.

EMILY: I know, I used my analysis as a crutch.

VINCENT: Exactly. Boy oh boy, just because you're in analysis, it doesn't mean you're that sick, it means you have problems.

EMILY: All right, darling. So?

MARSHA: I have to go to bed soon, I have a headache.

VINCENT: Did you take an aspirin? That's what the doctor said to me, he said you come to me without taking aspirins? Should I get it for you, Marshie? I'm in such torment, such crisis, you have no idea, no one knows. If Emily and I went to bed together, would you be very upset?

MARSHA: Yeah.

EMILY: Did I show you this picture of my father? Be very careful, it's the only one I have.

VINCENT: Ooooh! I've got some bad news for you, darling, and you better accept it. He looks just like Nathan Fass. I'll bet you didn't even see it—I'm the only one here who thinks of *any*-thing.

MARSHA: Vinnie's getting very cocky.

VINCENT: That's not true and don't say it either. That's horrible.

MARSHA: But you're constantly saying how you know everything about everything.

VINCENT: I do. I know everything about what I know about.

EMILY: What do you think of the picture? Do you love it?

VINCENT: It's gorgeous. No, Marshie, I mean it and I'm angry. You know I love your cat, Emmy, I love your cat.

EMILY: You really think he looks like Nathan Fass?

VINCENT: I think the cat looks like you, around the nose. Here's the aspirin.

MARSHA: No spoon?

EMILY: Spoon? Are you four years old? Seriously, how old do you think you are emotionally, Vinnie?

VINCENT: In certain ways I'm very old.

EMILY: Marsha thinks she's about nineteen.

VINCENT: She's adorable.

EMILY: In certain ways I'm about thirty, but basically I'd say about twelve. How long did you go to Yale?

VINCENT: I went to Yale for two years. You're very involved with status, aren't you, and names. That's because you don't think much of yourself. Have you ever thought that women having to put on makeup makes them less than men? It's true, isn't it, in a certain kind of way?

EMILY: Yes.

VINCENT: Just look at this gorgeous limb. She's got gorgeous legs.

EMILY: I love Marsha's legs, she has very pretty legs.

19. EMILY APPROACHES HER BIRTHDAY

MARSHA: Happy birthday to you,
            Happy birthday to you,
EMILY: Oh no, please, not yet! It isn't time! Did I tell you what Sick Joan said the day after her birthday? The first words out of her mouth when she woke up were I've decided to extend my birthday for another day. That's giving me the idea of extending mine. Not that it should begin before it begins—God knows I don't want to punch thirty any sooner than I have to —but once I start punching, I might as well keep going. I'm serious.

MARSHA: Have a good time.

EMILY: What was I going to tell you? Oh yes, about my sister. This is the theory she's been traipsing around town with, she's been doing political canvassing.

MARSHA: Who for?

EMILY: Lindsay. At the same time, she's been doing some birthday canvassing. What she comes up with is she thinks it's a crying shame that at some point in a child's life, whether he be ten or forty-five or whatever, the birthday parties and the fuss over that special day completely come to an end.

MARSHA: Canvassing for Lindsay she found this out? She asked people at the same time about birthdays?

EMILY: She said I really think it's a crime and we should initiate a whole new law that adults continue to have birthday parties with favors and baskets of candy. I swear to God she said that. It's very sad. Now what have we here? A little Jonquil? A black and white creature from Mars with bad breath and a yellow collar? You were really sweet to let me bring her out here, Marshie. Now please let me talk about something dear and important to my heart—my birthday. August 19th, 1935. August 19th, 1965. Thirty years separating those two dates. I'm scared.

MARSHA: I just realized that a minor present I sent away for you never arrived.

EMILY: From the looks of my other presents, it's probably pretty major. Marshie, remember you sent me letters in France saying will you be here to hold my hand on the seventeenth of May?

MARSHA: Yes, and *were* you?

EMILY: Where *was* I, darling? Struggling for my life and my survival.

MARSHA: What's that compared to my birthday?

EMILY: But you weren't really depressed about punching thirty, were you?

MARSHA: I certainly was, and nobody paid me any attention, either.

EMILY: I paid you a label-maker machine. That was this year.

MARSHA: Last year you didn't give me anything for my thirtieth birthday.

EMILY: You didn't give me anything either.

MARSHA: You haven't had it yet.

EMILY: I mean my twenty-ninth. You just gave me a couple of hand-me-down books.

MARSHA: I was trying to re-educate you.

EMILY: I only read about 404 books when I was in Europe.

MARSHA: I made the gesture.

EMILY: You did, you've always been very kind and generous to me, it's true. I still haven't figured out who you represent in my life.

MARSHA: Do I have to be someone else?

EMILY: One thing you do is that you listen. I think you're the only person I know who does. Do I listen?

MARSHA: Yes.

EMILY: I do? I feel very cut-off when I listen.

MARSHA: Vince doesn't listen.

EMILY: I know, he doesn't hear word one.

MARSHA: Except when he's listening.

EMILY: Go to your Marshie, Jonquil babes. How long were you with Vinnie in Europe that first time?

MARSHA: About four months.

EMILY: Was it all set up beforehand that you would stay with him?

MARSHA: I was invited there for two weeks, I stayed four months.

EMILY: That's when you got so close to each other?

MARSHA: We had a fantastic time. He was much more mature then, seven years ago.

EMILY: Vinnie's very immature, but his immaturity's important.

MARSHA: To whom?

EMILY: All around. He's really unique. I don't think there's another young man in the world like him. I absolutely don't think he's queer, by the way, and he's getting panic-stricken about it. You know why I was screaming this morning?

MARSHA: Why?

EMILY: Because he was raping me. He had to put his hand over my mouth.

MARSHA: Are you serious? Weren't you scared? I get terrified.

EMILY: I get scared, but do you know he had an erection? Got scared out of my wits.

MARSHA: You or he?

EMILY: Both of us. Don't forget *you* let him look at your breasts last night. Now that's a very erotic thing to do.

MARSHA: I think he's done it before.

EMILY: Remember what he said when Joan was here about what the relationship is? That what we all love about him is that he treats us badly by not fucking us, that everyone thinks it's about safety, but it's really about masochism.

MARSHA: I don't think of it as safety. In fact it's the sexiest relationship I've ever had, isn't it?

EMILY: It *is* very sexy. Do you and Vinnie want to sleep with each other?

MARSHA: No, I don't think so.

EMILY: I don't either, but I *do* think it's a sexual relationship and you could get married. Yes? No?

MARSHA: No. Did you tell him you think he's not queer?

EMILY: No, I don't want to put the pressure on him, because then he'll use it with his doctor. The reason he doesn't want to continue with that doctor is because her thesis is to make him healthy and making his healthy means making him straight.

MARSHA: You know I get a very scary feeling sometimes that I'm pushing myself into a corner—all of a sudden I'm beginning to find everyone except you and Vinnie very dull. We've set up such a stimulating, total, free, hysterical, intimate, intense relationship that I find it impossible to relate to other people, they leave me completely cold. If someone else comes into the house, I get annoyed because they cut down on our communication. I haven't met one person all summer that I'd want to spend a single evening with.

EMILY: Yes you have.

MARSHA: I *haven't*. Who?

EMILY: If you didn't know Merrill Johnston, you might want to spend an evening with him.

MARSHA: He's not fun, I'm talking about people who are fun.

EMILY: Serious people can be fun.

MARSHA: They have to be both, that's the whole thing.

EMILY: Michael Christy isn't fun really. He *can* be, but he's not. Was Zeke fun?

MARSHA: Zeke—may I speak the truth now after all is said and done?—bored me most of the time.

EMILY: Michael bored me a lot too.

MARSHA: Really?

EMILY: Yeah, when he was turned off, like the next morning he would bore me, until he warmed up.

MARSHA: That's the thing, you always have to warm these guys up, keep the fires burning, have the blankets ready and the hot tea, all these spiritual heating pads. Who needs it?

EMILY: Forget it. As far as getting ourselves into a corner though, I know exactly what you're saying, but it's misleading because there are other *very* interesting people. They aren't interesting instantly the way Vinnie and I are because you know us so well.

MARSHA: I hope you're right.

EMILY: You certainly don't begin to imagine that we're the only interesting people in the world, do you? Pretty scary thought.

MARSHA: That's the thought I've been having.

EMILY: Then let me ask you something. When you've been in love, didn't you feel like that person had all the qualities, that combination of rare properties, that you would never find again? It's exactly the same thing.

MARSHA: I've never thought that all the couple of men I've loved had the great properties. I thought I'd be linked to them for life, but I never imagined they were the most fantastic people in the world.

EMILY: Oh I *did*, you see. I thought Emil Reinhardt, for example, had absolutely everything I'd ever want in a man.

MARSHA: I always knew Eliot was lacking certain things—a heart, a soul, a couple of things.

EMILY: The only thing I thought Philippe lacked was money. I thought he had everything else, brains, sensitivity, I loved his looks, I was sexually attracted to him, he interested me—the fucking bore.

MARSHA: He was very boring.

EMILY: *God*, was he boring!

MARSHA: He came over one afternoon and bored the hell out of me, talking about the bomb or space or something.

EMILY: Poor Philippe, he's very boring. You know there's one thing about Philippe and Michael Christy that scares the shit out of me. They sit exactly the same way, with their legs wrapped like this, that double wrap.

MARSHA: It's very faggy.

EMILY: I thought Michael Christy was queer when I met him. As a matter of fact, when I was in London creating a scandal with him, I told everyone including Philippe it wasn't possible because he was queer. It was a defense, I was terrified that I wouldn't get out of Europe alive with my belongings, my packages, my pots, my pans, my letters. I'm not sure I *did*. I guess Michael Christy was the most interesting man in my life.

MARSHA: I'm tired of talking about Michael Christy.

EMILY: I am too. He's a bore because he's a big baby.

MARSHA: They all are. Zeke is the biggest baby who ever lived, he's like a three-year-old child.

EMILY: There is almost *nothing* mature about him.

MARSHA: Except his old-age potbelly.

EMILY: I wonder how mature *I* am.

MARSHA: I'm a baby too, but at least I'm trying to grow up a *little* bit. Wait a second until I'm out of the bathroom.

EMILY: Why is the door suddenly being closed? Are you shagrugging or something? You know when you think of it, you've actually got a very weird list.

MARSHA: Why?

EMILY: They're all people you can't stand. The only one you ever talk about with any semblance of feeling is Zeke. Certainly not Eliot.

MARSHA: I *do* have a semblance of feeling for Eliot, I still chew his chewing gum.

EMILY: You can't stand him.

MARSHA: I know it. You're right, once again.

EMILY: I, on the other hand, am quite fond of a lot of people on *my* list.

MARSHA: I'm friendly with more of mine than you are.

EMILY: I'm not friendly with any of them, I'm fond of them. I'm also fond of this ketchup trying to get out of the bottle. Which ones are you friendly with?

MARSHA: Tim.

EMILY: Oh, he's already in the past, relegated to oblivion?

MARSHA: Sure.

EMILY: Poor bastard. Can you do the list of my boyfriends?

MARSHA: No.

EMILY: You really can't? Try to get a couple.

MARSHA: Lord Alistair Brooke.

EMILY: Very good start.

MARSHA: Alfred Dreyer, Michael Christy, Philippe Rocheau, Nathan Fass, Ted McCortney, Howard Nelson, Von Huffedicker.

EMILY: Who's Von Huffedicker?

MARSHA: Von something, from last year.

EMILY: Oh yeah, that guy.

MARSHA: She doesn't even remember her own men.

EMILY: There's an obvious one you're forgetting.

MARSHA: Roy Imber. Then there's Merrill Johnston which you never told me about.

EMILY: Uh-oh.

MARSHA: There are some early ones I won't possibly get.

EMILY: Armand Pascal, even though we didn't have actual intercourse.

MARSHA: Did I leave out any of the recent ones?

EMILY: You left out a lot of them—Keira, Ted Mosher, John Orwell. I can't remember any others.

MARSHA: I didn't do that badly.

EMILY: I don't think there are any others. It's not possible, is it, that that's it? I have the list somewhere.

MARSHA: I hate my list, I'm bored to death with it.

EMILY: It's not that I'm bored, it's just that if that's what my thirty years are all about, I could puke.

MARSHA: It's so fucking meaningless the way I can recite those names.

EMILY: I could puke. You know Joan analyzed why you make all those lists of the men, she said by doing it, you completely castrate them, they all become equalized, one is just as important or unimportant as any other.

MARSHA: That's interesting.

EMILY: It is. I can't do your recent list, except for Tim Cullen. I can't think of anyone else.

MARSHA: There *is* nobody else.

EMILY: I don't remember who my last bout was with.

MARSHA: What's a bout?

EMILY: My promiscuity bout.

MARSHA: How many were there in it?

EMILY: Exactly fifteen in the batch-bout.

MARSHA: Boy, you really scored them up. Were there ever two in one night?

EMILY: Well, there were many night after night. I slept with a lot of men then, Marsha, and they're all like meaningless empty faces now, I don't remember them. I know their names, but they don't mean anything. That was very hard for me, you know, because I'm not promiscuous by nature. I feel very little guilt about it, but it was definitely part of my masochism. Another thing that's been on my mind is how did I get to all the parties I went to last year? What was I doing?

MARSHA: You were going to parties. Emily, we've got to figure out something for this year to avoid that. It's okay for you with your Wars and your Hols and your Roys and your Rays, but I'm really not interested. It's a dead end.

EMILY: It's *not* a dead end, darling, nothing is. I met a great many people this past year, Marsha, but I was so sick and so closed that it didn't mean anything. Like there's no reason in the world why we couldn't have met someone at that John Orwell party.

MARSHA: There was one reason.

EMILY: Because there was no one to meet?

MARSHA: No.

EMILY: Because we were with Vinnie?

MARSHA: We absolutely clung to him, you were hovering around him just the way I was.

EMILY: There was no one else to hover around.

MARSHA: If you stood by yourself, there would have been.

EMILY: All right, so what do we do? I have so much anxiety as it is about this year. There's nothing in the theatre world, I'll tell you that.

MARSHA: Do you think I'd want to marry an actor?

EMILY: No, but there are certain people, television writers, producers, those kind of guys, who are very interesting.

MARSHA: Yeah, but how do you get to them?

EMILY: Well let's see what I do with my career, honya, let's see how I hustle. There's also the literary world—there are a lot of men in the literary world.

MARSHA: Hi, Jonquil darling, you love me more than your Emmy, don't you?

EMILY: What do you think's going to happen this weekend?

MARSHA: Very little, I have a feeling.

EMILY: Listen, darling, there are going to be a lot of parties.

MARSHA: Yeah, and we won't hear about them until the following day.

EMILY: Jonquil, where are you, sweetie? Come here. She's so fucking feminine, it's heartbreaking. I love her little chirping.

MARSHA: Why don't you get a bird and save yourself a lot of trouble?

EMILY: It's ridiculous, she really chirps. I was sure you'd fall in love with her. It took you a long time, but you finally succeeded.

MARSHA: You know I'm a slow starter.

20. A DIFFICULT DINNER

VINCENT: That thing last night about being cocky was very cruel, darling.

MARSHA: It's just that you don't word things very nicely, and they *do* come out cocky.

VINCENT: We're supposed to look beyond words. I was trying to tell you what a rare moment it was, because you inspire me to feel things I haven't felt since I was an adolescent, and then you say you're getting cocky and presumptuous.

MARSHA: I'm going into the other room to work a little before dinner. Don't start whispering about me.

VINCENT: Marsha, Merrill Johnston is right around the corner. If you continue like this, I'll call him up and we'll take your head to Southampton Hospital. I'll tell you one thing I hate, Emily, this cat's food all over the place. You know I'm a reasonable man.

EMILY: You really are, but please don't pick on me when it's only two days away from my thirtieth birthday.

VINCENT: Emily, all this stuff about your thirtieth birthday is very very weird. I'm really getting sad.

EMILY: You were in a beautiful mood before you came.

VINCENT: I was, I was in a rare mood, and then I was treated very shabbily when I got here.

EMILY: Not by me. I love you very much.

VINCENT: I was in such a rare mood.

EMILY: You know I'm beginning to get just a little bit tired of your rare mood. How about me? I was in an even rarer.

VINCENT: You were crude, you were absolutely raw, you were so rare. See how I'm helping you around the kitchen? Mommy's little helper. Do you think part of my relationship with you and Marsha these days is like my two sisters? It is.

EMILY: You have two sisters?

VINCENT: You know it's brilliant what you said about my painting, about the honesty involved. It *is* more honest than anyone else's work.

EMILY: That's why Nathan Fass, when he says it's obscene, he's attaching to you a certain kind of social awareness.

VINCENT: He hates homosexuals. Don't get angry at me, Em, I can't bear it.

EMILY: What's the matter, darling?

VINCENT: I'm so sad.

EMILY: *Why?*

VINCENT: Because that's what being alive is.

EMILY: I know it, I'm sad all the fucking time, you have no idea.

VINCENT: I heard something last week about what makes humans different from animals, some gorgeous basic thing, like that humans have memories, but it's not that.

EMILY: What is it?

VINCENT: Something absolutely beautiful. Are you putting garlic powder in too? Wow, is that cheap. Why use *fresh* garlic then?

EMILY: Completely different tastes. They are, as one might say, complementary.

VINCENT: Marsha darling, I can't bear it when you're sad.

MARSHA: I'm not, I've just got a lot of work to do.

VINCENT: Who hasn't? I began a new painting today.

MARSHA: Yes, and were *you* interrupted?

VINCENT: Yes, continually, by my memories. Do you want to get married, Emily?

EMILY: When?

VINCENT: Not when—*do* you?

EMILY: You're looking at me and wondering if I ever could, right?

VINCENT: Boy are you sick. You want to know what I was thinking? I was thinking how alive and beautiful I feel and how alive and beautiful you are, and I was thinking of all the people we know who are married and how in their eyes we're lost.

EMILY: They don't think that.

VINCENT: Yes they do.

EMILY: I'm testing the broccoli to see if they're right.

VINCENT: Marshie, we're going to eat in five minutes, you and I. Get in there and work in the meantime. Emily, you're looking at me with love and I can't bear it. Marsha's falling in love with me sexually and now you are too, and I'm falling in love with both of you. Doesn't Marshie look good in those colors? Shall I tell her to come have the soup now?

EMILY: Yes.

VINCENT: Come have the soup now, Marshie.

MARSHA: Oh no, it's not five minutes.

VINCENT: Oh yes it is. Should we have it in cups or little saucers? You know something, I'm very elegant. But I'm really not. You know what I am?

EMILY: What?

VINCENT: I'm basically a good kid. Give Marshie her scotch broth, will you please?

EMILY: One scotch broth coming up.

VINCENT: Marshie, you don't know how much you hurt me last night about the cockiness.

MARSHA: You hurt me twenty times a day.

VINCENT: Can we have that lesson now of teaching you how to eat soup?

MARSHA: I know how.

VINCENT: No you don't. First of all you don't start there. Put it down, you're not going to eat until you do it right. Like this.

MARSHA: Oh no, that's wrong. You don't shovel it like that.

VINCENT: Yes you do, you scoop it up. The American way to drink soup is not to put anything in your mouth, like this. We're going to do it like the Italians.

MARSHA: Can I blow on it?

VINCENT: Don't *ever* blow on your food. And never show your teeth when you're drinking soup.

EMILY: When you're drinking anything. What's so good about this scotch broth? I'm tasting it.

VINCENT: Isn't it nice?

EMILY: Yeah, like you're a sick child.

VINCENT: It's homey, it makes it like a cold winter night outside. Do you think women are different from men? I do, and I think they should be. I think women are wonderful.

EMILY: Do you like women better?

VINCENT: I don't know.

MARSHA: I like men better than women.

VINCENT: What I like best is a man who has much of the woman's sensibility.

EMILY: Like you.

VINCENT: I know, I like myself.

EMILY: A healthy state of affairs.

VINCENT: Bring glasses for the wine, Cinderella. I suppose my meat will be done before the dinner's over. I'm sure of it, I just have that feeling.

MARSHA: Things were so calm here before he came.

VINCENT: Why did you invite me over then, if I'm such an uncalming influence? Let's be honest, you *didn't* invite me over, I invited myself. But no one made you say yes, you could have had courage for once in your life.

MARSHA: I get what you're trying to do, you know.

VINCENT: What?

MARSHA: Sever your dependency on me before the summer's over, so it won't be such a harsh blow in the fall.

VINCENT: Can I ask you a question? Do you *really* think I'm more dependent on you than you are on me? The car aside, do you really think so? You're a pathetic little bitch, you really are, with your mechanical appliances, your credit cards, your rich Mommy and Daddy and your car, you're absolutely crazy. Just because your

Daddy made some money during the war, you act like a society deb. It could make a person puke at the dinner table. You know she really got upset about what I just said, Em? I gave her a whole cataloguing of what her life is about, and it completely discoveted her.

MARSHA: That is *not* what my life is about.

VINCENT: Tell me what it *is* about, princess.

MARSHA: I'm not interested in talking to you.

VINCENT: So mature. You must have been terrific with Dwight MacDonald the other night.

EMILY: Are these the kinds of discussions you two have?

VINCENT: No, let me follow this through. You really think I'm dependent on you? And you *like* being in that position, don't you? That's why you're treating me so badly these days.

MARSHA: May I have the bone if no one's eating it? I'm ignoring you, I refuse to play into your whims.

VINCENT: What kind of Victorian prose is this? 'I refuse to play into your whims.'

MARSHA: You better behave yourself.

VINCENT: Why?

MARSHA: Because you're getting me angry.

VINCENT: Why am I getting you angry?

MARSHA: Because you're not behaving yourself.

VINCENT: You know I helped her out of two very important things this summer, and now *I'm* dependent on *her*. First with her whole reaction about the fact that her analyst happens to be sleeping with women, and then her crying and clinging with Tim Cullen. How much have you helped *me* out of?

MARSHA: Nothing.

VINCENT: You've driven me to Riverhead three times for driving tests, that's all.

MARSHA: Right, I'm not a giving person.

EMILY: Can I tell you something about the nature of your relationship which you seem to forget?

VINCENT: Go on.

EMILY: That Marsha's a girl and you're a boy.

VINCENT: I'll tell *you* something about our relationship—it's getting into a very precarious position. I mean it, it's gone too far.

MARSHA: You know what I said to Emily today? We were talking about Italy, saying how well we got along, and I said you were much more mature then.

VINCENT: Are you serious? Marsha, I love you more than anyone in the world, I really do, except for one thing: you're very dumb. Don't you realize I was half a person then? What you cannot accept about me—you think it's immature and you think it's sickness and you think it's defense—is that I am the only person you know who is absolutely willing to expose his wounds, and to show what he's not. I don't care if you call this immaturity, but don't call that *maturity*. That was someone who was guarded, someone who was just growing up. I wasn't mature then, I was frightened. And just because I'm open now—you know there are very few people as open as I am? Don't get cocky, I know.

MARSHA: You're right.

VINCENT: Emily, considering you're serving the meal, you really should wash your hands after you go to the bathroom.

MARSHA: But how about the way you walked out of my room last night?

VINCENT: I'll tell you about that. You were already asleep, lying on your right side with the sheet over you, and your tanned arm was on your hip, overlapping your body. It was absolutely beautiful, and I had so much affection for you and warmth. Do you call that dependency or do you call it warmth and affection?

MARSHA: Warmth and affection.

VINCENT: Yes, and that's what wanting to be with you this summer has been about, because I know that it's a rare time for us. I mean it. That's what infuriates me about you. You never see beyond the surface of things; that's your major obstacle.

EMILY: Your sensitivity is very sweet and touching, Vinnie, but you sure don't know how to make a dressing for tomatoes.

VINCENT: Lousy, absolutely lousy, I admit it. I only had apple cider vinegar in my house, that's why.

EMILY: You never put vinegar on tomatoes.

VINCENT: Do you know why I have to constantly defend myself against the two of you? Why I get so uncalm and panicky and completely frenetic when I'm here? Because I'm with the most like-myself people in the world, so this chemical thing happens, a substantiation of myself, which absolutely drives me crazy. It's like everything I always hold back because I'm against the world I'm confronted with in two other human beings. So maybe it's best we don't see each other anymore if I offend you. You didn't hear what she said before, Emily, when you were fixing the broccoli. She said it was so nice here without me.

MARSHA: No I didn't.

VINCENT: You said we were so calm here without you.

MARSHA: That's *right*.

VINCENT: It was definitely a comparative thing and a put-down of how alive I was.

MARSHA: We were alive when we were calm.

VINCENT: Listen to her, she is so ready to be angry with me and hate me. When I walked in here I was like a schoolboy coming home from school and finding the mother angry. I spend an hour searching for a picture today to do a painting for you, Marsha, I bring it, I show it to you, and you are so un-aristocratic that you say you're angry without even acknowledging the picture.

MARSHA: I didn't want a blonde picture.

VINCENT: It's not a blonde, there's sunlight in the sky.

MARSHA: It's a blonde.

VINCENT: You know you're having hallucinations—you take too much LBJ.

EMILY: I'd be happy to make some coffee, but I must say I'd really love some chocolate cake with vanilla ice cream.

MARSHA: I'm not going out for anything.

VINCENT: It's nine o'clock now, I'm leaving. I have to take the car for tomorrow morning, 8:15 mass. You know I'm very sad tonight. I came in completely happy, in such a rare mood.

MARSHA: A healthy person doesn't let someone else affect him to that extent.

VINCENT: Healthy people don't *have* moods, because all moments to them are the same. Anyway, I never said I was healthy.

EMILY: I make fantastic homemade pie.

VINCENT: Oh Em, let's go over to the other side of the island and get peaches?

EMILY: Okay, but I don't want to get into a whole homemade pie-making scene.

VINCENT: Emily's gotten so healthy. From above the waist. You know what I think of when I think of women? The breasts, not the vagina.

EMILY: You really do?

VINCENT: Oh look at her, trying so hard to be elegant, peeling the skin. You think putting that peach juice on the floor is making anyone happy? You think it's some sort of Johnson's wax? I'll just tell you one thing.

MARSHA: One thing.

VINCENT: What I was talking to you about last night was rarity.

MARSHA: How rare can it be when you feel it every two seconds?

VINCENT: I don't—only when I'm with you. I never use that expression with other people. But I won't feel it much longer, I'm beginning to feel very alone here. These peaches were not washed, I can feel the dirt on each one. There's water at the bottom of the bowl, but they were not washed.

EMILY: Vinnie, please don't start getting paranoid and alone. It's too sad. Because God knows your life compared to mine at this point is just so much better and so much sweeter. If you're going to start getting depressed when I'm punching thirty so fucking soon, just shut up.

VINCENT: You know you're pathetic, you're really pathetic.

MARSHA: There he goes.

VINCENT: You really are, you're so self-indulgent.

EMILY: Boy, if I could just count the times this summer you've said

I'm pathetic. *I'm* self-indulgent, but you're talking the whole fucking night about being alone. You are *not* alone, you're self-indulgent.

VINCENT: That's why I recognize it in others.

MARSHA: This is one of the most difficult meals I've ever had.

VINCENT: You really consider this a difficult meal? If your stomach is full at the end of it, it wasn't a difficult meal.

MARSHA: This is a whole act, you know, a complete act.

VINCENT: Let's have some more wine, Emily, and get drunk.

EMILY: No, darling, I don't drink anymore. It's a habit I've given up.

VINCENT: Course you have.

EMILY: Thank you, Marshie my love.

MARSHA: Let me touch your hair, Em. We have a very good relationship.

VINCENT: That exchange of looks between you was terrible just now. This is so Jules and Jim, you two are in love with me. I wonder what Nico's doing, alone with all those people wanting to go to bed with him, alone with Nureyev and Margot Fonteyn at dinner. You know going to bed with someone is a fantastic thing. That's why promiscuity is such a horrible word. I think going to bed with many, many people is very beautiful, I really do, if it's done with a certain kind of sensitivity and sensibility.

MARSHA: That's the point—going to bed with a lot of people tends to dull sensitivity. And don't forget, you *don't* go to bed with a lot of people.

VINCENT: No, I don't. But I'll tell you, one of the reasons why the people I go to bed with once fall in love with me—and I always know they do—is because I look them in the eyes. I do it not out of loving or of liking their eyes or anything, but because it's rare for me and I want to know exactly what I'm doing and who I'm with.

MARSHA: I look at them in the eyes too.

VINCENT: Yeah, but you don't go to bed with strangers.

MARSHA: I do so, I get to know them afterwards.

VINCENT: Have you ever met someone at a party and gone to bed with them that night?

MARSHA: A lot of people I've gone to bed with the night I met them.

VINCENT: I'm talking about people you had no idea you were going to bed with, and you also knew during the bed that you'd never see them again.

MARSHA: No.

VINCENT: And so you look at them to hold on to the experience.

EMILY: I can't go to bed with someone for once anymore because I see through it, I see through to the end and I see too much, I know too much.

VINCENT: I think with a man it's different.

EMILY: Unless I'm drunk and insensible, it's too terrible.

VINCENT: If I were either of you, I wouldn't go to bed with a man for a long time.

MARSHA: I think that's the new policy.

EMILY: It's not such a new policy—I haven't slept with a man in three months.

MARSHA: You haven't met anyone you *wanted* to sleep with.

VINCENT: It's the same thing, darling. If she were hoping to go to bed on any night, she'd find someone.

EMILY: Right.

VINCENT: And I'm saying maybe it's a good idea to hold it off.

EMILY: That's what my analyst says. But Nathan Fass says you can't tell anything about anyone until you've been to bed with them. I do think it's a bad idea, doing it immediately, but how can you avoid it? You want to do it, you know he wants to do it, and yet you have to go into some prudistic ethic, to say I believe in waiting three and a half weeks, we don't know each other well enough?

VINCENT: You mean you think you have to do it the first night? I'm sorry, I see men that I don't even do it with the first night, or the second or the third. I don't mean to be cocky, but I *do* know what it's about. Going to bed in our society as it's set up now means for the woman to give herself up completely to the man. But the thing is she *can* go to bed the first night and remain independent. But if you surrender totally like Marshie does, then it's no good.

EMILY: What do you mean?

VINCENT: The morning after she makes him a big breakfast and gets very upset if he doesn't call two hours after he leaves.

MARSHA: The first night is the only time I *do* care about them, because it's a new name on my list.

EMILY: No, let's say I meet Michael Christy, right? And I fall madly in love with him and he falls in love with me.

VINCENT: We're not talking about a Michael Christy, we're talking about casually meeting someone you're attracted to, who's attracted to you.

EMILY: You *don't* go to bed with him, you're absolutely right, because you don't want to make it serious before you know where you are. That's a safeguard. But what about someone who is obviously going to be meaningful?

VINCENT: I don't believe there *is* anyone who's obviously going to be meaningful. I think it's all chance and what you bring to a thing. Loves aren't made in heaven, you know.

EMILY: I'm not talking about loves made in heaven, I'm talking about the whole gestalt.

VINCENT: The gestalt of it is that it's completely what one does with it.

EMILY: Yeah, but what one *does* is what one *is*.

VINCENT: And one is many, many people, so what one does is many different kinds of things. Like if you decide to stay at one party instead of going to another one, if you stop at one street corner or another, you're going to meet someone else, and that person can be the person of your life. I met Nico completely by chance, I met Clem completely by chance. Anyone you've ever been involved with, you've met completely by chance, and that doesn't mean if you hadn't gone to London last year and met Nathan Fass and Michael Christy, you might not have gone someplace else and met two other people who would have been just as meaningful. We've all got this fantastic capability, that's the whole myth about love. Love is a completely fake idea, and it's one more thing that's ultimately going to go. Love is based on fears and irrational things, people's needs; it's got to do with one's self, it has nothing to do with the other person and it's absolutely foolish to think it does. All love can do is help one be productive and get through life.

EMILY: Yeah, but you're leaving something out.

VINCENT: What?

EMILY: There is also love. I don't mean romantic love, I mean Zen love, love on a larger level.

VINCENT: I'm not leaving it out. My point is that there is love, but there is no one love.

EMILY: I don't believe in destined romantic love either. When you can really love, you can love anyone, the object is almost anonymous.

VINCENT: In the city of New York, with its ten million people, there are at least—

EMILY: Ten thousand.

VINCENT: Ten thousand, that was the figure I was going to say, there are at least ten thousand people in any minute that you could fall in love with, who would be equal to your love and who would really be the person that you *should* love. Like if you went to Henry Geldzahler's party for Andy last year, that was a group of let's say six hundred people throughout the evening.

EMILY: Three hundred.

VINCENT: All right, then I'll just half my figure. There must have been at least three new people there who, if I had been independent and alone, I could have made it with for at least seven months in a love relationship. And you too and you too.

EMILY: So the art world isn't as closed as we thought.

VINCENT: The only thing about the art world which isn't good for you and Marshie is that the men in it are too much like yourselves. Oh, if only I hadn't eaten all those gingersnaps last Friday night. Remember when you arrived last Friday night, Em? It seems like so long ago.

EMILY: Vinnie, was that really last Friday?

VINCENT: Look at Jonquil, she's so elegant. She unnerves me, she's so elegant. Are raisins fattening? Tell me the truth.

EMILY: They're fattening as hell, they're 100% carbohydrates. Ten raisins are about twenty carbohydrates, loaded with sugar. You're not allowed to have any.

VINCENT: Thanks for all the milk, cheap bitch. Did you ever see a color like this coffee? It's raw umber. You could learn a lot about being a woman from Jonquil. Very independent, but when she wants to be, she's very affectionate.

EMILY: I want to hear Dionne Warwick, I really do.

MARSHA: I'm sorry.

VINCENT: What is this, Marsha, you're braindraining us? I'll bet you don't even know what the brain drain is.

MARSHA: What?

VINCENT: No one understands anything here. The two of you may be marvelous women, intuitive intelligences and all that, but you don't know anything about the outside world. Really ignorant. The brain drain refers to the scientists leaving England because they get higher wages from universities here.

EMILY: Very interesting.

VINCENT: Just because there isn't a name personality involved, darling, it *can* be interesting. You know you're a very beautiful person, Emily. I can't get involved with you because you're too beautiful.

EMILY: Who the fuck wants you to get involved with me?

VINCENT: Maybe I *want* to.

EMILY: Then don't warn me, I don't need preludes and prefaces.

VINCENT: What do you want? Epilogues?

EMILY: Either commit yourself or don't, but don't give me a four-act play about it.

VINCENT: Anyhow, I wouldn't want a woman who's slept around the way you have and who uses the word fuck so much.

EMILY: What he says in jest, does he mean in jest?

VINCENT: What I say in jest, I mean in jest.

EMILY: Vinnie, did you ever hear the story of how Marsha and I got to Stromboli? Listen to this. I was dead sick in Positano, the doctors were coming every day and Marshie was bringing me rice with butter. I was dying, but I knew if we didn't get out of there pretty quick, she'd kill me first, because she was so unhappy and I was too. Someone told us to go to the Stromboli Islands, they said they're like deepest Africa, Greek, passionate, blabla, so we said okay. The next day I went to call Philippe and I fainted in the telephone office, they had to carry me out on a stretcher. But in the morning I woke up, I said Marsha don't worry, we're leaving. We got to Naples, we had lunch in some place where there was an air-conditioner backwards, it was blowing this shit smell into our noses.

VINCENT: Was it really a shit smell?

EMILY: It was unbelievable. We got onto the boat—I had lost about twelve pounds—big huge boat, I'm falling on the floor every here and there, dragging the big rubber what-do-you-call-it, *materassino*.

MARSHA: We carried it from town to town.

EMILY: And at some point, Marsha's in the bar asleep, and I blow the thing up to lie near the water, because I'm so fucking sick, Vinnie, you don't know.

VINCENT: Yes I do.

EMILY: And in the middle of the night, some marino shakes me on the shoulder. I wake up and I go huh? He says *vieni con me*. He wants to fuck me, I should go with him to his cabina. That's all I need, I'm almost puking over the side of the deck, with the sharks and the fins and the dolphins swimming around. Then a little later I'm sound asleep and all of a sudden I get it into my head I've got to find my Marshie.

VINCENT: Why?

EMILY: Because I miss her. I'm sick, it's three o'clock in the morning, I find my Marshie curled up with her bowlegs around some bar stool and I say Marshie, come out onto the deck. She walks out and immediately falls back to sleep on my *materassino*. Then I'm talking to a Milanese journalist and the Milanese journalist falls asleep. So I'm all alone again on the fucking side of the ship because I've been so sick, dawn is slightly coming up, I look and I see a black cone jetting out from the land, from the sea, into the gray sky. I say to myself this is incredible, it's Stromboli. I wake Marshie up and we look, the boat comes a little bit closer and it's the scariest fucking thing I've ever seen, this black volcanic island.

MARSHA: I'm giving these pants into the laundry.

EMILY: You know, Vinnie, I just decided that I'm never listening to you again, I'm serious.

VINCENT: *She* interrupted you, I didn't.

MARSHA: He didn't. It was my fault, I'm sorry.

EMILY: It has nothing to do with interruptions, it has to do with straight brown hair in front of a tanned forehead and an open mouth and a lying soul.

VINCENT: And very good teeth.

EMILY: Nice teeth. Are you listening to my story?

VINCENT: I'm not carrying your extras to the laundry, Marsh.

EMILY: I think it's important to discuss your laundry, much more important than Stromboli.

VINCENT: Marshie, the pictures in this album don't look anything like you, you look much older younger.

MARSHA: Can I ask you something? If I haven't been to the beach in a week, how come I'm full of sand?

EMILY: Because you haven't been to the beach in a week.

VINCENT: Marshie, you are unbelievable. Your face changes from hairstyle to hairstyle. What was this dark mark you used to have on your face? I'm sorry, it's no longer there.

MARSHA: It is so, it's my mole, hon. I pluck it every Thursday.

VINCENT: When you look at this album, do you think the things you wrote in it were a lot of hogwash and bullshit?

MARSHA: I can't stand them.

VINCENT: Boy, we've all changed so much. That's why when I look at teenagers, I admire them because of their youth, but I know that their minds are shy. Marshie, you look horrible in these pictures. You've gotten so beautiful. Look, Clem lifting you up. In Siena, they must have thought Clem and I were gorgeous.

EMILY: What a time to go through her album. It's such a bore.

VINCENT: You know I just looked at this picture of Clem and I got sad for the first time since we broke up. This is where all the zinnias were planted, Marsha, next to the herb garden. And look at this picture of little Sam Gold.

EMILY: Not so little.

VINCENT: He was the most intelligent man you were ever involved with.

EMILY: Can we name our men and their professions and what they looked like?

MARSHA: Okay, Number one: Jewish ne'er-do-well.

EMILY: Stanley Siskind. It has to be *real* number one, not guys who just put it near but never really got it inside, it has to be a real prick going into a real cunt, not any fooling around like coming between the breasts. I had about three of those.

VINCENT: You have such big breasts to come between?

EMILY: All right, you start. Number one?

MARSHA: I told you, Number one: Jewish blond ne'-er-do-well.

EMILY: Number two, I have no matches.

MARSHA: Number two, Sam Gold. You?

EMILY: Handsome man with a huge head.

MARSHA: Roy Imber.

VINCENT: This is a very hostile game, because I'm left completely out of it.

EMILY: Aren't you looking at the fucking album and not saying anything to anyone? Number three?

MARSHA: Catholic on call at Mount Sinai Hospital.

VINCENT: You slept with Bill Meehan? What kind of dick did he have?

MARSHA: I just remember there was a big scar above it.

EMILY: I'd like to sleep with Bill.

VINCENT: Would you *really?* Would you like to suck him off too? Have you ever had sperm go into your mouth?

MARSHA: Of course.

VINCENT: I asked Emily, not you.

MARSHA: I suck Tim Cullen off.

VINCENT: No wonder he doesn't respect you.

EMILY: Why, is it wrong to suck a man off?

VINCENT: You shouldn't do it too often. Don't forget in English there's an expression "you dirty cocksucker."

EMILY: Michael Christy made me do it all the time.

MARSHA: So does Tim.

VINCENT: Then you're both involved with the wrong men.

EMILY: *All* men want it, Vinnie, they all want everything, and so do we.

MARSHA: I don't get that much out of it though.

VINCENT: She's adorable. Can you swallow it? Don't you gag?

MARSHA: I gag.

VINCENT: I love this cat. You know what she is? She's the feline you when you realize yourself.

EMILY: Jonquil! Get down on the floor and play your games, Jonquil.

VINCENT: She loves me, she loves me because she knows I'm a man. Animals do know, that's why Gide was so wrong.

MARSHA: What did he say?

VINCENT: He looked to animals and tried to make an argument about homosexuality.

EMILY: Yeah, animals *are* very homosexual.

VINCENT: No they're not, just bees and ducks. Look at this cat— has it ever loved anyone quite as much as me? She understands the whole secret of what Marshie doesn't understand with men. I didn't pay any attention to this cat for twenty-four hours, none whatsoever. Then at the end it happened.

EMILY: Why is that the secret? I don't get it, Vinnie—what are we supposed to do with these men? You know when my doctor was teaching me how to let go and give and love with Philippe, I achieved all those things, but look at the object I had chosen. I still owe that doctor five hundred dollars.

VINCENT: You do? And you're lying there? Why aren't you working as a waitress somewhere, getting the money to pay him?

EMILY: Because I worked as a waitress for two years and put myself through thirteen, fifteen thousand dollars' worth of analysis.

VINCENT: Let me tell you a very quick story. I had an analyst once named Dr. Herne, I never knew his first name.

EMILY: Just tell Jonquil you're not rejecting her.

VINCENT: She knows it, cats are fantastic. Look how symmetrical she is in the chair. Anyway, I had been going to this analyst at the N.Y.U. clinic for bright, talented children, where I had this other doctor who went into the service. I had dreamt I fell in love with him—I was eighteen years old and I didn't know about transference or anything.

EMILY: Shrinking at eighteen, huh?

VINCENT: Of course, darling, I was an extraordinary child. That's what's wrong with American civilization; we think at eighteen you're still a child. So anyway, I told him this fantastic dream I had, and at the end of the session, he announced that he was drafted and would have to leave in three weeks. It was horrible. It set up one of the basic patterns of my life. Then they found a substitute for me, this Dr. Herne. I was going there because I couldn't speak in my art history class and I was failing. Oh, parenthetically, Johnson, in his press conference today, did an unbelievable thing. He announced that anyone married after midnight tonight would not be exempt from the draft. Isn't that awful, giving people eight hours' notice?

MARSHA: You can't even get your blood test.

VINCENT: That's a dirty trick, I'm sorry, he should have warned them. Anyway, see, I have this deep problem of not being able to talk in school. The doctor comes in, after I had had this marvelous green-eyed brown-haired Jewish East Side Salinger-type analyst, this new doctor comes in, he says mmmmmmmy nnnnnnnnname is uhuhuhuh Docdocdocdoctor Hhhhhherne.

EMILY: And you said mmmmmmmmy nnnnnnname is Ppppppppatient Mmmmmmmiano.

VINCENT: So there are two things I want to tell you about him. The first is I walked out of my last session during Christmas vacation that year, I'm two blocks away, it's winter, very cold but not snowing or wet, and I hear someone calling Vincent! Vvvvvincent! I didn't even turn my head, I just stopped in my tracks, and there he was with this Christmas present for me. It was a ballpoint pen in a box, and it had Merry Christmas Vincent written on it.

EMILY: Oh my God, it's so sad!

VINCENT: Very sad. I'm not even going into the other thing, it's even sadder. I'm getting bored. I'm the only one all evening who's had any vitality.

MARSHA: That's not true—I've been flipping it in.

VINCENT: Have you ever had to show a man how to get to your vagina? I mean take his penis and push it in?

MARSHA: Yeah, just the other week.

VINCENT: Boy, Tim must be such a sad guy.

MARSHA: He's half a person.

VINCENT: You have no sympathy for him. All of a sudden he's half a person. A couple of weeks ago he was three times a person. You know I like this room, it's got good proportions.

EMILY: The walls are a nice color.

VINCENT: Yeah, you couldn't have them in the city this color, but it's nice out here. By the way, last Thursday night, I didn't really go to a friend's house, I went to a gay bar.

MARSHA: I knew you did when you said you were going to visit a friend in Water Mill. I know how many friends you have in Water Mill.

VINCENT: It was a beautiful thing, it took about a half hour to get there, through side roads and potato fields. I think we should go there tonight. They do line-up dancing and there are beautiful girls.

EMILY: I'm not going anywhere. I'm relaxing here and I have things to do in the morning.

MARSHA: What was it like? All boys?

VINCENT: No, I just told you, beautiful girls.

MARSHA: Lesbians?

VINCENT: No.

EMILY: Were there a lot of people? Attractive people?

VINCENT: A news commentator from NBC was there. What's his name? Very thin, with blond hair?

MARSHA: Did you meet anyone?

VINCENT: No. There was one guy there who looked just like Eliot Simon. I'll tell you something about Eliot Simon—he's really ugly.

EMILY: No he's not.

VINCENT: He is, with his loafers and white socks and short green pants.

MARSHA: That's not what ugliness is. Besides, he's changed his style. He wears black socks now with shiny black shoes.

EMILY: He has no class, but he's a lovely guy.

MARSHA: He's a horrible guy.

VINCENT: By the way, Emily, you know that's a beautiful thing, the fact that the Reinhardts took Sick Joan to the insane asylum. How did that happen? Did you get in touch with them?

EMILY: I called Joan a couple of times, she wasn't home. Finally *she* called *me*, and she was out of her mind. I talked to Diana Reinhardt and told her I wasn't too interested in taking Joan to the bin.

VINCENT: So you called Diana to ask her to take her?

EMILY: Diana called *me* to ask *me* to take her.

VINCENT: You're very hostile to me tonight, don't think I'm not noticing it. And don't tell me that you're calm either.

EMILY: I don't feel related to you or Marsha, but it has nothing to do with hostility.

MARSHA: I don't feel well.

VINCENT: You know you're both very bad at relating if you don't have total love.

MARSHA: I need total love.

EMILY: So anyway, are you listening? What am I talking about?

VINCENT: Sick Joan.

EMILY: Oh, so I said I'd take her even if I didn't want to. I knew that if she didn't get in, I would have to deal with her not getting in and that's what I was afraid of, the aftermath of her being rejected from the hospital. Not only that, I just didn't want to go; I was all alone, I was feeling good, I wanted to do something for myself. But I went anyway, the Reinhardts picked me up and we all took her to the hospital. Apparently she belongs in one because after all the interviews and everything they wanted to accept her. If they want to accept you, you must belong.

VINCENT: Sometimes they accept you just to calm you down.

EMILY: They thought she was in very bad shape. We said we didn't want to accept the responsibility and the doctor said I don't blame you for a minute.

VINCENT: You know what the guy I went to the gay bar with asked me that night? He said if I called up Emily, would she come here and dance with me?

EMILY: I don't like to be used as an escort in that way, Vinnie.

VINCENT: I know that.

MARSHA: I don't either, except I am.

VINCENT: By me? I never used you that way.

MARSHA: Never, except on Ischia.

VINCENT: That was terrific.

MARSHA: You know that story? When Vinnie used me as *Suddenly Last Summer*? When I was his pimp?

VINCENT: This will be very interesting for me, because I'll finally hear her version of it.

EMILY: Can I have your version of the ashtray?

MARSHA: You want to hear the story? You know I had had this beautiful Sienese summer with Vin and Clem, my ideal of romantic love? I thought they were the perfect couple, they would never break up, they were going to come back and live in Bucks County from here to eternity? All winter we corresponded, and the following summer they invited me over again because I had been such a good guest.

EMILY: Where was this?

MARSHA: They were living in Rome, they had left Siena. So I get there, I see my ideal couple, and after about ten minutes, the news starts to filter through that they're not so ideal anymore, they're not even a couple. I had a complete internal breakdown. I mean their union was my whole security against the world at that time. I had never really thought of them as homosexual, you see, just as a happily married couple, because they were very private, their bedroom door was always closed and everything else. Even though their bed *did* have a white wedding veil over it in Siena.

VINCENT: Oh wait a minute.

MARSHA: Mosquito netting, they called it. So anyway it was a total shock to me.

EMILY: Vinnie's so sunburned. Look at him.

MARSHA: Vince was a nervous wreck, both of them were, all they did was comb their hair. They were constantly combing their hair. I had never seen them with a comb in their hands before, now they were never without one.

VINCENT: Is that really true?

EMILY: I'd like to take a photograph of your hands, Vinnie, they are not to be believed.

MARSHA: And the phone calls were pouring in, Alberto, Paolo, Cici, all these guys calling up night and day, with liaisons and rendezvous and everything else. I was a wreck, Vince was a wreck, so we decided we should go away, take a little trip together to Ischia.

EMILY: Jonquil!

MARSHA: Oh stop it, let her sleep. Boy, you're going to be some mother. Anyway, to make a long story short, we were there, we hated Ischia, it was very ugly.

VINCENT: She's not listening to a word you're saying. She's got venom in her ears.

MARSHA: Are you listening to me?

EMILY: Ischia.

MARSHA: We were staying at separate places for some reason, and the maid in my pensione kept winking at me and saying don't worry, he can stay over anytime he wants to. I was quite a distance from the center of town, it was an area where they were building, sort of lonely, deserted, with workmen and things. Dig we must.

EMILY: For a growing Ischia.

VINCENT: Avec Edouard. Con Ed.

MARSHA: I just realized this isn't even the right story I'm telling.

VINCENT: I know it. What was the original one?

MARSHA: On the beach.

VINCENT: Walking you home is a horrible story, please don't tell it.

MARSHA: Can't I tell it?

VINCENT: Sure, tell it.

MARSHA: It's halfway finished anyway. He was walking me home and some guy, some trick catches his eye. He's looking at Vinnie and Vinnie's looking at him. It's dead of night, late, no moon, and suddenly Vince says to me, Marshie, you can get home alone, can't you? I've got to follow that man, I *have* to go with him. I said all right, darling, if you must, you must. Dig. So he leaves me there in the middle of nowhere, I didn't even know how to say "help" in Italian in those days.

VINCENT: That's all right, there was no one on the street to say it to.

MARSHA: And off he went.

VINCENT: She told me to, Em. Actually I didn't *go* off, I *ran* off.

MARSHA: Ran off, clopped off on his cloppy clodhoppers. And I just stood there, watching his white shirt disappear into the night. But all of a sudden, as I'm watching it, the shirt, instead of receding, seems to be coming towards me. It's Vinnie, racing back, I think he was crying.

VINCENT: I was.

MARSHA: He grabbed me in his arms and said darling, how could I have done that to you? It'll never happen again, I promise, and he escorted me home as a proper escort should. But that wasn't the story I wanted to tell.

EMILY: It's beautiful though.

VINCENT: It was the beast overtaking the civilized man, and then the civilized man taking over the beast.

MARSHA: Of course the guy rejected him, but he won't go into that. The story of *Suddenly Last Summer* was on the same island, on the beach. We were sitting there, Vince and I, and there was this awful-looking boy with broken gold teeth.

VINCENT: But he had a fantastic torso.

MARSHA: Who was interested in me.

VINCENT: I didn't know it though.

MARSHA: Vince kept saying lure him over, lure him over, he's queer, he's queer, he's queer. So together we lure him over and he starts flirting with me, he's in love with me and everything else, and Vince says to him let's take a walk.

EMILY: With the gold teeth and the broken teeth?

VINCENT: Yeah, but gorgeous. A fantastic crotch and a beautiful light torso.

MARSHA: Vinnie tells him he's my half-brother and our mother has been married eight times. Tells it to this simple Italian fisherboy who's horrified, thinks it's the most awful story he's ever heard.

EMILY: And Vinnie's trying to prime him for himself?

VINCENT: What does prime mean? Putting white gesso on?

MARSHA: Somehow we made a date with him for the next day.

VINCENT: He was going to take us on his boat, remember?

MARSHA: But he stood *us* up and we stood *him* up. Vinnie and I have had adventures through hell and high water.

VINCENT: Marsha was so good to me in the hospital. She wouldn't do it again though, she told me.

EMILY: You're still talking about that hospital. I never got to tell you the Strindberg-Bergman dream I once had about my father. We were riding a bicycle and I was holding on to him, my head up against the back of his shoulders. We were going down this dirt path beautifully, there was a soft wind blowing, and there were different turn-offs which I kept thinking we were going to take, but he kept going straight down the hill. The next thing I know we're riding through high grasses in the field, and in the distance I can see my mother and my sister coming toward us. They had long white gowns, flowing gently through these tall leaves. They looked at me and I waved, but I said to my father let's ignore them. That's the dream, my favorite dream that I ever had.

MARSHA: My favorite dream was having a conversation with a fish in a beautiful bubbling brook.

VINCENT: My favorite dream was the first dream I had in analysis. When I was growing up, you see, I didn't believe that I was the intelligent kid I am, and this dream showed number one that I was intelligent and number two my decision to be a homosexual. I went to Riis Park....

MARSHA: That's where Tim Cullen goes every day to the beach.

EMILY: Tim Cullen isn't at all queer, is he?

VINCENT: I don't know, only Marsha can answer that. Is he sexual, Tim?

MARSHA: No.

EMILY: He's not, he's all closed up.

MARSHA: But he thinks he's the most sexual person alive.

VINCENT: Marshie, do I have to get up at 8:15 to go to the laundry?

MARSHA: Before.

VINCENT: Oh that's horrible.

MARSHA: Why? It's only eleven. You better get home.

VINCENT: Who me? I know it. Have you learned a lot about me this weekend?

MARSHA: Yeah. When did the weekend begin?

VINCENT: Last night.

MARSHA: Can I come over and hug you, Vincie?

VINCENT: No.

21. ANOTHER GAME

EMILY: If this person were a color, what color would he be?

MARSHA: Sort of yellow on the outside and some darker one inside that you can't see. Not too obvious, am I?

EMILY: A person who on the outside seems bright, but is really serious. Okay, what time of day is he?

MARSHA: Ten-thirty at night.

EMILY: What kind of food?

MARSHA: Canned chop suey. Are you getting anything?

EMILY: I'm getting a sort of phony person.

MARSHA: That's not what you should be getting.

EMILY: What kind of plant?

MARSHA: Rubber plant.

EMILY: Sturdy and healthy. It's a healthy kind of person, more serious than he appears, who likes good food but won't go out of his way for it.

MARSHA: What's good food about canned chow mein?

EMILY: What kind of drink would this person be?

MARSHA: Colka-colka.

EMILY: Jesus Christ, one of those young health ones. What character in literature?

MARSHA: I can never think of anything when that question's asked, I go completely blank.

EMILY: Any character, it can be in movies.

MARSHA: In a very crazy way which you'll say I'm wrong about, the guy in *l'Avventura*.

EMILY: What was his name?

MARSHA: I don't know. What's the difference?

EMILY: I think I'm giving up. I don't know this guy. What kind of music?

MARSHA: Rock-n'-roll.

EMILY: What kind of a party?

MARSHA: A loft party that doesn't quite make it.

EMILY: Zeke Sutherland.

MARSHA: No.

EMILY: Don't tell me it's Timothy Cullen.

MARSHA: Why not?

EMILY: Okay, I have one. Ask.

MARSHA: If this person were a country in Europe.

EMILY: Germany.

MARSHA: It's someone I hate immediately.

EMILY: Here's a good question for you to ask—would this person take tranquilizers or pep-ups?

MARSHA: No, that's not allowed—you have to ask what *kind* of tranquilizer he would be. What kind?

EMILY: Bufferin.

MARSHA: If he were a dessert?

EMILY: Doesn't that man over there in the green trunks look like a desexualized Picasso?

MARSHA: A cross between Stravinsky and Picasso. You didn't answer my dessert question.

EMILY: A sliced apple.

MARSHA: Just one slice of apple without any trimmings?

EMILY: A peeled, sliced apple.

MARSHA: I have a feeling it might not even be a man. If this person were an object like to make love on, what would it be?

EMILY: Very good question—okay, gynecologist's table.

MARSHA: I hate this person.

EMILY: That may be the best answer I've ever given.

MARSHA: If this person were a shoe.

EMILY: If this person were a shoe, a fur boot with a heel.

MARSHA: I hope it's a lady. I hate this person. If he were an animal, what animal would he be?

EMILY: Oh, very good—a groundhog.

MARSHA: I think I know who it is.

EMILY: Then guess; otherwise it's no fun.

MARSHA: Clem Nye.

EMILY: Are you kidding? Clem's not any groundhog.

MARSHA: Is it Nathan Fass?

EMILY: Nathan Fass it is.

22. MARSHA INTERRUPTS A DISCUSSION OF HERSELF

VINCENT: You know you're unbelievable? You're a pathetic thing, Emily, and I'll tell you why.

EMILY: I'm a pathetic thing and you're drunk on vodka.

VINCENT: I'm not drunk. Let me tell you something.

EMILY: Enough of the preludes.

VINCENT: Preludes nothing—preludin, that's what you need, because you're very ill. Preludin is a very strong tranquilizer which my daddy took when he was in such pain.

EMILY: Preludin is a diet pill. Go ahead, tell me why I'm a pathetic person, it's one of the greatest compliments I've ever been paid.

VINCENT: You're a pathetic person because you cannot accept criticism and what's even more pathetic is that you think it *is* criticism.

EMILY: Darling, I am *the* person of all time who accepts criticism. Do you think Marsha does, or you?

VINCENT: No, seriously, we were talking about Fitzgerald.

EMILY: Right—Fitzgerald says to Laurette Taylor: "My God, you beautiful egg, you beautiful egg, you beautiful, beautiful egg." And Laurette Taylor turns to her husband and says, "Oh Hartley, I've just seen the doom of youth. Do you understand? The doom of youth itself, a walking doom."

VINCENT: Now that's gorgeous. And do you know what made that gorgeous which the other thing you read didn't have? A beginning and an end.

EMILY: Oh you and your art, you and your related images, you and your no one thing stands by itself; you, you, you.

VINCENT: Marsha's coming back. Let's close the door and show them we're alone.

EMILY: Can we analyze a little about her and Tim Cullen?

VINCENT: No, can we be honest about ourselves?

EMILY: I want to tell you a story about my sister.

VINCENT: All right, but make it short?

EMILY: My sister's a lot like me on certain levels.

VINCENT: Aw, let's talk about ourselves.

EMILY: This is very interesting. My sister said I'm having trouble with my older little boy, and I went to the school psychologist —my sister was telling me this story on the street.

VINCENT: Is it going to be long or short?

EMILY: Very short. She said you know we very often don't listen to our children; we hear them and we give them answers, but we don't really listen.

VINCENT: Um.

EMILY: And as my sister was telling me this story, I said what? Because *I* wasn't listening to what *she* was saying.

VINCENT: Beautiful.

EMILY: I have a great deal of difficulty really listening to people.

VINCENT: Not with me.

EMILY: No, because I feel very secure with you and I also respect you, I know what your mind is.

VINCENT: You mean you don't listen to other people because you feel insecure?

EMILY: No, I cut off. I'm very fantasy-ridden, you know, I have a fantastically active fantasy life. But my dreams are getting very realistic. The healthier I get, the more realistic my dreams become.

VINCENT: The more your life becomes a fantasy.

EMILY: Did you ever hear my Ingmar Bergman dream of my father?

VINCENT: Your Gertrude Berg dream? Yes, you just told it the other night. Besides, I don't want another story; I want repartee.

EMILY: Should I read you one of my poems?

VINCENT: You know you're crazy? I just said we want repartee, a thing going back and forth between two human beings, and you say do you want me to read a poem? What has that got to do with communication?

EMILY: Communication is that you're a human being with crazy beautiful brown eyes and I'm looking at them.

VINCENT: Hazel in the sunlight, you told me last week on the beach.

EMILY: In the sunlight, in the light in the window, the key is in the sunlight.

VINCENT: You can only function when you've had a drink.

EMILY: Do you know what my father left me when he died? I've never told this to anyone but my analyst, what he left me in his will. He left me his undying love. That's very scary, isn't it?

VINCENT: It's beautiful.

EMILY: That's just what he had written in his will.

VINCENT: Only for you?

EMILY: No, for his children. "And to my children, my undying love." It's very sick, but it's also very beautiful.

VINCENT: I don't think it's sick at all. And if you do, you're crazy. It's a beautiful, abstract thing, a very substantial, complex thought. And do you know something? It's all that remains with you of him. If he had left you a hundred thousand dollars, you would have spent it like that girl did, Sick Joan. But he left you his undying love. It's a fantastic thing, something you hold.

EMILY: Yes, darling, but undying love from a father who didn't love you the right way when he was alive is very dangerous.

VINCENT: I'll tell you something about a child's reaction to his father's or his mother's love. As an adult, one looks back on the love of his parents as a child, and that child, I am *sorry*, does not know what love is about. That's what's wrong with most adults, they're judging whether or not their parents have been good to them in terms of a child looking at his parents.

EMILY: No, in terms of an adult looking at his parents.

VINCENT: No, because what they're analyzing are their childhood responses. It's not facts they're looking back on but feelings and remembrances.

EMILY: But that's what's true. Facts don't mean anything, darling. On that level, facts mean very little.

VINCENT: You're wrong. Truth is involved with facts, I'm sorry. If you say to me the sun is out now and I look and it's cloudy, then it's not sunny.

EMILY: Of course not.

VINCENT: So what I'm saying is how the parents were to the child is not necessarily, underline necessarily, as the memory of it is, because the memory was through the child's eyes.

EMILY: Of course, of course. That's what I said about chemical states and perceiving reality, about the nature of it being subjective. My problems do have a lot to do with my father. Now Marsha, you see—I've thought about this a great deal from what I know about psychoanalytic theory, I mean in the Chekhovian sense I know, I know how the present and the past are like life and art, how they're so much a part of each other—Marsha's relationship with her father, I would say, was permanently damaging.

VINCENT: You mean cannot be undone.

EMILY: Cannot be undone and *will* not be undone. At some point, at the crucial threshold of becoming a woman, her father rejected her, or, as you would say, she *felt* he rejected her, so she shut him out and shut herself off. So now, when she has someone like Tim Cullen, she can seduce him, get him into bed, and get the intimacy, but then she arranges for him to shut it off, just at that moment where nuance, identity and relationship start. Her relationships are all beginnings, they never get past that.

VINCENT: That's where I disagree. I think they're all conclusions, I don't think there are any beginnings or growth.

EMILY: Well it's exactly the same thing, just as what happened with her father was either a conclusion or a beginning, however you want to interpret it.

VINCENT: No, no, with her father it was a conclusion because there *had* been a beginning—that's why it was so painful and there was the shutting off. So what she does now is begin at the conclusion, where the father left off, the point of intimate love relationship and deep intense feelings. You know I'm saying something very profound.

EMILY: I'm listening, I'm just getting my cigarettes.

VINCENT: I didn't know you had them there. Is that where you hid them, you bitch?

EMILY: I didn't hide them; they were on my bed and someone kicked them off. I'm listening, darling.

VINCENT: It's true, you need someone to treat you badly, you all do.

EMILY: All right, go ahead, darling.

VINCENT: The thing is this, Marsha begins at the point where her father let her down. She gets him though, now in the form of a lover, into bed, and then she starts to devour him.

EMILY: Does she really?

VINCENT: Yes. She's outside so I better whisper—she's probably within earsight if she keeps this quiet.

EMILY: I think she's in the car.

VINCENT: No, they came in.

EMILY: Can I look out the window and see? Go ahead, I'm listening to what you're saying because I'm actually amazed by it.

VINCENT: It's absolutely brilliant.

EMILY: They're still out there in the car.

VINCENT: She begins to devour these men, she clings, she hangs on, she's inseparable, she sucks, she's parasitic.

EMILY: Does she care?

VINCENT: She panics.

EMILY: Does she care?

VINCENT: And she does all this not to *win* the man, but to *lose* him. It happened at such a crucial point, the thing with her father, that it's not something she can get over, she wants it repeated because she's a masochist.

EMILY: You know what masochism is, don't you? It's a striving for pleasure.

VINCENT: Do you know what sadism is?

EMILY: It's a striving for pleasure, they both are. Masochism has nothing to do with pain; pain is recognized as an area of pleasure.

In other words, Marsha gets pleasure from rejecting the man and being rejected by him—you have to understand that.

VINCENT: Here she comes—she's listening. I wouldn't listen to this if I were you, because it's the truth about you, Marshie.

EMILY: Being rejected is love, it's as simple as that, it's the way the father showed love.

VINCENT: Exactly. However, it's neurotic because she thinks she doesn't want it and it becomes unpositive and clogged as a flow. It's not a love flow.

EMILY: It's not, it's a need flow.

VINCENT: A hate flow, a way of getting even.

MARSHA: What are you saying about me?

EMILY: Shall we play her the last part of the tape?

MARSHA: Play it—I can take it.

EMILY: Okay.

> VINCENT: *The thing is this, Marsha begins at the point where her father let her down. She gets him though, now in the form of a lover, into bed, and then she starts to devour him.*
>
> EMILY: *Does she really?*
>
> VINCENT: *Yes. She's outside so I better whisper—she's probably within earsight if she keeps this quiet.*
>
> EMILY: *I think she's in the car.*
>
> VINCENT: *No, they came in.*
>
> EMILY: *Can I look out the window and see? Go ahead, I'm listening to what you're saying because I'm actually amazed by it.*
>
> VINCENT: *It's absolutely brilliant.*
>
> EMILY: *They're still out there in the car.*
>
> VINCENT: *She begins to devour these men, she clings, she hangs on, she's inseparable, she sucks, she's parasitic.*
>
> EMILY: *Does she care?*
>
> VINCENT: *She panics.*
>
> EMILY: *Does she care?*
>
> VINCENT: *And she does all this not to* win *the man, but to* lose *him. It happened at such a crucial point, this thing with her*

*father, that it's not something she can get over, she wants it
repeated because she's a masochist.*

EMILY: *You know what masochism is, don't you? It's a striving
for pleasure.*

VINCENT: *Do you know what sadism is?*

EMILY: *It's a striving for pleasure, they both are. Masochism has
nothing to do with pain; pain is recognized as an area of pleasure. In other words, Marsha gets pleasure from rejecting the
man and being rejected by him—you have to understand
that.*

VINCENT: *Here she comes—she's listening. I wouldn't listen to
this if I were you, because it's the truth about you, Marshie.*

EMILY: *Being rejected is love, it's as simple as that, it's the way
the father showed love.*

VINCENT: *Exactly. However, it's neurotic because she thinks she
doesn't want it and it becomes unpositive and clogged as a
flow. It's not a love flow.*

EMILY: *It's not, it's a need flow.*

VINCENT: *A hate flow, a way of getting even.*

MARSHA: That's very interesting because it's more or less just what I
was talking to Tim about in the car.

VINCENT: What did he say?

MARSHA: Nothing, he just agreed with everything I said.

EMILY: He had no reaction?

VINCENT: It wasn't about him, why should he have a reaction?

EMILY: There *is* something I'm sure he feels, that in a way all this stuff
sounds very pat, almost as if there were no room to say anything.

VINCENT: But why should he have something to say? This is about
Marsha.

MARSHA: Isn't he involved with me?

EMILY: Vinnie, you're saying a crazy thing—why *shouldn't* he have
anything to say?

VINCENT: I mean there are certain things people have nothing to
say about. You talk about a baseball game and what will I have to
say about that?

MARSHA: Am I a baseball game? This is supposedly a subject he has some interest in. I asked what he thought the dynamics were, if I reject the man or if I work it so that he rejects me and he said I probably do force the man to reject me, but that I have to be aware of what other things are going on in the mind of the man. But I think all men are the same and they can all be manipulated.

VINCENT: Oh, you don't manipulate, darling.

MARSHA: You can make *any* man reject you if you want to be rejected.

EMILY: Isn't it a chemical thing? I mean can't you make each man reject you in a different way?

MARSHA: Sure, I'm very clever about it. I've dealt with each man differently, but I've gotten them all to toss me out.

EMILY: Your dealing with Tim isn't that.

MARSHA: I'm suffocating him.

VINCENT: Now wait a minute—some of them *you* tossed out.

MARSHA: Listen, I may have made the final gesture of tossing Eliot out, but he had been tossing me for four years. I had worked that rejection to the bone.

EMILY: I just don't understand how your relationship with Tim is suffocating him.

MARSHA: You want to know how I'm doing it? With a lot of affection, with what he imagines are tremendous demands upon him, possessiveness, getting upset if I know about the other people he's sleeping with. And he also has the feeling I'm thinking about marriage all the time. I asked him when he got here yesterday if he missed me and he found that tremendously suffocating.

VINCENT: You know what it is? It's not all those words you're saying. It's that the man responds to the demonstration of your undisciplined feelings; it's not because you said did you miss me, it's the subtext. You give yourself up completely to the man and that's too much for any human being to take. As soon as Tim came, Marsha turned into a completely different person. And this has nothing to do with competition on my part, no matter what you think. I'll tell it to you in a basic animal way. He came in sick, he was like an animal who is ill goes over and lies in a corner, which he did, alone, out in the backyard. He's lying there, and you interpret what you as the woman must do for the man, heal and console and caress. So you went over, a physical action which put you almost on top of him.

MARSHA: He told me to get down on the blanket because he couldn't see me with his sore neck.

VINCENT: All right, then everything I'm saying is wrong. But it's not, it's a total thing I'm talking about. There is no area in which the man is safe. As I once said to you—this is something famous from our very first close conversation, Emily—I have always maintained that in a love relationship, a relationship which is on a bed physical and in public erotic because it can't be expressed, the one area of independence between the two people has to be the bathroom. Like for someone to be taking a shit and the other one to come in to wash or talk is very very bad, because the civilized animal has got to have the sense of freedom and privacy.

MARSHA: That's what Tim was saying. He said he has the feeling that wherever he is, whether it's at a party or on the beach, he's under my eye the whole time. If he's dancing with another girl, he looks over and sees me watching him dance with the girl.

VINCENT: It's true, you *are* watching him, you *are*.

MARSHA: It's true. He said he came in a wounded animal yesterday, very conscious of the pain in his back and sort of hoping to get it healed here. He was happy he'd be able to take a bath, that I would help him through this thing etcetera, but that suddenly I began to make his pain a psychological rejection of me, which I know it *was*.

VINCENT: No it wasn't, you see, and if it was, it became that because you wouldn't be content with it unless it was.

MARSHA: At the beginning of the relationship, you know, *he* was suffocating *me*. His eyes were always on *me*. I couldn't stand it, I was ready to run out of the room.

VINCENT: All right, then he leaves, he loses interest and you go after him. So what is the lesson to be learned? The lesson to be learned is to always be cool and leave loveplay for the bed. Love is not play; love is hard work and it's strategy and it's not being yourself, not giving vent to every feeling you have.

EMILY: No, you're making a mistake, darling; you're talking about edifice, you're not talking about structure. There are certain structural things that go on between man and woman that have to do with elegance, all those things we talked about when Joan was here, that kind of deep, personal subjective respect. You know Marsha has a tremendous need for freedom, much stronger in a way than Tim's.

MARSHA: That's true.

EMILY: So when she's watching Tim on the dance floor, it's not about checking out the areas in which he's unfaithful, it's like her almost making checkpoints on her new freedom list. I think if you ever looked at Tim Cullen dancing with another girl, Marsha, and found him totally loyal to you, you'd be suffocated out of your mind.

MARSHA: I would, I'm definitely looking for him to be unfaithful.

VINCENT: But he has been faithful, he's been terribly faithful and loyal.

EMILY: Even if he slept with other women, he's been very faithful.

VINCENT: In his friendship, in his love, fantastically loyal. I'm talking about spiritual love loyalty.

EMILY: He's very innocent.

MARSHA: He said one thing that really got to him last night was when he went into the bedroom to lie down and I came in and turned on the phonograph, then he went into the other room, and I followed him in there. I lay down beside him, knowing full well he can't sleep when anything is really touching him. We both tried to take a nap, then I started jumping up and down dancing to the music.

VINCENT: You see on both sides it's absolute panic. In the face of a love object, she panics in a very assertive, physical advancing way; he panics in just the reverse way. I don't know Tim that well, but

I know myself and I know lots of other people, so I've learned certain things, and I think one of the basic reasons he withdraws from her, besides his basic need for independence, is that he doesn't think that much of himself. I mean he knows he's a good sculptor and everything, but he has great doubts and insecurity, and he's shy, he had a late beginning. You know I'm crazy about him, but the fantastic tension in his back yesterday showed me he's not a flowing thing. So he meets a person, and he loved her at the beginning when she was distant because this made sense to him, just as all his parental love figures were distant and not loving. But then after a while she's all over him, she can't be away from him for one second, and so he thinks she must be less than me if she thinks I'm this fantastic guy I know I'm not. Therefore she must be nothing, so how can I love her? I better find someone who's cool and distant again—I mean how can I love someone who loves an untruth?

MARSHA: That's also something I share.

VINCENT: Well, for that matter of fact, almost all sensitive, advanced people have something of it, but in your two cases, it's exaggerated.

EMILY: But Marshie, you know very well that in our relationship, which is basically a love relationship too, you're completely non-smothering and independent, very ungiving essentially. It's a totally autonomous relationship.

MARSHA: Something else interesting came up with Tim this morning. I asked him what he thought I liked about him, and he said his forgiveness, and he was right, because the one moment when I really loved Timothy Cullen was when he forgave me.

EMILY: Forgave you for what?

VINCENT: When she threw him out on the Fourth of July and he was willing to come back and forgive and forget.

MARSHA: I was flowing over with love for him when he came back that next day and forgave me. Something came up with my doctor once about this—I had had that pat theory of my father rejecting me at some point, turning off without my knowing why, and so all my life since, I've had the feeling that if only some man would come along and punish me once and for all—that's why I let Eliot hang me on the wall probably— then the guilt would be expiated and my father would love me again. And Merrill Johnston said maybe the same thing could be accomplished if you were forgiven instead of punished. I think it must be true, because when Tim forgave me, I really felt the most freeflowing love I've ever felt. It wasn't any of that hysterical stuff—it was a moment of pure true love.

EMILY: That's marvelous. Vinnie, are you going to stay and eat with us?

VINCENT: No, I have to go home. To paint, now that it's dark.

23. EMILY AND MARSHA REACT TO AN ATTACK ON VINCENT

MARSHA: We never should have let Nathan Fass come over here last night.

EMILY: It was really incredible. Vinnie said he felt he was attacked by him on the most crucial, primary level as a man, that his *life* was threatened.

MARSHA: What do you mean, his life was threatened?

EMILY: That his free spirit as an artist was in danger, that Nathan was cutting it down, this soaring spirit that he doesn't know anything about.

MARSHA: What have you got in there?

EMILY: Tea.

MARSHA: That's a very expensive antique pitcher and you put tea in it?

EMILY: It's very pretty, isn't it a nice thing to put tea in?

MARSHA: Yes. So what's going to happen to Vinnie today? Will he be able to paint?

EMILY: He's out of his skull. Look, let's discuss it on this level: you and Vince both seriously threatened with the end of the friendship. Vinnie lost his father just before the summer, he's afraid of losing Nico because of the heterosexual shift with his doctor; he's being threatened with the loss of love objects all around, and last night Nathan Fass comes along and threatens to kill you off too. That's why Vinnie feels he was stabbed in a life way.

MARSHA: Have you told him what you think?

EMILY: No, I'm still working it out. I talk a lot, but I think a lot too.

Last night, Vinnie was really threatened with the loss of you, which your eventual marriage will mean to him someday, just as it will to me. When I was with Philippe, darling, you had to give up a great part of *me*. Our relationship changed, didn't it?

MARSHA: Certainly. So what Nathan said was the most obvious thing in the world.

EMILY: Of course. What did he say?

MARSHA: That when I get married, I'm not going to be spending night and day with Vinnie. Doesn't Vinnie know that?

EMILY: What do you think would happen to him if you cut off your relationship?

MARSHA: According to what he said last night, he'd just find him another Marsha.

EMILY: Bullshit. I know how *I* function without *my* friends: I break down, but I get through. Like when I was in Europe, we were writing each other letters and you were sending me tubes of toothpaste, but that wasn't supportive, it wasn't structural. One thing your relationship with Vinnie and me does is make you know who you are.

MARSHA: Yeah, sure, it all has to do with identity. Because in the early days, when I used to go to Vinnie's first apartment with Clem on 89th Street, I would feel that I was going to visit myself, to find my identity. When I was there I was myself and when I left I wasn't. I was constantly looking to Vinnie to establish who I was. There's also a very strong Pygmalion thing: Vinnie created me, in a sense.

EMILY: Do you have any honey in the house? I've got to get some honey for my cold, that's the first thing I've got to get today. Let me ask you an important question: what do you think would happen if you and Vinnie slept together?

MARSHA: I think it would end the relationship. But on the other hand, it could conceivably be very unimportant.

EMILY: If going to bed with Vinnie's unimportant, it's only part of your whole problem of going to bed with men being unimportant.

Do you think for one minute that if you finally went to bed with Vinnie, the two of you are alone in a room and he makes love to you ...

MARSHA: I think I'd burst out laughing.

EMILY: I bet you both would.

MARSHA: No, actually it would become deadly serious—that's what happens when we look at each other now and he's got his hand on my breast or something—it gets deadly serious. You know I had one moment of absolute terror last night.

EMILY: What was the moment of terror?

MARSHA: When Nathan came out and said I wouldn't be able to have a marriage until this relationship with Vince ends.

EMILY: What he was saying was as long as you have Vinnie, why do you *need* a husband? Of course that's too pat, life isn't about things getting that simple. But what *do* you really want in another man? The only other relationships you have with men are fucking relationships, they don't have any of the range that you have with Vinnie, right? You have purely sensual relationships with the other men.

MARSHA: They're not sensual, they're sexual. There's very little sensuality in those relationships.

EMILY: This bread is too thick to fit into the toaster. Look, any man coming close to you must feel fantastically threatened by Vinnie.

MARSHA: Of course, he's a powerhouse, a knockout.

EMILY: Not only that but he's madly in love with you.

MARSHA: *Is* he?

EMILY: He is, but you can also say I'm madly in love with you. Let me ask you, are you closer to Vinnie than you are to me? After all he *is* a man with cock and balls.

MARSHA: No, I think I'm closer to you, even though *he* thinks I'm closer to him.

EMILY: I asked you that not in a competitive way.

MARSHA: I know. They're both very close—I think it shifts. With Vinnie it's such a delicate balance of picking and criticizing and then building up and love. They're *both* very strange relationships. Do you really think he *is* madly in love with me? In any sense of the term?

EMILY: It's very hard to say. What do you think?

MARSHA: I'm not sure I know what it means.

EMILY: It doesn't mean anything.

MARSHA: Nathan was really relentless with him though, he kept sticking the knife in and in and in.

EMILY: What knife, darling?

MARSHA: That Vince is ruining my life.

EMILY: He didn't say that.

MARSHA: Yes he did, he said that this relationship is screwing up my life, and as long as I cling to it, I can't have any other.

EMILY: Yeah, but then he said that *Vinnie* was the one getting done in.

MARSHA: That was an afterthought.

EMILY: No, it was a second thought that became very important. You don't have all your important thoughts first.

MARSHA: What role *does* Vinnie play in my relationships with other men? With Tim it was certainly very blatant—he almost couldn't go to bed with me because of Vinnie. He kept saying I was Vinnie's girl, it wasn't right for us to go to bed together because I was Vinnie's girl. Almost every time I'm in bed with someone, Vince is there too.

EMILY: You know Vinnie's encouraging you with all these different men, but I'm sure it's partly because he has no faith in any of them sticking. He can encourage you with Tim Cullen because he knows it doesn't stand a chance. About 70% of his feeling is absolutely genuine, I'm sure, but there's that other percentage that's more selfish. He knows that if you go with this one and that one, he can still maintain what *he* has with you.

MARSHA: Which is much stronger.

EMILY: And he's happy to have that final fulfillment done by this one or that one. But Nathan was right to some extent— there *are* few men who could feel complete enough against this strong relationship you have with Vinnie. Which doesn't mean the relationship has to end. In time you'll change, Vince will change, and the other man who comes along will be a different man. But I think you *always* will have a relationship.

MARSHA: Is there more tea?

EMILY: Yeah, in the antique pitcher. Okay, so the thing is that on a certain level, your relationships with me and Vinnie are not constructive, they're camouflages and excuses and props. We both serve. I won't go into what you and Vinnie serve for *me*. I'm also interested in the affect thing, that you said you didn't feel anything while all this combat was flying around your head. You still don't feel anything now?

MARSHA: Who knows?

EMILY: I get this very often myself—someone says something to me and I get two contradicting, conflicting feelings, so I end up feeling neither and nothing, I end up feeling zero.

MARSHA: Is that me?

EMILY: Well, you say you don't feel anything.

MARSHA: What I felt last night was locked, I felt such walls of defense around me. I just wouldn't let myself enter into it, I was very cool. Tim Cullen would have been proud of me, I was so cool.

EMILY: What did he say to you that time? Cool it?

MARSHA: Yeah, and it's funny because in a sense I'm the coolest person in the world, right?

EMILY: Right, 100% right. That's what's so ridiculous. But let's talk about this for a second. What do you think your relationship with Vinnie's really about? Take it on a very ordinary level, not the soaring love level of it.

MARSHA: I don't know. I've never known what was going on.

EMILY: You have to have some sneaky hunchy clue, you have to have some idea. Like in my friendship with Joan, I know what's going on *there*. But I also don't.

MARSHA: I assure you that what you *don't* know is much more important than what you know.

EMILY: But at least I'm able to talk about the relationship and seemingly what it is.

MARSHA: I hope you're being very careful with the disposal of the tissues. You know in a sense last night was like listening to the voice of the public, condemning my relationship with Vin.

EMILY: You also have to bear in mind that some of the things Nathan said are true, and the question remains how do you handle those things?

MARSHA: Those are the things to handle.

EMILY: Right. After all, Vinnie can be fantastically honest about himself, incredibly open and honorable, but he also has a tremendous facility for turning things to his own advantage.

MARSHA: But it didn't work that way last night—he broke down at the end and his mind was flailing out in every direction. Emily, what do you think the mock sex business with Vinnie is really all about?

EMILY: I'll tell you about the mock sex if you put up some more mock tea. Mock sex, that's a soup made with mock genitals and mock come, and as far as I can see, mock sex is more fun than real sex. When is the moron coming over here anyway? I don't get it. How come he wants to go out dancing tonight all of a sudden?

MARSHA: I have no idea, it must be some kind of inverse reaction. I mean here he is, destroyed and distraught and drained, his legs aching, he can't paint, and then he wants to go out dancing.

EMILY: He's not getting any chicken because I'm having a whole half of it.

MARSHA: And I'm having the other.

EMILY: Jonquil, come here. God, I'm in love with her. I'm not just fond of Jonquil, I'm in love with her.

MARSHA: I'm damaged, Jonquil, I'm damaged goods. Come on, Emily, *please* tell me about mock sex.

EMILY: OK, what do *you* think it's about?

MARSHA: I think it's about real sex.

EMILY: That's your comprehensive answer to such an incredibly complex question? No, what mock sex is is heterosexual groping, like testing the water with your toe. Vinnie's feeling things out. See, when he shows his penis, he's exposing himself, but it's still very passive aggression. He's not showing you an erected penis, he's just showing you a penis, right? Don't you have these kinds of insights? I mean don't you ever correlate what you do on the outside with Merrill Johnston?

MARSHA: Sure, didn't I immediately when I threw Tim Cullen out on the Fourth of July correlate it with Merrill Johnston?

EMILY: Did you?

MARSHA: Of course. But I do sometimes get the feeling that I'm very dumb. I seem not to allow myself any perceptions—but maybe they're not even there. Like last night, I just sat like a dumb animal.

EMILY: Well, it may be lucky that you *are* dumb in that sense. Come on, Jonquil, *giù, giù, giù!*

MARSHA: Catholic, Catholic, Catholic!

EMILY: She's very hungry but I think this meat's too cold for her to eat.

MARSHA: Put it on top of the tea kettle for a second.

EMILY: Good idea. My Marshie's such a smart person, my Marshie's really not dumb after all.

MARSHA: You know you can't say my analysis has stopped this summer. It's continuing on and on and on right under our noses.

EMILY: Analysis doesn't stop.

MARSHA: No, but I mean it's not like going off to Europe and having a real vacation from it. Uh-uh.

EMILY: I'm calling Vinnie right now and telling him he has to bring me some honey for my cold when he comes. Maybe we should all go to the beach for a little while and relax.

24. VINCENT HAS A SEIZURE ON THE BEACH

VINCENT: Psychoanalysis is a crock of shit.

EMILY: What are you saying, darling?

VINCENT: I'm saying we're living in some kind of medieval time where analysis is all we have, it's probably the most intelligent thing we can do at the moment, but certainly in a hundred years people will look back on it like we look back on the naiveté of the past. And I'm also saying another two or three days of this wild kind of group therapy we've been going through would be permanently damaging.

EMILY: It can only be damaging if the truth is damaging. Look at that little girl over there in the polka-dot bathing suit. She's so beautiful she's breaking my heart. She's going to be a first-class beauty.

VINCENT: She's gorgeous. How old? Ten?

EMILY: To be so beautiful at that age is scary.

VINCENT: The thing is, I just don't know how good it is to go into such fantastic analysis of your closest friends. I can't tell you how on edge I feel with Marsha right now because of the Nathan Fass episode, I feel all the implications of the complexity of our relationship.

MARSHA: But don't you think they're things we should try to understand?

VINCENT: No, because they weren't hurting us. It was someone outside who brought us to the damaging point, to our tether's end. That's where we are, at the end of our ropes, our summer's ropes. You just can't get down to these really basic feelings without an analyst to protect you from certain pitfalls. I'm sorry, I found myself, with the help of that man last night, digging a kind of grave for our relationship. It's like LSD, if you don't take it with a doctor or someone who can guide you, it's very dangerous. Or it's like if you want to improve your muscles and you start using barbells without any preparation, you can break your muscles.

EMILY: But we're all highly equipped to deal with these things. It happened you were victorious last night, you emerged very strong, you were *not* beaten.

VINCENT: Let me just finish what I was saying. I, only in the last few weeks, have really been anxious to get back to my analysis. Marsha has too, especially seeing her doctor on the beach all the time. It's been a long hot summer and it's been a very important one for all of us. But we've been trying to substitute our own analysis for the real thing and that's why we've gotten into trouble. My doctor, when I asked her shall I remember my dreams this summer, she said no, try not to get too involved in them.

EMILY: Why?

VINCENT: Because of just this, the misinterpretation and the feeling that you're in over your head. This is a time for me which is very crucial and very meaningful and very, very loaded and confused and raw. And right now, all my anxieties are about Marsha, she has become for me a terrible figure.

MARSHA: Why have I?

VINCENT: I don't know, I just feel it. I'm filled with a tremendous antagonism.

EMILY: I have one more thing to say about last night. First Nathan attacked Marsha and then he attacked you. You came to *her* defense, and I'm sure you expected her to do the same for you.

VINCENT: She never did.

EMILY: Right, and so you're angry. I told Marsha to expect that, but the point is she didn't stand up for your friendship because she wasn't standing up for anything, she wasn't participating on any level. It wasn't about you, it was about her reaction to the whole situation.

VINCENT: Yeah, but I'm talking in a very deep way right now. This summer, because Nico's been away so much, my love relationship has essentially been with Marsha. And it was coming to a very serious point, like last Friday my getting her on the bed and everything, even *before* the thing with Nathan. So that in a completely feeling way, my relationship is out of control with you now, Marsha. I have been continually hurt by you in the last two or three days, really terribly, terribly hurt, like this morning when you wouldn't speak to me on the phone.

MARSHA: When I was trying to work?

VINCENT: Yes, it hurt me to the quick.

EMILY: That's the paranoia that was aroused by the whole attack.

VINCENT: No it wasn't, it was my total anxiety about loss. But we've been through all that. God, I'm anxious today. I'm anxious because on one level I want the sun and on another level I really want to paint. Did all those things I just said frighten you, Marsh? She hasn't uttered one word, Em.

MARSHA: I guess they did.

VINCENT: And you totally withdrew, didn't you?

MARSHA: It doesn't matter. I'd rather know about it, I don't want any bullshit I love you I love you I love you when you're really feeling antagonism. I can't live that way.

VINCENT: You see, she doesn't understand a thing. That's why it's impossible to talk to her.

MARSHA: What don't I understand?

VINCENT: That what I'm talking about *is* love, and when I say I love you, I mean I love you. From everything I said, all she got was that I was antagonistic.

MARSHA: No! All I'm saying is I'm glad you expressed that too.

VINCENT: Okay, okay. Look at that man over there. He's very old, but he still has a fantastically tight body.

EMILY: He's not old, he's about forty-three, Nathan Fass' age.

VINCENT: How can you mention that name? Look at your doctor over there, Marsh, how skinny he is. He probably has an enormous complex about it. He's the skinniest man I've ever seen.

EMILY: Oh he is *not*. Philippe's skinnier than that.

MARSHA: I like that kind of body.

EMILY: You never did before. You like hairy Eliot-bodied muscular men.

VINCENT: Merrill Johnston is one of the handsomest men I've ever seen.

EMILY: He's got a real pre-Columbian face—you were right about that, Marsha.

MARSHA: Should I go over and tell him he's needed here?

VINCENT: What do we need him for?

MARSHA: I have to remember to get gas on the way home.

VINCENT: We should all read that book about games. We're all terrifically involved in them, particularly you two. You diminish everything to games.

EMILY: No, we start *out* with everything as games.

VINCENT: No, I mean diminish in terms of sexual interests, people interests—everything becomes name games.

EMILY: That's true, it *is* on a very childish level.

VINCENT: It's really a very ego thing, like to see which of you is cleverer, it's a continual competition back and forth.

EMILY: No it's not. Marshie and I are in cahoots, we're on the same team against whoever the opponent happens to be, Tim Cullen or whoever.

VINCENT: I'm sorry, I see it as a kind of love play, I really do, a performance thing. It's the way athletes, without being openly homosexual, a lot of their playing on the same team is that.

EMILY: Am I heavier than that girl over there?

VINCENT: Definitely, your ass is twice as big. You have an enormous ass.

EMILY: And as fat as my ass is, your face is twice as fat. I don't think I'll ever get over what you just said.

VINCENT: It's true, Emmy. Nico said you should absolutely get a reducing machine. Concentrate on that. You can't walk across a stage with that ass. By the way, did I tell you what Clem said to Tim? He said Vince isn't as nice as he used to be, and it's all because of his analysis. And that's true, I know I'm going to lose many, many friends this year.

EMILY: That's marvelous.

VINCENT: I'm even going to lose Clem and it will hurt him terrifically.

MARSHA: You've essentially lost him already, darling.

VINCENT: Not really, I'm still very committed to him emotionally.

EMILY: Why do you think you'll lose him, Vinnie?

MARSHA: Because he doesn't give enough in return.

VINCENT: That's part of it, but basically it's because I'm in this fantastic state of growth, I'm in an accelerated state of growth, which I have been all my life. That's why I have a tremendous fear of death, because of the speed I'm going at and the speed of feelings I've *always* gone at. I'm not exalting myself either.

EMILY: I understand that because I'm exactly the same.

VINCENT: Also the fact that I'm an artist and my structure has to do with growth and movement—starting a painting, finishing it and starting another one, you always move a step ahead, you never repeat yourself. And the fact that I'm in analysis and really want to go all the way back into things in terms of truth. I think anything you undertake you have to do completely and well.

MARSHA: You know how many friends *I've* rejected this year?

EMILY: Practically everyone you've ever known.

MARSHA: Right, and it's one of the best things that's happened to me.

VINCENT: That's what I was talking about last night, when I said all these years I have encouraged Marsha to get a feeling of herself within herself. That's when I was most hurt, when you didn't acknowledge that positive aspect of our friendship.

MARSHA: I know.

EMILY: Besides, very deep and full and varied experiences can only come from relating to a few select people. For instance, when I made the analogy of your replacing Joan, Vinnie, I didn't mean in terms of particular qualities, but in total meaning in my life. Because people are really quite unique.

VINCENT: Oh, I just got the most terrific pain right here. What is it? Is it my heart? Is it my heart, Marsha?

EMILY: Don't talk, darling, I'll tell you how to get rid of it. Completely relax, stretch your legs out and breathe very deeply and slowly. That's right—very, very slowly. Make an effort to relax, it'll go away.

MARSHA: Is it going away?

VINCENT: Very slightly. It's where my heart is, I'm sorry, it's exactly where my heart is.

EMILY: Darling, there's such a thing as heart pain, you know. Just make an effort to completely relax. You don't want to contract with the pain, you want to relax with it.

MARSHA: Natural childbirth.

VINCENT: Don't touch me, that's all. Oh, the pain!

EMILY: Just relax and it will go away. Believe me, I deal with this every single day that I study acting. I promise it will go away if you relax.

VINCENT: Put that hat over my face—I need shade.

MARSHA: Should I hold it for you?

VINCENT: Just be quiet.

EMILY: Lee Strasberg is all about dealing with these things. People do exercises in class and the sensory work opens up the instrument so that certain parts of the body start to let go like on a Reichian level. It has nothing to do with anything being wrong with you—nothing.

VINCENT: I'm so frightened of death.

MARSHA: This happened just after you said that. We were talking about death and five minutes later you get this pain in your heart.

VINCENT: Am I turning into some sort of a nut? Am I? Tell me the truth, I can take it.

EMILY: No, it's not you, it's your body. Your body's been doing this for thirty-two years.

VINCENT: What, having heart attacks?

EMILY: No, the body expresses itself independent of the mind. If you have anxiety, like over Nathan's attack and all the analyzing, the body's going to let you know; it'll shake, it'll do whatever it's going to do. The body can say to hell with you—that's exactly what it's doing.

VINCENT: I think it's letting up. Maybe we should take a walk—it might relax us a great deal, a little bit of a walk by the water. Then later we have to go out dancing.

25. EMILY AND VINCENT GO OUT DANCING

EMILY: No one's going to believe it in a million years.

VINCENT: Emmy, let's go back there.

EMILY: Turn around, Vinnie, we've got to go back. I'll never get over this as long as I live, so help me Christ oh God.

VINCENT: I'm sorry, this is a fantastic experience.

EMILY: Did it ever happen to you before?

VINCENT: Never. Can we go back to the gay bar as though we'd never been there?

EMILY: No, darling, you don't understand the importance of this.

VINCENT: Of course I do! What do you think I am—some sort of slunk?

EMILY: Can you *believe* that we just saw four reindeer? I don't care what anyone says, I'm never going to get over this. It might have been the most moving experience of my entire life.

VINCENT: It was right in this field and now they're nowhere to be seen.

EMILY: Vinnie, put your brights on, sweetheart.

VINCENT: They *are* on, darling. I wish they were brighter.

EMILY: Are you sure this is the field? That was one of the most tragic experiences of my entire life.

VINCENT: Unbelievable. Did you see how they were looking at us? I'll tell you, if we had had a gun, we could have gotten them all in a minute.

EMILY: Who would have wanted to? You don't really understand.

VINCENT: Tell me about it. Why was it so important to you?

EMILY: Because deers are the wildest and purest of animals, they are the combination of virile and beautiful, that exact combination of great valor and great sensitivity.

VINCENT: Emmy, do you think we're going to sink in the mud?

EMILY: I think we're going to be raped and killed on this road. Vinnie, nobody would believe what happened to us.

VINCENT: There was only one guy in that whole place who was attractive, I don't care what you say, that boy in the purple sweater.

EMILY: It wasn't purple, it was gray.

VINCENT: It was a washed-out purple. Emmy, what do I do now?

EMILY: Don't turn your wheel, baby. Let me do it, darling, please. You're turning your wheel too much, sweetheart, you're turning your wheel too much.

VINCENT: No I'm not, I'm doing it right. Emmy, I'll tell you something—we were very stuck there for a minute. Wait a second— what's that?

EMILY: It's a beer can.

VINCENT: Some beer can—it's blinking.

EMILY: Vinnie, I'm going to tell you once and for all, we saw four reindeer tonight, and it just beat my heart in twain.

VINCENT: Mark that, Emmy, mark that. Get it?

EMILY: I mean who in a million years would think there were deer around this part?

VINCENT: I know there were some in Montauk, but I thought they only came out in the winter.

EMILY: I've never seen a deer before.

VINCENT: Look, there's someone necking there.

EMILY: Should we pull up and watch? No. How come you know where you're going?

VINCENT: Because I've been here before and I have a fantastic sense of humor. Emmy, did we have fun tonight?

EMILY: I had a very good time; I loved it.

VINCENT: The whole thing was unbelievable in terms of a complete experience—first the Puerto-Rican-Hawaiian element of the

Out-of-the-Ordinary Inn, then going to this gay bar with all those low-class people. And then seeing the four deer which made us realize who we were.

EMILY: It did, really, it completely sobered us up, it brought us back to a certain kind of spiritual purity.

VINCENT: Emmy, you're a wonderful woman. I'm sorry, it's raining, I don't care what you say.

EMILY: Put your wipers on.

VINCENT: I love you for letting me drive. But why do these things that are cleaning the windows go so slow?

EMILY: You can whip them off too, you know. Learn a little something about your car.

VINCENT: I don't want them going slow, I like action. Emily, I'm going to take four aspirins when I get home. Do you think that will kill me?

EMILY: I don't know, but I'll give you a couple of quotes from Lawrence Durrell and you see whether or not you'll want to read *The Alexandria Quartet* this week.

VINCENT: Want to go back to the gay bar?

EMILY: No.

VINCENT: Want to go to the gay beach?

EMILY: No. One quote is "We all lead lives of selected fictions."

VINCENT: Brilliant.

EMILY: Another line is "We always fall in love with the love objects of the person we love."

VINCENT: Beautiful.

EMILY: Vinnie, I'm telling you you've got to read it. "We use each other like axes to destroy the ones we really love"—something like that. I've been thinking a lot about Durrell lately and I'm coming to the conclusion that I don't think novels can be written without the very sad and pitiful knowledge that they are totally self-conscious and ridiculous and untrue. I'm curious to see what Marsha does with hers. At least it'll be true.

VINCENT: They're all passing me, Emmy.

EMILY: It's just as well, you don't have your license yet.

VINCENT: That's right. You taught me from the very beginning that it doesn't matter how fast the others want to go. Maybe they're on their way to the city and they have to get there in a hurry. Emmy, you've taught me so much.

EMILY: I really have. I'm one of your great mentors.

VINCENT: Mentor health. Let's pick up some boy and suck him. I don't know why I talk to you this way, I don't even suck boys.

EMILY: I have no idea why.

VINCENT: Emmy, are you at all in love with me?

EMILY: Deeply.

VINCENT: And I'm terribly in love with you because you're so pretty and versatile.

EMILY: Marsha told *you* I looked beautiful, but she wouldn't say it to me. That's my Marsha.

VINCENT: Marsha has a fantastic affection for you, and I think she's very demonstrative, I really do.

EMILY: She's patting my head all the time these days. Very touching. I think Marsha's in good shape.

VINCENT: Wouldn't you love to drive to Idaho or someplace tonight?

EMILY: Let's go.

VINCENT: It's silly though, because we don't have any money.

EMILY: And we don't have any licenses. And we're in Marsha's car.

VINCENT: We could get through the entire country on her free Mobil credit.

EMILY: We certainly could.

VINCENT: And take tomatoes and corn from farms.

EMILY: But how long could we last?

VINCENT: We could last forever.

EMILY: And what about the opening of your show?

VINCENT: Oh, I don't care about that; I hate it.

EMILY: How do you like the way I gauged the gas situation?

VINCENT: Fantastic, but we're not home yet. You know I'm very happy, are you?

EMILY: I have to teach you something about psychodynamics, Vinnie. You must have asked me a hundred times tonight if I was having a good time. That just means you were projecting *your* anxiety about having a *bad* time, right?

VINCENT: I kept saying it because you were so reluctant to go.

EMILY: I wasn't reluctant, I was ready from the start.

VINCENT: To the gay bar?

EMILY: To the gay bar, I was reluctant, yes I was. I was reluctant not because I was afraid, but because I wasn't sure I'd have a good time, that's all.

VINCENT: And instead we had a *very* good time. It's always that way dancing in gay bars.

EMILY: That's right, because there are no inhibitions.

VINCENT: And there's no threat for you. If anything, you were performing fantastically. You were performing for the nature of gay men, which is like the positive, open part of straight men.

EMILY: Exactly. I even liked the line-up dancing.

VINCENT: What's lilac dancing?

EMILY: Line-up dancing, sweetheart.

VINCENT: I *love* line-up, I think it's terrifically orgiastic.

EMILY: Keep on the inside of the road, it's raining again.

VINCENT: Thank you. I love you because you're so sober when you're drunk.

EMILY: I'm not at all drunk. I had nothing to drink.

VINCENT: I know. How many drinks did we have? You had a dry martini.

EMILY: I had one dry martini.

VINCENT: Two of them, darling, it was filled for two.

EMILY: No, it was one shot in a small glass. Listen, if you have some honey, you should take a couple of spoonfuls when you get home.

VINCENT: Really?

EMILY: It sobers you up, it restores Vitamin B to the system, which is what the alcohol consumes in digestion.

VINCENT: You know all things well.

EMILY: All things well and true.

VINCENT: You believe in me driving, don't you?

EMILY: I believe in your driving, you're a marvelous driver.

VINCENT: Shall I drop you off and then take the car home? I'm not saying that because I'm threatened by the fear of going to bed with you, either. I've got such a headache you wouldn't believe it. What time do you think it is?

EMILY: About three.

VINCENT: Is it really that late? We've been out for five hours?

EMILY: Sure. We didn't get to that Out-of-the-Ordinary until about 12:30, right? I mean to the Out-of-the-Gay. Vinnie, it was so beautiful when we didn't leave that guy a tip.

VINCENT: That waiter was so hostile.

EMILY: So queer and so hostile, I couldn't stand it.

VINCENT: He was much more hostile than queer.

EMILY: I also loved it because we saved fifty cents.

VINCENT: That's something I learned from Nico. He said if people aren't nice to you, don't be intimidated by them.

EMILY: Yeah, but why didn't that waiter like us, Vinnie? We're perfectly nice personages. I think he was attracted to you and he knew nothing was going to come of it.

VINCENT: We can't ever go back there now.

EMILY: I wouldn't *want* to go back, would you?

VINCENT: No. I can go back next year and he won't know I'm me.

EMILY: Without me, nobody will recognize you. You know I walked in there as a teenager, not as a woman who's just punched thirty.

VINCENT: We should have found some rich people and had them pay everything.

EMILY: Did I ever tell you about the night of Michael's official opening in the gallery? Let me tell you exactly what happened.

VINCENT: Is there any reason to scream?

EMILY: No. That night I went to the gallery, from there I went to the Plaza for a drink, then I met Michael, who took me to the Guggenheim opening, from there we went to a party, and from there, it was about four in the morning, we went to the Brasserie. This is his taste—he ordered three bottles of champagne and two or three dozen snails.

VINCENT: Who paid?

EMILY: When Michael called for the check, the waiter came over and said the check has been taken care of, sir.

VINCENT: By who?

EMILY: He refused to tell us.

VINCENT: And you never found out?

EMILY: We never found out. We were sitting there kissing each other.

VINCENT: You kiss each other in the Brasserie?

EMILY: Yeah. So Christy pulled out a ten-dollar bill and gave it to the waiter as a tip, and the waiter said I'm sorry, sir, but it's *all* been taken care of.

VINCENT: You're kidding. Now that's very high class, that's beautiful. But you mean there was no one in that room you knew?

EMILY: There obviously must have been.

VINCENT: Yeah, but you didn't identify him as such?

EMILY: Well we certainly didn't stand up and start searching to see who it was. We were madly in love, we kept looking at each other and kissing.

VINCENT: I bet it was some old person who just liked the idea of your young love. But isn't it interesting that you fall right back into the Michael Christy pit as soon as you have a drink?

EMILY: I know. Vinnie, what about that thing you told me about Ursula Andress coming to New York and Nico getting me into her movie and everything?

VINCENT: We will, we'll have a small party for you.

EMILY: Oh, for *me*, not for Ursula, I see. And what's she going to do? Say oh, you're such a lovely girl I want you to star in my next picture?

VINCENT: You have to start hanging around fancier people for your career. Emmy, if I didn't get my license, I'm going to be morose.

EMILY: Oh you're going to get it, there's not a doubt in my mind.

VINCENT: I really hope I passed, because I love to drive. For me it's one of the great sensual pleasures, like brushing your teeth.

EMILY: Vinnie, I'm sure you did pass. The inspector said fine, didn't he? He never would have used that word, it wouldn't have slipped off his tongue otherwise.

VINCENT: That's what I told Marsha, but she just passed him off as courteous. You know, Emmy, I love your stories about Michael and everything, but to me it's just a sad love affair, sad because it's a love affair that's over.

EMILY: Vinnie, do you realize that we saw those four deer?

VINCENT: I can't get over it. But why was it so important?

EMILY: It was just so moving, so unusual, so extraordinary. Remember when we came out here once with Nico and saw a water rat?

VINCENT: Oh that was so long ago, the Fourth of July weekend. My Nico's coming back tomorrow night; then I'll be a different person, mature and adult.

EMILY: But he knows you're *not*, right?

VINCENT: Want to go back to the gay bar?

EMILY: No. I'm hungry.

VINCENT: You're hungry too? I am *starved*. I haven't had any dinner yet. You know there are an awful lot of people out at this hour.

EMILY: What time is the hour?

VINCENT: I don't know. Are we glad we went out?

EMILY: I am.

VINCENT: I am.

EMILY: You're not hungry, huh?

VINCENT: I'm starved.

EMILY: I'm so hungry I'm suffering.

VINCENT: There isn't even a delicatessen out here to go to.

EMILY: I'm suffering from hunger, I really am, and there's nothing to eat but cold chicken soup. I made a fantastic salad tonight —you want to hear what it was?

VINCENT: Oh God, that's all I need.

EMILY: Cucumber, tomatoes, scallions and lettuce, fresh dill and blue cheese dressing.

VINCENT: Are you impressed that I got you home on time?

EMILY: What do you mean, "on time"?

VINCENT: In one piece.

EMILY: I'm impressed by you in every way.

VINCENT: We were very drunk tonight.

EMILY: *You* were—I was never drunk. Really, I swear to God.

VINCENT: All right—I'll put it all on my shoulders: I was completely drunk. Look, Marshie left the light on for you. Isn't that adorable?

EMILY: She left the light on and it's adorable, except that that's not her house.

VINCENT: My breath is so horrible.

EMILY: So is mine.

VINCENT: Yours is not, yours is beautiful.

EMILY: Vinnie, you drove me home.

VINCENT: Oh Emmy, I'm so exhausted.

26. MARSHA AND EMILY'S LAST DAY ON THE BEACH

MARSHA: I'm not coming back here next summer, you know.

EMILY: I don't blame you, but where else can you go? You don't like Fire Island.

MARSHA: Oh no. Maybe I'll go back to Europe, get a house. It's just as cheap. It all comes down to the same old problem, being a woman alone. I mean I'd love to get a place in Norway, which Clem Nye said was the most breathtakingly beautiful landscape he's ever seen, but I'd go nuts by myself, right?

EMILY: Nuts.

MARSHA: And I wouldn't go to some arty Positano or Spoleto.

EMILY: They're so faggy and terrible.

MARSHA: Decadent and stupid.

EMILY: But obviously it's not the end of East Hampton. A lot of people are going to stay on, the ones who've bought houses and made all that fucking investment.

MARSHA: They're the ones who ruined it.

EMILY: Let's quickly dissect what the East Hampton beach scene is. First of all, there are those perennial people who come out every summer, the couples with babies who have a certain amount of money, and when they're on the beach they're with friends who are just like them, couples with children, and if they have guests for the weekend, they're men who bring their girlfriends. That's one category. Then there's the thirty-year-old woman who's fucked around, maybe she's been married, she has a house out here with a girlfriend and she's beachcombing the weekend guests, she's looking for a man up the wrong tree. Then there are the single men who come out here in groups.

MARSHA: I haven't seen any of that.

EMILY: I'm buoying myself up here in the sand for great action, lest I sink. He's not bad, this bald midget with the orange shirt and the orange cigarette.

MARSHA: He's leaving.

EMILY: That's what's not bad about him.

MARSHA: Do you like bald men?

EMILY: My father was bald.

MARSHA: I didn't ask you that.

EMILY: You mean just as a sensory thing? No, do you?

MARSHA: I'm beginning to.

EMILY: It's a good thing too. You know Vinnie's right about this definitely being a middle-class family, coupled situation. I think the real emotional, intellectual upper class are people who don't group to begin with. But the beach is still a nice collection of people, basically very varied, very heterogeneous. It's nothing like say Jones Beach, where people are strangers.

MARSHA: No, it's a personality beach.

EMILY: It's a party, with the pretense of being a beach, a kind of fantasy charade of people's projections. Like when I see Keira walk by, what I see is a poster-flyer of his show. Look at him. He's walking up and down like he's at a cocktail party. He only makes contact with people to revitalize the image he has about himself. It becomes so-and-so, Painter, or so-and-so, Author, not so-and-so who may have problems with his wife. But you still very well might meet somebody when you're out here by yourself.

MARSHA: Yeah, if there's anyone here to meet.

EMILY: Uh-oh, there's what's-her-name—Merle.

MARSHA: Who?

EMILY: Philippe's sister-in-law. Over there—to the left and to the water. Look, her kid's crying and she's giving him one of her talks.

MARSHA: Man-to-man.

EMILY: "We are all grown-ups and we must be mature," blablabla. Don't look. She knows enough not to come over here, doesn't she?

MARSHA: Of course.

EMILY: Meanwhile she's coming over. You're what they call *in piena vista*.

MARSHA: Where is the water coming from?

EMILY: Probably the shithead's giving me a spraygun. This guy over here's got an erection.

MARSHA: All right, so tell me about the life you're going back to.

EMILY: I'm getting sprayguns like crazy here. I may be lying down any minute, I have a feeling it's warmer down there. You want to know about my life in New York?

MARSHA: Yeah, don't you?

EMILY: Well, I'm going to get the money people owe me, number one. I'm going to hit class and hit an agent. I'll see what's happening, put out feelers, find out what the story is, go up for things. Meanwhile I don't have a dime, meanwhile I'm seeing my doctor, meanwhile I'm thinking of getting a nine-to-five job along with everything else. Meanwhile I'm spending a lot of time alone.

MARSHA: You are? You're out of Sick Joan?

EMILY: Totally out of Sick Joan. I'm going to be spending a lot of time in my apartment, in my darkroom, typing up my letters. These are things I can do, that I'm interested in doing. I'm not going to run away from them, but you know I *do* have a fantastic facility for running away. You might call me the genius kid.

MARSHA: I well might.

EMILY: I knew Joan would never stay in that hospital. But why was she calling me out here? What was in the heart that was being poured into the phone? How did she sound?

MARSHA: Sober. I hated lying to her that you weren't here.

EMILY: I know. When she used to call me in Europe, I very often wouldn't talk to her. She'd call me at five o'clock in the morning, after she'd been drinking all night or all week.

MARSHA: I bet Philippe loved the calling.

EMILY: Drove him wild, wall-to-wall crackers. I still don't know whether she belongs in a hospital. You know she has a facet to her sickness, I don't know how common it is, but it's very alienating, and that is she plays on it all the time, the tune of her sickness, that's the song she sings, I'm sick, I'm sick, I'm sick, I'm an alcoholic, I'm drinking myself to death, I'm suffering, I know all about pain. To spend a lot of time with her when she's like that is to get ultimately very depressed.

MARSHA: Immediately, I'd say.

EMILY: You get immediately depressed. You know I was thinking something very interesting about your trusting me now, knowing I won't get drunk, the way I did before Woods Hole. It was that the demon in me, that terrible thing that had to be expiated, was made visible in the form of Joan, which is why we had to drive her out when she was here. It's almost true, isn't it?

MARSHA: It is.

EMILY: I think that on so many levels, almost anything can be true.

MARSHA: What language are those guys speaking?

EMILY: I'm trying to figure it out. It sounds like Afghanistan or something. Marsha, say you got married to a man who lived very far away, like in Japan or Africa, and you went off with him, maybe you'd come home once a year for a visit. I'm sure you *would*, because your father, if nothing else, would *pay* for you to come home once a year. Can you imagine how your relationships would change? To me, to Vinnie, to everyone?

MARSHA: I'd like it.

EMILY: You *would?* That's very positive. I couldn't ever marry a person who didn't speak English, not for anything. I suffered like a lunatic with the language when I was in Europe, you know.

MARSHA: I know. You just have a conversation with words and you really can't tell what people feel about themselves or about you.

EMILY: That's very true. I remember, because I'm a person who first of all, aside from being very verbal, tends to be expansive and my use of words is very peculiar to me, I was completely frustrated in French. I almost preferred to say the simplest things. It's such an entirely different sensibility anyway. I sometimes get the feeling that in a way the pain of analysis in us is the equivalent of the war experience to the Europeans.

MARSHA: What do you mean?

EMILY: Well, the American sensibility is fairly flat, the nuance of it, the cadence, the depth; it doesn't have the tradition or the culture or any of the things of history that the European has, right? But what we do have is a certain kind of psychological awareness that somehow corresponds. I'd like to know who that man with the moustache is.

MARSHA: He keeps looking over here every minute.

EMILY: I'm definitely suspicious of men who hide behind moustaches and beards from now on.

MARSHA: Darling, that man has five children—what do you want from him?

EMILY: I was talking philosophically, generically. I'm steering clear of them, except that my analyst has a moustache.

MARSHA: What kind?

EMILY: Completely uneducated and unpretentious; the kind of moustache a man just has on his face, that looks like it's part of it.

MARSHA: Do you really think they have a beautiful life, that gorgeous beard and his wife?

EMILY: I wouldn't want to be her, but at the same time there *is* something beautiful about it, that she's married to him and they have those children they love, that he carries into the water on his shoulders. I need that, I want it desperately.

MARSHA: I don't want it desperately anymore.

EMILY: I never wanted it desperately before.

MARSHA: She's horrible, that wife. Did you see her hit the little boy?

EMILY: I don't have to, darling, I know that girl from years ago. She just wrote a book on Chekhov.

MARSHA: What could she possibly know about Chekhov? Emily, your hair is turning white, golden white. What I have to do is get to work on the whole superego area.

EMILY: I was the first person to point it out, wasn't I?

MARSHA: Yeah, but at the same time Tim had put this big

photograph of me up on his wall and said it was like his conscience looking down on him.

EMILY: But I stated it very simply, that you function as a superego.

MARSHA: All I do is tell him what he should do, what he should do, what he should be doing.

EMILY: Yeah, you're fantastically critical. And the sun's really playing games.

MARSHA: Can I borrow your sunglasses?

EMILY: Yeah, but I'm going to take them off pretty soon.

MARSHA: I'll wear them while you have them on.

EMILY: You want me to tell you what I think about the superego thing?

MARSHA: I thought we weren't getting into that shit anymore, but we'll get into it.

EMILY: No, not on a depth level. First of all, your being so critical has to do with anger and disappointment. It's almost as if you're making some kind of moral judgment, because the degree to which you get involved is completely out of proportion to reality.

MARSHA: I *am* very moral, I'm scared to do anything wrong.

EMILY: That's not moral, that's scared.

MARSHA: Maybe most morality is based on fear.

EMILY: Most morality, like puritanism and stuff like that *is* based on tightness and fear, sure. And anxiety.

MARSHA: I'm afraid to lie, afraid they'll find out.

EMILY: You *do* lie though, don't you?

MARSHA: Very rarely.

EMILY: You see, this all goes together with the superego stuff. You don't lie, you don't steal, because you're afraid to be caught. You have this big censor thing, like irresolute judge, judger, judgment.

MARSHA: I don't think it's a good idea to steal.

EMILY: It's a very *bad* idea.

MARSHA: But you're criticizing me, you say I'm not free enough to steal.

EMILY: No I'm not. I'm saying it goes together with your other superego things.

MARSHA: Do you have a pimple here that you picked?

EMILY: No, I must have scratched it in my sleep—I don't pick my pimples. I'm not saying you should steal, Marsha. I don't think stealing and lying are good, but I think they're bad for the right reasons, not because of being afraid. Joan steals.

MARSHA: So do you.

EMILY: Not anymore.

MARSHA: You did, you stole from Bloomingdale's.

EMILY: Macy's. I certainly did. But it's very bad to steal because of how it makes you feel. If you were a man, what kind of bathing suit would you wear?

MARSHA: Depends on my body.

EMILY: I think Emil Reinhardt wears the right kind. I don't like those short things with the jock straps underneath, I think they're disgusting. Who's got the nicest body here?

MARSHA: Who cares?

EMILY: I'm curious to see what Nathan Fass looks like in a bathing suit. He says he can't keep the women off him.

MARSHA: He's got a tight body.

EMILY: Yeah, he must do very well on this beach; he's the only man available.

MARSHA: Here comes your boyfriend, Emil, without Diana. Talk to me, quick, so it isn't so obvious that I'm staring at him. He's ignoring us and walking over there.

EMILY: How do you know he saw you? Chances are he didn't, he doesn't see that well. Hey, where are all these people running? It's beautiful, isn't it, all the people running?

MARSHA: I just figured out what's making the spray—the ocean.

EMILY: I know, it's spraying our freshly shampooed, freshly non-set hair. They're all running—it must be a sea animal.

MARSHA: Shark. Now they're coming back and grabbing their children.

EMILY: They're all shadows, everybody running. Do you think it's a whale?

MARSHA: Shark. I love the sunshine that's not here.

EMILY: It's terrific. *Ma vie que continue.* You know this dream I had last night was really weird. Some incredibly rich guy asked me to marry him and I realized after about maybe fifteen minutes that that was exactly what I was going to do, and I was going to do it in direct relation to the rejection I had just gotten from Michael Christy. Then I thought about the things I was going to do for my mother, I was going to buy her things, take care of her. Where's that fucking Nazi?

MARSHA: Who?

EMILY: Reinhardt, with his towel and everything. He's looking around, I don't know if he sees us. You know why I'm really on the beach, the main reason? Therapy for my cold.

MARSHA: Bullshit, the same sun is in back of my house.

EMILY: Completely different sun; this is white sun. Meanwhile the kids have just ruined the whole Emil Reinhardt setup. I can't see thing one.

MARSHA: Shall we take a little stroll around?

EMILY: Around every which where?

MARSHA: Yeah, down to the water.

EMILY: He could really see me now if he had normal eyes and if the kids weren't blocking his total view. If he was Clark Kent with X-ray vision, he could see me. Oh, there's a woman who looks just like Mike Christy. See, with the pink robe and the big sunglasses?

MARSHA: Hey, I don't blame you for liking this guy, the guy with the nose.

EMILY: Yeah, he's great, isn't he? One of the nicest guys on the beach.

MARSHA: If not *the*.

EMILY: He's not too hairy, he's not too old. The new ideal man: he shouldn't be completely bald, he shouldn't have to wear glasses *all* the time, he shouldn't be too tired after dinner, he shouldn't lose too many jobs inside of a year, shouldn't smoke more than six packs of cigarettes a day, shouldn't forget your name more than every now and then, shouldn't be too queer. Shouldn't have too many alcoholic binges, too many crying jags.

MARSHA: Shouldn't have too much possessive resistance.

EMILY: Too many pairs of the same tassel loafers, too many La Costa shirts.

MARSHA: What's that?

EMILY: Those tennis shirts with the alligators on them. Shouldn't have too many friends named Shep, Myron,

MARSHA: Armand. He shouldn't wear white socks with his tassel loafers.

EMILY: He shouldn't smoke pot all day and sleep until five in the afternoon. You know I'd really like to talk about love for a second, Marshie, because I've said a lot of very twenty-nine-year-old drunken things this summer. But I can say right now that I don't want any more married men and I don't want any weak men and I don't want any men that I've ever known before. I think I'm just about ready to find someone who's healthy enough to take the chance of getting married to me.

MARSHA: Amen.

27. MARSHA AND VINCENT DRIVE BACK TO NEW YORK

MARSHA: I'm beginning to think that everything in my life happens offstage, it's all reverberations and echoes and filters, and that's exactly what my book is too. Essence is always avoided.

VINCENT: Yes, but that isn't a defect of the book. If anything, that's what's beautiful about it. I think all great art comes from people's inabilities to do what they want to do, and your book is completely organic to what you are, it's a very dependent book on other personalities, on the people close to you.

MARSHA: Right.

VINCENT: It's a very passive book on your part, and yet it's very positive, just as you are positive but passive. This book is completely you. We all laughed while you sat on the beach knitting while Emmy and I taped your book—you *do* lie back and let people do things for you. And I'm not saying this to knock you, I'm saying that because you *are* this way, and because you're also a writer and a creative spirit, you're making something new and valid out of your own defect, which is what all great art does. Do you think the Beatles know how to drive a car?

MARSHA: Sure.

VINCENT: They must have learned before they got famous, don't you think? They wouldn't have had time since. You know I've really gotten cool on Clem. And it's not because I'm hurt or anything either, I've just begun to find him unattractive as a person. Isn't that awful?

MARSHA: Why is it awful? The same thing happened to me—you won't think it's the same—but it happened to me very suddenly with Eliot Simon. For all the years after I stopped seeing him, my feelings were still colored by an emotional residue, but then finally I was able to see him for what he was—not a particularly good or exceptional or even interesting person.

VINCENT: It's really very funny.

MARSHA: Six months' time heals all wounds. I had a dream once where I went cross-country in a toll booth. It had wheels. You're in a terrible mood, aren't you?

VINCENT: State or mood?

MARSHA: State. You just used a certain tone which I know I have only when I'm completely tense, you have to force the words out, there's a cut-back in the voice, it's way down in the back of the throat. Did you ever have any physical psychological things? When I was going with Eliot, I had pains in my legs all the time. I couldn't sleep because I was so conscious of my knock-knees knocking into each other all night.

VINCENT: Nico says I should never wear sunglasses because they hide my eyes. There was an awful lot of garlic in that chicken yesterday.

MARSHA: Just two cloves.

VINCENT: Have you ever cooked anything that really came out well? I've never tasted one dish that you made right, never.

MARSHA: Darling, that's a very rude thing to say. You always give me stringy stringbeans and scrambled eggs with brown edges.

VINCENT: Wouldn't it be awful if you spent your whole life believing you loved white meat of chicken and vanilla ice cream, then you reached the age of thirty-two and suddenly realized that you loved dark meat all along and chocolate ice cream and you hadn't ever had them, and you felt that the years had passed you by?

MARSHA: But you must have liked vanilla too if you were eating it all that time.

VINCENT: I'll bet you anything it's psychological types, liking only white meat and vanilla ice cream.

MARSHA: No, I like chocolate and white meat. When I was a child I despised anyone who liked chocolate and now it's the only kind

I like. Slow down, I want to see the dwarf in the back of that truck.

VINCENT: It's not a dwarf, he's got the size face of a normal man.

MARSHA: Is it a person or a bundle?

VINCENT: A person.

MARSHA: It's not blinking.

VINCENT: Why should it? The sun's not in its eyes.

MARSHA: Last autumn, Zeke was making pumpkins in my house for his children.

VINCENT: Did you just fart? You did, didn't you? Marsha, I'm asking you please not to do it.

MARSHA: How can I stop?

VINCENT: You can hold it in until we get to New York.

MARSHA: That's ridiculous.

VINCENT: You're so self-indulgent, and then you look at me with some sort of sweet face. Do you really think the sweetness of your smile can possibly make up for the acridity of that smell?

MARSHA: Yeah. Did I ever tell you the dream I once had about Nathan Fass, that he farted and a great orchestrated rhapsody came out? You can smile even though you hate him.

VINCENT: I don't hate *him*, I hate what we've been through.

MARSHA: Look, look at the sun!

VINCENT: It's split by a cloud, it's beautiful.

MARSHA: You know where Zeke lives now is closer to L.A. than New York.

VINCENT: So?

MARSHA: So that's where he belongs, that's more what he is. He has a surfing sensibility. He hated your big painting, you know.

VINCENT: You never told me that. How much did he hate it? Let's be open about it. I'm very open.

MARSHA: You're not that open.

VINCENT: Are you kidding? I'm one of the most open people I know.

MARSHA: Besides, I thought we weren't getting into these things again, picking each other apart.

VINCENT: No, we're just being honest, it's as simple as that. When it goes wrong is when one of the parts can't take it and lately I haven't been able to take it, so this ride may end up the same way.

MARSHA: Well I don't want it to, I can't go through it. I only meant you're not just some simple, sweet open person.

VINCENT: What's it got to do with sweetness? Because you're open doesn't mean you're good. I'm not a good person.

MARSHA: Sick Joan thinks she's one of the most open people in the world.

VINCENT: To her way of thinking, she is.

MARSHA: She's open to her way of thinking, but she's closed in terms of a circle. She says she drinks to communicate, but when she drinks she communicates zero.

VINCENT: I'll tell you—I think I'm open, I think I'm direct, I think I give, but I don't feel I necessarily give the truth.

MARSHA: Maybe the truth isn't what has to be given.

VINCENT: Exactly, that's my whole point in life. But I want to know how much Zeke Sutherland hated my painting.

MARSHA: Very much. He stared at it for hours and hours. Of course he couldn't avoid it, it filled the room.

VINCENT: He could have looked the other way. Why did he hate it?

MARSHA: He thought you had hopped on the pop bandwagon.

VINCENT: Everyone thought that. Besides, we know about boyfriends criticizing other boyfriends' work. He was right though; it *was* closer to the bandwagon than what I was doing before, but that was because it was transitional. Now I'm very singular, there's no one in New York doing work like mine. I had to go through that to get where I am. That's why it was such a fantastically painful period. I'll tell you one thing about this summer, Marshie, and you're not going to believe me, but I'll tell you anyway—at the beginning of the summer, I thought of you and me as boy and girl, and now I feel of us as man and woman.

MARSHA: Really?

VINCENT: Yes, definitely, I mean it, and it's a very important thing.

28. MARSHA UNPACKS FROM THE SUMMER

EMILY: Can I buy this light bulb from you? It's crucial—my big bulb just broke.

MARSHA: Yeah, how much is it?

EMILY: Two for sixty-two; thirty cents.

MARSHA: Thirty-one in my book.

EMILY: Your book is the book of the crooks.

MARSHA: You know I've completely forgotten about Vincent Miano? I haven't thought about calling him once since I've been back. I'm cured, I can go on to real-life mock sex.

EMILY: You didn't forget about him—you just remembered. Vinnie's a very pure person, you know, but don't think for one minute he's not a cool operator, because he is. I didn't realize that he had never said word one to Michael Christy.

MARSHA: I've never met him either, even though he plays such a leading role in my book.

EMILY: Well finally Vinnie did, talked to him for five minutes last night and said he's a great guy. You know sex with Michael Christy was very strange, but I better not talk about it.

MARSHA: Why?

EMILY: You shouldn't talk about those things. Do you have hair on your toes?

MARSHA: Yeah.

EMILY: I do too, and it's disgusting. I feel like chewing it off. When I was a child, I used to be able to bite my toenails. I must say, it's not every day you go to your best friend's house and get served warmed-over scotch.

MARSHA: Darling, have some fresh scotch.

EMILY: I don't want any, darling, I'm not drinking, believe me.

MARSHA: I'm not believing you.

EMILY: You know I had a boyfriend once who owed me five dollars, so he sent me a check. But I loved the signature so much that I didn't cash it for a long time. When I finally succumbed, got rid of my romanticism and cashed it, he had closed his account.

MARSHA: Zeke gave me a check once and it broke my heart to cash it. Oh no, I wrote *him* a check—that's more like it.

EMILY: And it broke his belly to cash it.

MARSHA: And I treasured the countersignature on the backside.

EMILY: I've got a countersignature from Emil Reinhardt dating 1956. How could that be? I didn't marry Roy until 1959. I guess it's dated 1959.

MARSHA: All this work is getting me depressed.

EMILY: I'm surprised you're not depressed about the summer being over.

MARSHA: I am.

EMILY: Who helped you move all this stuff?

MARSHA: Tim.

EMILY: He's a very good boy. What's the name of this Sutherland sculpture?

MARSHA: Alice. You know the full name, don't you?

EMILY: Alice, the Dawn is Breaking?

MARSHA: No, Zeke named it for me and what I represented to him: "A my name is Alice and my husband's name is Alfred, we come from Alabama and we sell apples."

EMILY: Oh I love that, it's beautiful. Here comes the army of underpants, the army of drips, back into action. Onions she moves in from East Hampton, onions and a carton of Gauloises.

MARSHA: You're what?

EMILY: Oy, the deafness, it could drive a person buggy. That's definitely not your strongest sense, the sense of hearing. I lost mine with my ear infections, but I used to hear brilliantly, they would test me all the time.

MARSHA: Did you pass? What's Vinnie doing tonight? Staying home?

EMILY: I think so.

MARSHA: I told Merrill Johnston today I feel very cool toward Vinnie, very unclingy.

EMILY: You feel that way toward everyone. You know your relationship with Vinnie did get a little weird this summer, you know that.

MARSHA: Yeah. Sick.

EMILY: I'll tell you, Marshie, I still have some very bad problems and I don't know what to do about them. Like the way I felt glad to see Michael again the other night? I did, Marsha, it's like you with Tim, because they're men we've gone to bed with and we're certain they can function that way, they're still alive. You know I really don't have any opinions anymore, I just have ideas. From drugs and a lot of pot, the big thing I'm trying to find out now is what I feel, not what other people feel or what they think about me, I'm trying to find out what I feel vis-à-vis any particular stimulus or situation. For instance, in a love affair, in a relationship with a man, if I'm afraid of doing something because of being rejected, then I'm not dealing with my own feelings. I don't see human behavior anymore in terms of passive and responsive; I see it only as active. And that's maybe one crucial, definitive step I've been able to make towards being a woman. And I think that's our business; if we have any business being anything, it's being women. All I can say is I want a man in my life and I need one very badly. I'm lonely and I'm frail, but I think I'm strong enough to take on someone else's demands, because I'm beginning to know what my own are. It's very tough, Marshie.

MARSHA: It is. I don't know where to store everything, Em.

EMILY: You definitely need a larger apartment.

MARSHA: Did I tell you my sister's my new best friend?

EMILY: Is she really?

MARSHA: Sweet as sugar. She dragged all over town with me today, on buses, on foot, little pregnant baby. You know the saddest thing? The other night, when I was getting dressed at her house, she sat on the bed watching me like a little girl watching her older teenage sister. And there she was with a baby in her belly.

EMILY: Yeah, but you know babies in bellies don't mean anything. As you well *know*, my Marshie, babies in bellies don't mean very much at all. Is your sister bright?

MARSHA: I don't know.

EMILY: She has a lot of the qualities of bright people, she's sort of cynical and bored, negative, quick, but I've never heard any sustained thoughts come out of her head. What am I supposed to do about Joan now?

MARSHA: I don't know, get rid of her, tell her we decided to go to the movies and she can't come.

EMILY: Yeah. This chicken has a very Jewish smell. My mother used to make fricassee with meatballs thrown into it.

MARSHA: My mother did too, only with a brown sauce.

EMILY: That's what this is—brown sauce. If you want me to throw in the meatballs, I will. I think I'm getting a maid. My apartment is so clean right now, so meticulous, it's so neat and beautiful, just like this, it's in exactly this kind of shape. But I don't have time to keep it that way.

MARSHA: Who does?

EMILY: Nobody. I don't want to shit away my evenings anymore, Marshie, I'm feeling extremely positive about life. Tiny little meatballs she used to put in. You know how many years it's been since she put in those tiny meatballs?

MARSHA: Maybe she still does.

EMILY: My mother's madly in love with me these days. I was going with my doctor today through the fantasies I have about being a star. You want to hear them? They're so sad. I come out onto the stage, and all of a sudden this big hot wet black womb full of love, this theatre, bursts into applause. And who's in the audience? You're there, all my friends are, all the friends who love me and think I'm brilliant and talented but basically a flunky failure, they're all in the audience. Michael's in the audience, Nathan's in the audience, my mother's in the audience, the whole family scene is out there in the audience. Guess who isn't?

MARSHA: Sick Joan?

EMILY: My doctor, he's not in the audience. Why should he be? After all, I only have a limited amount of tickets for opening night. I was describing to him the nature of my present life being amorphous and plastic and without form and he said but it has great form; your masochism is its shape. And it's true, my dollar-a-day allowance, my twenty-seven-dollar-a-month rent and my stealing, my incredibly impoverished sense of self have been so neatly and compactly worked into my mental bloodstream, it's unbelievable. Before the summer, Marshie, I felt I was what my masochism was, that was the only identity I had, the fact that I was a loser. I had no hope. I never told you, but I was very suicidal. And you have to admit I had a lot of good company, a lot of sick people to keep me happy and on the swing. Pushing to the left was Sick Joan and pushing me to the right was that gorgeous series of deprived and risky men, Nathan, Michael, Philippe. I'm glad it's over, Marsh. You know something? You look just like a little girl right now.

MARSHA: Tim Cullen said I look pretty in yellow. First compliment he's given me since last February.

EMILY: What does he know?

MARSHA: He knows I look pretty in yellow.

EMILY: You do, it happens that you look very well in yellow, I wouldn't shit you. Guess what color the sauce of the fricassee is?

MARSHA: Yellow.

EMILY: Completely brown, brown as a witch's tit.

MARSHA: Oh lordy, here we go again. You know when I went to my doctor today, I told him how sick I think I am.

EMILY: Why?

MARSHA: Because I have no feelings, or at least I don't come into contact with them, they're all buried. It's funny because I thought I was going to go in and tell him I had had such a constructive summer of working and studying myself and this and that. Instead all I did was qvetch about what a horrible person I emerged as on the tapes and how all the three of us talk about is sex and food and yet how I felt we were the only people who communicate in the whole world, blablabla. He said it must be very isolating.

EMILY: What must be isolating?

MARSHA: Just having you and Vinnie as people I can talk to.

EMILY: What's this thing about not having any feelings?

MARSHA: Well, he asked me what I would feel like if I got married and had to give up Vince, and I said I wouldn't feel anything.

EMILY: You told him what happened with Nathan Fass, didn't you?

MARSHA: Yeah, but I blocked most of it out, I couldn't remember the details. I had already told him on the beach anyway. I did say if I don't care about Vinnie, who ultimately is the closest person in the world to me, who *do* I care about?

EMILY: He is? He's closer to you than me?

MARSHA: In a way, yeah. He *is* a man. I mean you both are close, but actually, I think in terms of influence, he's more important in my life.

EMILY: You were with him a lot more this summer.

MARSHA: Let's not compare; you're both terribly close to me.

EMILY: Yeah, okay.

MARSHA: But in the end, do I really give a shit about either of you? Do I give a shit about anything? I don't think I do. I had just described the feeling I had for Tim, getting so overwhelmed with emotion when he forgave me, and Merrill Johnston said what was that, just sham feeling? I said I brought it up because it was so rare for me to have such a big feeling. I said maybe it's because I spend my time with people like Sick Joan, who goes to a psychotic extreme, and Emily, who goes to a neurotic extreme of feeling, feeling, feeling; maybe only by comparison with them don't I feel.

EMILY: You definitely have a problem with feeling.

MARSHA: That's a pretty big problem.

EMILY: I think it's very healthy that you're worried about this.

MARSHA: Then after telling him I had no feelings, I came home and burst into tears.

EMILY: Darling, we know that you *have* feelings, you're a very complicated person. But you *did* have a very positive summer in certain respects.

MARSHA: The whole purpose of the summer was to write a book.

EMILY: And you did that.

MARSHA: I wrote the book and everything I missed in the summer as well as everything I gained was because of it. I set the summer up so that I could be out of bed at seven o'clock every morning. I set it up so I wouldn't meet a lot of distracting people, even though he admitted there weren't any people to meet.

EMILY: Merrill Johnston admitted that?

MARSHA: Yeah, I said can you name one available man and he said no.

EMILY: My sister thinks I'll be married with children within the year.

MARSHA: How many children?

EMILY: So does Joan, they both really think I'm going to be married.

MARSHA: You know we're getting right back into the Zeke season. Last year at this time he was making pumpkin faces here for Hallowe'en.

EMILY: And I was off in my whirl.

MARSHA: Zeke is an empty bucket.

EMILY: A seedless raisin.

MARSHA: A bottomless pit.

EMILY: Oh, she's wearing one slipper red and one slipper green. Is that typical? We're back where we started; when you were packing you were wearing one red and one green.

MARSHA: Was I really?

EMILY: Of course, I was hysterical over it. You know you can tell all about everything just by looking at these fucking photographs of the summer. First of all, my tongue is sticking out on every picture.

MARSHA: So is Tim's. But you want to see pure symbolism? Look, here are my two best friends laughing and talking, and I'm all alone between them.

EMILY: All Antonionied up.

MARSHA: All Antonionied up.

EMILY: It's so sad. Okay, honya, the fricassee's ready. Do you want to dole out the dish or shall I?

TITLES IN SERIES

For a complete list of titles, visit www.nyrb.com or write to:
Catalog Requests, NYRB, 435 Hudson Street, New York, NY 10014

J.R. ACKERLEY Hindoo Holiday*
J.R. ACKERLEY My Dog Tulip*
J.R. ACKERLEY My Father and Myself*
J.R. ACKERLEY We Think the World of You*
HENRY ADAMS The Jeffersonian Transformation
RENATA ADLER Pitch Dark*
RENATA ADLER Speedboat*
AESCHYLUS Prometheus Bound; translated by Joel Agee*
CÉLESTE ALBARET Monsieur Proust
DANTE ALIGHIERI The Inferno
DANTE ALIGHIERI The New Life
KINGSLEY AMIS The Alteration*
KINGSLEY AMIS Ending Up*
KINGSLEY AMIS Girl, 20*
KINGSLEY AMIS The Green Man*
KINGSLEY AMIS Lucky Jim*
KINGSLEY AMIS The Old Devils*
KINGSLEY AMIS One Fat Englishman*
KINGSLEY AMIS Take a Girl Like You*
WILLIAM ATTAWAY Blood on the Forge
W.H. AUDEN (EDITOR) The Living Thoughts of Kierkegaard
W.H. AUDEN W.H. Auden's Book of Light Verse
ERICH AUERBACH Dante: Poet of the Secular World
DOROTHY BAKER Cassandra at the Wedding*
DOROTHY BAKER Young Man with a Horn*
J.A. BAKER The Peregrine
S. JOSEPHINE BAKER Fighting for Life*
HONORÉ DE BALZAC The Human Comedy: Selected Stories*
HONORÉ DE BALZAC The Unknown Masterpiece *and* Gambara*
SYBILLE BEDFORD A Legacy*
MAX BEERBOHM The Prince of Minor Writers: The Selected Essays of Max Beerbohm
MAX BEERBOHM Seven Men
STEPHEN BENATAR Wish Her Safe at Home*
FRANS G. BENGTSSON The Long Ships*
ALEXANDER BERKMAN Prison Memoirs of an Anarchist
GEORGES BERNANOS Mouchette
ADOLFO BIOY CASARES Asleep in the Sun
ADOLFO BIOY CASARES The Invention of Morel
CAROLINE BLACKWOOD Corrigan*
CAROLINE BLACKWOOD Great Granny Webster*
NICOLAS BOUVIER The Way of the World
MALCOLM BRALY On the Yard*
MILLEN BRAND The Outward Room*
SIR THOMAS BROWNE Religio Medici and Urne-Buriall*
JOHN HORNE BURNS The Gallery
ROBERT BURTON The Anatomy of Melancholy
CAMARA LAYE The Radiance of the King

* *Also available as an electronic book.*

GIROLAMO CARDANO The Book of My Life
DON CARPENTER Hard Rain Falling*
J.L. CARR A Month in the Country*
BLAISE CENDRARS Moravagine
EILEEN CHANG Love in a Fallen City
EILEEN CHANG Naked Earth
JOAN CHASE During the Reign of the Queen of Persia*
UPAMANYU CHATTERJEE English, August: An Indian Story
NIRAD C. CHAUDHURI The Autobiography of an Unknown Indian
ANTON CHEKHOV Peasants and Other Stories
GABRIEL CHEVALLIER Fear: A Novel of World War I*
RICHARD COBB Paris and Elsewhere
COLETTE The Pure and the Impure
JOHN COLLIER Fancies and Goodnights
CARLO COLLODI The Adventures of Pinocchio*
IVY COMPTON-BURNETT A House and Its Head
IVY COMPTON-BURNETT Manservant and Maidservant
BARBARA COMYNS The Vet's Daughter
EVAN S. CONNELL The Diary of a Rapist
ALBERT COSSERY The Jokers*
ALBERT COSSERY Proud Beggars*
HAROLD CRUSE The Crisis of the Negro Intellectual
ASTOLPHE DE CUSTINE Letters from Russia*
LORENZO DA PONTE Memoirs
ELIZABETH DAVID A Book of Mediterranean Food
ELIZABETH DAVID Summer Cooking
L.J. DAVIS A Meaningful Life*
VIVANT DENON No Tomorrow/Point de lendemain
MARIA DERMOÛT The Ten Thousand Things
DER NISTER The Family Mashber
TIBOR DÉRY Niki: The Story of a Dog
ARTHUR CONAN DOYLE The Exploits and Adventures of Brigadier Gerard
CHARLES DUFF A Handbook on Hanging
BRUCE DUFFY The World As I Found It*
DAPHNE DU MAURIER Don't Look Now: Stories
ELAINE DUNDY The Dud Avocado*
ELAINE DUNDY The Old Man and Me*
G.B. EDWARDS The Book of Ebenezer Le Page
JOHN EHLE The Land Breakers*
MARCELLUS EMANTS A Posthumous Confession
EURIPIDES Grief Lessons: Four Plays; translated by Anne Carson
J.G. FARRELL Troubles*
J.G. FARRELL The Siege of Krishnapur*
J.G. FARRELL The Singapore Grip*
ELIZA FAY Original Letters from India
KENNETH FEARING The Big Clock
KENNETH FEARING Clark Gifford's Body
FÉLIX FÉNÉON Novels in Three Lines*
M.I. FINLEY The World of Odysseus
THOMAS FLANAGAN The Year of the French*
SANFORD FRIEDMAN Conversations with Beethoven*
SANFORD FRIEDMAN Totempole*

MASANOBU FUKUOKA The One-Straw Revolution*

MARC FUMAROLI When the World Spoke French

CARLO EMILIO GADDA That Awful Mess on the Via Merulana

BENITO PÉREZ GÁLDOS Tristana*

MAVIS GALLANT The Cost of Living: Early and Uncollected Stories*

MAVIS GALLANT Paris Stories*

MAVIS GALLANT Varieties of Exile*

GABRIEL GARCÍA MÁRQUEZ Clandestine in Chile: The Adventures of Miguel Littín

ALAN GARNER Red Shift*

WILLIAM H. GASS In the Heart of the Heart of the Country: And Other Stories*

WILLIAM H. GASS On Being Blue: A Philosophical Inquiry*

THÉOPHILE GAUTIER My Fantoms

JEAN GENET Prisoner of Love

ÉLISABETH GILLE The Mirador: Dreamed Memories of Irène Némirovsky by Her Daughter*

JOHN GLASSCO Memoirs of Montparnasse*

P.V. GLOB The Bog People: Iron-Age Man Preserved

NIKOLAI GOGOL Dead Souls*

EDMOND AND JULES DE GONCOURT Pages from the Goncourt Journals

PAUL GOODMAN Growing Up Absurd: Problems of Youth in the Organized Society*

EDWARD GOREY (EDITOR) The Haunted Looking Glass

JEREMIAS GOTTHELF The Black Spider*

A.C. GRAHAM Poems of the Late T'ang

WILLIAM LINDSAY GRESHAM Nightmare Alley*

EMMETT GROGAN Ringolevio: A Life Played for Keeps

VASILY GROSSMAN An Armenian Sketchbook*

VASILY GROSSMAN Everything Flows*

VASILY GROSSMAN Life and Fate*

VASILY GROSSMAN The Road*

OAKLEY HALL Warlock

PATRICK HAMILTON The Slaves of Solitude

PATRICK HAMILTON Twenty Thousand Streets Under the Sky

PETER HANDKE Short Letter, Long Farewell

PETER HANDKE Slow Homecoming

ELIZABETH HARDWICK The New York Stories of Elizabeth Hardwick*

ELIZABETH HARDWICK Seduction and Betrayal*

ELIZABETH HARDWICK Sleepless Nights*

L.P. HARTLEY Eustace and Hilda: A Trilogy*

L.P. HARTLEY The Go-Between*

NATHANIEL HAWTHORNE Twenty Days with Julian & Little Bunny by Papa

ALFRED HAYES In Love*

ALFRED HAYES My Face for the World to See*

PAUL HAZARD The Crisis of the European Mind: 1680–1715*

GILBERT HIGHET Poets in a Landscape

RUSSELL HOBAN Turtle Diary*

JANET HOBHOUSE The Furies

HUGO VON HOFMANNSTHAL The Lord Chandos Letter*

JAMES HOGG The Private Memoirs and Confessions of a Justified Sinner

RICHARD HOLMES Shelley: The Pursuit*

ALISTAIR HORNE A Savage War of Peace: Algeria 1954–1962*

GEOFFREY HOUSEHOLD Rogue Male*

WILLIAM DEAN HOWELLS Indian Summer

BOHUMIL HRABAL Dancing Lessons for the Advanced in Age*

DOROTHY B. HUGHES The Expendable Man*
RICHARD HUGHES A High Wind in Jamaica*
RICHARD HUGHES In Hazard*
RICHARD HUGHES The Fox in the Attic (The Human Predicament, Vol. 1)*
RICHARD HUGHES The Wooden Shepherdess (The Human Predicament, Vol. 2)*
INTIZAR HUSAIN Basti*
MAUDE HUTCHINS Victorine
YASUSHI INOUE Tun-huang*
HENRY JAMES The Ivory Tower
HENRY JAMES The New York Stories of Henry James*
HENRY JAMES The Other House
HENRY JAMES The Outcry
TOVE JANSSON Fair Play *
TOVE JANSSON The Summer Book*
TOVE JANSSON The True Deceiver*
TOVE JANSSON The Woman Who Borrowed Memories: Selected Stories*
RANDALL JARRELL (EDITOR) Randall Jarrell's Book of Stories
DAVID JONES In Parenthesis
JOSEPH JOUBERT The Notebooks of Joseph Joubert; translated by Paul Auster
KABIR Songs of Kabir; translated by Arvind Krishna Mehrotra*
FRIGYES KARINTHY A Journey Round My Skull
ERICH KÄSTNER Going to the Dogs: The Story of a Moralist*
HELEN KELLER The World I Live In
YASHAR KEMAL Memed, My Hawk
YASHAR KEMAL They Burn the Thistles
MURRAY KEMPTON Part of Our Time: Some Ruins and Monuments of the Thirties*
RAYMOND KENNEDY Ride a Cockhorse*
DAVID KIDD Peking Story*
ROBERT KIRK The Secret Commonwealth of Elves, Fauns, and Fairies
ARUN KOLATKAR Jejuri
DEZSŐ KOSZTOLÁNYI Skylark*
TÉTÉ-MICHEL KPOMASSIE An African in Greenland
GYULA KRÚDY The Adventures of Sindbad*
GYULA KRÚDY Sunflower*
SIGIZMUND KRZHIZHANOVSKY Autobiography of a Corpse*
SIGIZMUND KRZHIZHANOVSKY The Letter Killers Club*
SIGIZMUND KRZHIZHANOVSKY Memories of the Future
GIUSEPPE TOMASI DI LAMPEDUSA The Professor and the Siren
GERT LEDIG The Stalin Front*
MARGARET LEECH Reveille in Washington: 1860–1865*
PATRICK LEIGH FERMOR Between the Woods and the Water*
PATRICK LEIGH FERMOR The Broken Road*
PATRICK LEIGH FERMOR Mani: Travels in the Southern Peloponnese*
PATRICK LEIGH FERMOR Roumeli: Travels in Northern Greece*
PATRICK LEIGH FERMOR A Time of Gifts*
PATRICK LEIGH FERMOR A Time to Keep Silence*
PATRICK LEIGH FERMOR The Traveller's Tree*
D.B. WYNDHAM LEWIS AND CHARLES LEE (EDITORS) The Stuffed Owl
SIMON LEYS The Death of Napoleon*
SIMON LEYS The Hall of Uselessness: Collected Essays*
GEORG CHRISTOPH LICHTENBERG The Waste Books
JAKOV LIND Soul of Wood and Other Stories

H.P. LOVECRAFT AND OTHERS The Colour Out of Space
DWIGHT MACDONALD Masscult and Midcult: Essays Against the American Grain*
NORMAN MAILER Miami and the Siege of Chicago*
CURZIO MALAPARTE Kaputt
CURZIO MALAPARTE The Skin
JANET MALCOLM In the Freud Archives
JEAN-PATRICK MANCHETTE Fatale*
JEAN-PATRICK MANCHETTE The Mad and the Bad*
OSIP MANDELSTAM The Selected Poems of Osip Mandelstam
OLIVIA MANNING Fortunes of War: The Balkan Trilogy*
OLIVIA MANNING Fortunes of War: The Levant Trilogy*
OLIVIA MANNING School for Love*
JAMES VANCE MARSHALL Walkabout*
GUY DE MAUPASSANT Afloat
GUY DE MAUPASSANT Alien Hearts*
JAMES McCOURT Mawrdew Czgowchwz*
WILLIAM McPHERSON Testing the Current*
DAVID MENDEL Proper Doctoring: A Book for Patients and Their Doctors*
HENRI MICHAUX Miserable Miracle
JESSICA MITFORD Hons and Rebels
JESSICA MITFORD Poison Penmanship*
NANCY MITFORD Frederick the Great*
NANCY MITFORD Madame de Pompadour*
NANCY MITFORD The Sun King*
NANCY MITFORD Voltaire in Love*
MICHEL DE MONTAIGNE Shakespeare's Montaigne; translated by John Florio*
HENRY DE MONTHERLANT Chaos and Night
BRIAN MOORE The Lonely Passion of Judith Hearne*
BRIAN MOORE The Mangan Inheritance*
ALBERTO MORAVIA Agostino*
ALBERTO MORAVIA Boredom*
ALBERTO MORAVIA Contempt*
JAN MORRIS Conundrum*
JAN MORRIS Hav*
PENELOPE MORTIMER The Pumpkin Eater*
ÁLVARO MUTIS The Adventures and Misadventures of Maqroll
L.H. MYERS The Root and the Flower*
NESCIO Amsterdam Stories*
DARCY O'BRIEN A Way of Life, Like Any Other
SILVINA OCAMPO Thus Were Their Faces*
YURI OLESHA Envy*
IONA AND PETER OPIE The Lore and Language of Schoolchildren
IRIS OWENS After Claude*
RUSSELL PAGE The Education of a Gardener
ALEXANDROS PAPADIAMANTIS The Murderess
BORIS PASTERNAK, MARINA TSVETAYEVA, AND RAINER MARIA RILKE Letters, Summer 1926
CESARE PAVESE The Moon and the Bonfires
CESARE PAVESE The Selected Works of Cesare Pavese
LUIGI PIRANDELLO The Late Mattia Pascal
JOSEP PLA The Gray Notebook
ANDREY PLATONOV The Foundation Pit
ANDREY PLATONOV Happy Moscow

ANDREY PLATONOV Soul and Other Stories
J.F. POWERS Morte d'Urban*
J.F. POWERS The Stories of J.F. Powers*
J.F. POWERS Wheat That Springeth Green*
CHRISTOPHER PRIEST Inverted World*
BOLESŁAW PRUS The Doll*
ALEXANDER PUSHKIN The Captain's Daughter*
QIU MIAOJIN Last Words from Montmartre*
RAYMOND QUENEAU We Always Treat Women Too Well
RAYMOND QUENEAU Witch Grass
RAYMOND RADIGUET Count d'Orgel's Ball
FRIEDRICH RECK Diary of a Man in Despair*
JULES RENARD Nature Stories*
JEAN RENOIR Renoir, My Father
GREGOR VON REZZORI An Ermine in Czernopol*
GREGOR VON REZZORI Memoirs of an Anti-Semite*
GREGOR VON REZZORI The Snows of Yesteryear: Portraits for an Autobiography*
TIM ROBINSON Stones of Aran: Labyrinth
TIM ROBINSON Stones of Aran: Pilgrimage
MILTON ROKEACH The Three Christs of Ypsilanti*
FR. ROLFE Hadrian the Seventh
GILLIAN ROSE Love's Work
LINDA ROSENKRANTZ Talk*
WILLIAM ROUGHEAD Classic Crimes
CONSTANCE ROURKE American Humor: A Study of the National Character
SAKI The Unrest-Cure and Other Stories; illustrated by Edward Gorey
TAYEB SALIH Season of Migration to the North
TAYEB SALIH The Wedding of Zein*
JEAN-PAUL SARTRE We Have Only This Life to Live: Selected Essays. 1939–1975
GERSHOM SCHOLEM Walter Benjamin: The Story of a Friendship*
DANIEL PAUL SCHREBER Memoirs of My Nervous Illness
JAMES SCHUYLER Alfred and Guinevere
JAMES SCHUYLER What's for Dinner?*
SIMONE SCHWARZ-BART The Bridge of Beyond*
LEONARDO SCIASCIA The Day of the Owl
LEONARDO SCIASCIA Equal Danger
LEONARDO SCIASCIA The Moro Affair
LEONARDO SCIASCIA To Each His Own
LEONARDO SCIASCIA The Wine-Dark Sea
VICTOR SEGALEN René Leys*
ANNA SEGHERS Transit*
PHILIPE-PAUL DE SÉGUR Defeat: Napoleon's Russian Campaign
GILBERT SELDES The Stammering Century*
VICTOR SERGE The Case of Comrade Tulayev*
VICTOR SERGE Conquered City*
VICTOR SERGE Memoirs of a Revolutionary
VICTOR SERGE Midnight in the Century*
VICTOR SERGE Unforgiving Years
SHCHEDRIN The Golovlyov Family
ROBERT SHECKLEY The Store of the Worlds: The Stories of Robert Sheckley*
GEORGES SIMENON Act of Passion*
GEORGES SIMENON Dirty Snow*

GEORGES SIMENON Monsieur Monde Vanishes*

GEORGES SIMENON Pedigree*

GEORGES SIMENON Three Bedrooms in Manhattan*

GEORGES SIMENON Tropic Moon*

GEORGES SIMENON The Widow*

CHARLES SIMIC Dime-Store Alchemy: The Art of Joseph Cornell

MAY SINCLAIR Mary Olivier: A Life*

TESS SLESINGER The Unpossessed: A Novel of the Thirties*

VLADIMIR SOROKIN Ice Trilogy*

VLADIMIR SOROKIN The Queue

NATSUME SŌSEKI The Gate*

DAVID STACTON The Judges of the Secret Court*

JEAN STAFFORD The Mountain Lion

CHRISTINA STEAD Letty Fox: Her Luck

GEORGE R. STEWART Names on the Land

STENDHAL The Life of Henry Brulard

ADALBERT STIFTER Rock Crystal

THEODOR STORM The Rider on the White Horse

JEAN STROUSE Alice James: A Biography*

HOWARD STURGIS Belchamber

ITALO SVEVO As a Man Grows Older

HARVEY SWADOS Nights in the Gardens of Brooklyn

A.J.A. SYMONS The Quest for Corvo

MAGDA SZABÓ The Door*

ANTAL SZERB Journey by Moonlight*

ELIZABETH TAYLOR Angel*

ELIZABETH TAYLOR A Game of Hide and Seek*

ELIZABETH TAYLOR A View of the Harbour*

ELIZABETH TAYLOR You'll Enjoy It When You Get There: The Stories of Elizabeth Taylor*

HENRY DAVID THOREAU The Journal: 1837–1861*

ALEKSANDAR TIŠMA The Use of Man*

TATYANA TOLSTAYA The Slynx

TATYANA TOLSTAYA White Walls: Collected Stories

EDWARD JOHN TRELAWNY Records of Shelley, Byron, and the Author

LIONEL TRILLING The Liberal Imagination*

LIONEL TRILLING The Middle of the Journey*

THOMAS TRYON The Other*

IVAN TURGENEV Virgin Soil

JULES VALLÈS The Child

RAMÓN DEL VALLE-INCLÁN Tyrant Banderas*

MARK VAN DOREN Shakespeare

CARL VAN VECHTEN The Tiger in the House

ELIZABETH VON ARNIM The Enchanted April*

EDWARD LEWIS WALLANT The Tenants of Moonbloom

ROBERT WALSER Berlin Stories*

ROBERT WALSER Jakob von Gunten

ROBERT WALSER A Schoolboy's Diary and Other Stories*

REX WARNER Men and Gods

SYLVIA TOWNSEND WARNER Lolly Willowes*

SYLVIA TOWNSEND WARNER Mr. Fortune*

SYLVIA TOWNSEND WARNER Summer Will Show*

ALEKSANDER WAT My Century*

C.V. WEDGWOOD The Thirty Years War

SIMONE WEIL On the Abolition of All Political Parties*

SIMONE WEIL AND RACHEL BESPALOFF War and the Iliad

GLENWAY WESCOTT Apartment in Athens*

GLENWAY WESCOTT The Pilgrim Hawk*

REBECCA WEST The Fountain Overflows

EDITH WHARTON The New York Stories of Edith Wharton*

KATHARINE S. WHITE Onward and Upward in the Garden

PATRICK WHITE Riders in the Chariot

T. H. WHITE The Goshawk*

JOHN WILLIAMS Augustus*

JOHN WILLIAMS Butcher's Crossing*

JOHN WILLIAMS Stoner*

ANGUS WILSON Anglo-Saxon Attitudes

EDMUND WILSON Memoirs of Hecate County

RUDOLF AND MARGARET WITTKOWER Born Under Saturn

GEOFFREY WOLFF Black Sun*

FRANCIS WYNDHAM The Complete Fiction

JOHN WYNDHAM The Chrysalids

BÉLA ZOMBORY-MOLDOVÁN The Burning of the World: A Memoir of 1914*

STEFAN ZWEIG Beware of Pity*

STEFAN ZWEIG Chess Story*

STEFAN ZWEIG Confusion *

STEFAN ZWEIG Journey Into the Past*

STEFAN ZWEIG The Post-Office Girl*